TOTALLY
DECEASED

Published in the UK by Scholastic, 2023
1 London Bridge, London, SE1 9BG
Scholastic Ireland, 89E Lagan Road, Dublin Industrial Estate,
Glasnevin, Dublin, D11 HP5F

Text © Sue H. Cunningham, 2023

ISBN 978 0702 32585 4

A CIP catalogue record for this book
is available from the British Library.

Printed and bound in Great Britain by Clays Ltd, Elcograf S.p.A
Paper made from wood grown in sustainable forests
and other controlled sources.

MIX
Paper | Supporting
responsible forestry
FSC
www.fsc.org
FSC® C018072

1 3 5 7 9 10 8 6 4 2

www.scholastic.co.uk

TOTALLY DECEASED

SUE H. CUNNINGHAM

SCHOLASTIC

For Col,
who makes me braver

PROLOGUE

When they first tell me what's wrong with me, I think they're having a laugh. Nobody gets heart failure at my age, right? On the other hand, Mum doesn't think it's the least bit funny.

"Parvovirus? *Parvovirus?*" she shrieks at the consultant heart specialist. "You're telling me my only child might die from a disease that *dogs* get?"

What the hell? I'm struggling to breathe anyway, but this just about finishes me off.

Dad clocks my panicky face. "You're not going to die, Jess. Is she, doctor?"

"Not if I can help it," Mr Khan says, his deep voice inappropriately jolly. "Didn't you know you were unwell, Jess? Even with a rapid onset cardiomyopathy, you usually have some symptoms beforehand. Any flu-like illness recently? Shortness of breath, difficulty concentrating, fatigue?"

"I've been tired, I guess. Feeling pretty crappy." I pause

to catch my breath. "I thought it was just, you know, stress. Moving house, starting a new school and all the stuff with my mum and dad."

"Our conscious uncoupling," says Mum, fussing with my oxygen mask.

Dad puffs out his cheeks. "She means we're getting a divorce. So what's the treatment, doctor? Will Jess be all right?"

Mr Khan hesitates. "If we can find her a new heart, she has an excellent chance of recovery."

What?

Dad squeezes my hand, his knuckles white. "Our little girl needs a heart transplant?"

"As soon as possible. It's lucky she's so common." Mr Khan waves his hands in a placatory manner. "What I mean to say is that Jess has a very common blood type."

Dad swallows. "That's good, is it?"

"Very good. When we get on to tissue typing, it will be easier to find a donor. It is essential we get a good match." He scrolls through my medical notes and tilts the screen towards us. "O-positive, see? Very average indeed."

Average. That just about sums me up.

Sixteen years old and I'd never done anything memorable in my life until the day I fainted and fell off my chair in the middle of Mrs Ayodeji's careers presentation. Woke up to find the whole class leaning over me – who knew that Year 12's supposed sex god, Raz Fernandez, had so much nostril hair? Even worse was the total over-the-topness of the ambulance journey: blue lights flashing, sirens wailing and a cute guy in a green jumpsuit taking my pulse. If I hadn't been *mortified*, I'd probably have enjoyed that bit.

Three days later, I'm still stuck in this hospital bed, sucking in air like a dehydrated goldfish. Dad must have been pretty worried because he actually *phoned my mother*. He never does that. And Mum immediately cancelled her goat yoga retreat (she never does that either) and came straight here, stranding a shedload of corporate clients in darkest Wales.

As my parents converse across me in worried whispers, *not even arguing*, I consider the disturbing fact that not one thing about me is special.

A British, standard pear-shaped body: size twelve on the bottom and ten on the top. Khaki-coloured eyes which are neither green nor brown. Average mousy hair way overdue a cut and highlights, but I haven't sorted out a hairdresser here in Manchester yet.

Even my name's boring – there are, like, at least three other girls called Jess in my new sixth form class.

I pull off the oxygen mask to stare at my parents. "Am I going to die?"

Mum opens her mouth, but Dad gives her a warning look.

"No, love," he says. "You're not going to die. And when

you're better, we'll go on holiday – wherever you like. Barcelona, Venice, New York; we could go to Disneyland, swim with dolphins…" He sounds like an advert for the Make-A-Wish Foundation.

Bollocks. I really am going to die.

I'm going to die at the age of sixteen. I've achieved nothing in my life and even my roots need doing.

1

There's someone else in the bed with me.

I can feel breathing and someone's shoulder digging into my back.

Slight problem – I don't have a clue who it is. This isn't even my bed. It smells lemony and the pillow is super hard, which doesn't help my banging headache. But before you put two and two together and make twenty-seven, stop! I didn't get smashed at a party and get with some random guy. Or even crash at my best mate's house. My two besties are forty miles away in Sheffield, so no chance of a sleepover right now.

I keep my eyes shut and listen to the even breaths behind

me. Who the hell is it? The thin mattress dips as whoever-it-is fidgets, making my bum sink into the middle. I grab on to the edge of the bed, trying not to roll back.

Ow. *Ow.* Something tugs on my arm and a hot stabbing pain shoots through my ribs. I open my eyes to see Tinkerbell curtains and a Winnie-the-Pooh mural running around the walls. Not to mention a load of tubes running into my chest and a jumble of wires hooking me up to some sort of monitor. I try to lift my head but dizziness swoops in like a tidal wave. The curtains blur as Tinkerbell whooshes in and out of focus, scattering fairy dust in her wake.

I lower my head back on to the pillow. Now I remember where I am – in hospital, in Manchester, which means I've made it through my heart surgery. Phew. I'm not normally a drama queen (my mother doesn't leave room for anyone else), but it's a massive relief to think I'll actually make it to my seventeenth birthday. Even if this is a hospital bed though, it doesn't explain why there's someone else in it. I was feeling pretty rough before the surgery, but I vaguely remember a little girl in the opposite cubicle shouting for the nurse because she'd wet the bed. I seriously hope she hasn't got into mine.

"Go back to your own bed," I say, my throat dry and scratchy.

There's a pause before whoever-it-is gives a muffled sniff.

"Hey?" I say. "Are you crying?"

"Don't be ridiculous." She sounds well posh. "Of course I'm not crying."

No *way*. I recognize that voice. She was the one doing the running commentary when I was in Intensive Care. "Lie still, don't panic, go back to sleep." Blah, blah, blah. All the bog-standard phrases I guess student nurses have to learn before they're let loose on the bedpans and the controlled drugs.

"Why on earth would I be crying?" She seems irritated. Maybe she's not a nurse but a doctor. The junior ones you hear about on telly working a three-million-hour week or something. What's she doing in my bed? Did she come into work seriously knackered, find the nearest unconscious patient and whip the curtains closed so she could have a quick snooze?

"Aw. Were you on call last night?" I ask sympathetically.

"God's sake. Stop talking nonsense and go back to sleep, Jess," instructs the voice.

I'm desperate for a drink of water but my eyelids weigh a tonne. Maybe just another ten minutes then. I snuggle back down into the rubbery pillow.

"You'll feel better tomorrow," she adds doubtfully. The mattress springs up as her weight disappears and next time I wake, she's gone.

2

I open my eyes, completely disorientated to find I've switched beds again. This time, I'm in a sunny side room with pale green walls and a distinct absence of Winnie-the-Pooh. Suspended between floor and ceiling is a bunch of sad-looking deflated helium balloons with "17" in shouty metallic print. On the bedside cabinet, a pile of opened greetings cards confirm my suspicions.

No *way*. I've missed my bloody birthday.

I take an experimental breath to find my chest is super sore. Peering down the front of my nasty hospital nightie, it's a relief to see the wound's covered by a big white dressing. Somewhere underneath, my new (second-hand) heart beats unassisted. Tentatively, I slide my hand down until I feel a faint *thud, thud, thud* matching the blips on the monitor next to my bed.

How cool is that?

How *weird* is that?

The door swings open and Mr Khan, my heart surgeon, appears followed by a huge entourage. I yank my hand out of my nightie and struggle to sit up.

"Good to see you with us at last," he says as his minions straggle into the room. "How are you feeling, Jess?"

"OK, I guess." I hardly recognize my hoarse voice. "My chest hurts."

"That's to be expected." He nods to the junior doctors. "We have to crack the breastbone and open the ribs to get the old heart out and the new one in, you see."

Ew. Too much information. I zone out from the enthusiastic discussion around metal retractors and chest drains, tuning back in for the end credits. "You had us worried, young lady; it took longer than usual to wake you up, but you're doing very nicely now. Do as you're told for the next couple of weeks and we'll soon have you home."

"Where's my dad?" I ask, seeing his red United fleece slung over the arm of the chair.

"Perhaps he's gone to get a cup of tea with your mother?"

Mum's still here? Jeez, I hope the truce is ongoing.

Mr Khan taps at a handheld screen with long fingers

before passing it on to the nurse behind him. "Any questions, Jess?"

Only about a million.

I take a deep painful breath. "What about the donor? What happened to them?"

"You really want to do this now?" Mr Khan asks gently. I nod. "OK. It was a road traffic accident, I believe."

I feel like I'm going to puke. Someone got killed in a car accident so I could live.

"Can you tell me their name?"

"I'm sorry, I can't tell you anything." He scratches the side of his nose as he backs away. "I'll ask the transplant coordinator to come and have a chat with you, but it's all strictly confidential unless the donor's family agree to be contacted."

The door bangs closed as he leaves, taking most of the doctors with him. Only one remains.

"Her name was Tilly, if you must know. Your donor." It's her again, the girl with the posh voice. She doesn't look much like a junior doctor. She's tiny with super shiny straight hair, killer heels and a gorgeous blue jacket I've long coveted from the window of Zara.

"How do you know?" I ask, feeling mega scuzzy in my horrible hospital gown. I'll have to get Dad to bring me in some pyjamas.

"Oh, I know lots about her. I'll tell you something else if you like." I get a waft of expensive perfume as she approaches the bed, flicking long caramel hair over one shoulder. Shouldn't she have that tied back?

"Thought you weren't allowed to tell me anything." She doesn't look much older than me – too young to be a doctor. Maybe she's some kind of social worker? Whatever she is, she doesn't seem very professional.

The girl rolls her eyes. "God's sake. Do you want to know or not?"

"OK, yeah," I say. "I want to know."

"That car accident wasn't an accident at all. She was *murdered*." She drums French-manicured fingernails against her teeny hips. "Or should I say – *I was murdered*."

Okaaay. I grab the call button and press firmly. "The nurse is coming. And my dad. Better get back to your own room, yeah?"

She smiles before perching her tiny arse on the edge of the bed. "I'm not going anywhere," she says. "Not without you."

"You reckon?" I edge away from her. "Erm, do you want to explain what you were doing in my bed the other day?" *Keep her talking until they come and rescue you.*

"On it, not in it," she corrects, rolling thickly-lashed blue eyes.

"On it, not in it. Gotcha." There's no sign of the nurse but through the window of my side room, I see Dad ambling towards me. *Hurry up!*

The girl chatters on. "God, those plastic chairs are hard

11

and there's nowhere else to sit apart from the floor. *Total* health hazard. I'm glad you've woken up. It's been *sooo* boring just watching you sleep—"

Uh-oh. I shrink back against the pillows as she places a perfectly oval fingernail over the dressing on my chest. "Do you mind if I have a little feel?"

"Get off!" I screech, new heart pounding. "Dad. *Dad!*" I wave to get his attention, wincing as the pain shoots through my splintered sternum.

"Take it easy, Jessie, love," he says, barging through the door. "Phew. It's nice to see you awake at last."

"Not you as well. Look, can you get someone to take this girl back to her ward?" I lower my voice. "I reckon she's from Psychiatry or something."

"What girl?" Dad looks puzzled as he glances around the room.

"Her. *Her!*" I gesture towards the girl who's watching us with an amused expression.

Dad puts his arm around my shoulder, mindful of the tangle of tubes and drains. "There's no one else here, Jessie."

"What? But she's right there!"

"Don't worry, love. It's probably just the stuff they've had you on, heavy duty gear. It can give you hallucinations."

He'd know, if anyone would. He and Mum met as students at the height of the Manchester rave scene. *Mad*chester, people called it. Mum did drama at uni (in her case, more of a lifestyle choice than a degree) and Dad did geography (which usually means you end up working for an insurance company).

"You're OK." Dad rocks me against him. "There's no one here, I promise."

"Except me," sings the girl, dancing forward to wiggle her fingers in front of Dad's face. I try to fix on them as the room tilts and blurs out of focus.

"How come I can see you and he can't?" I sob, squeezing my eyes shut.

"Duh! Because you've got my heart and he hasn't," she says, pressing her hand against her chest. In response, my new heart speeds up, bumping against my rib cage. She leans in towards me. "Don't you get it? I told you, I'm Tilly. The way I see it, you owe me big time. And I'm going nowhere until you get off your fat backside and help me."

It's just as well Dad's already run to get the nurse because if this is the drugs wearing off, I seriously need a top-up.

No one goes around telling me I've got a fat arse.

Especially not a size eight dead girl.

3

God knows what they gave me but when I come round, woolly and headachy, it's growing dark. Dad's on one side of the bed and my mother sits opposite, reading my birthday cards. Spotting Nisha's neat handwriting and Bex's sparkly felt-tip scrawl, I'm seriously hoping none of my mates have written anything dodgy.

"Hey, Mum," I whisper, lifting my head from the pillow. No *way*. The posh girl – Tilly – is still here, frowning at me from the bottom of the bed. Dad was right about the side effects of the medication.

She's just a figment of your imagination, I remind myself. I blink super hard but she's still there, knees drawn up daintily to her chest and a fingertip to her lips in an exaggerated shush. She's pretty realistic for a hallucination.

"Not one word," she orders. "OK, maybe I shouldn't have broken the news like that, but I had no idea you'd totally lose it. Do you realize how much time we've wasted with you being off your face? *Don't* answer that. If they think you're bonkers, they'll never let us out of here."

I shake my head. *She's not real.* If I ignore her, she'll go away.

Mum leans across, silver bangles jangling, to stroke my brow. "However did you get yourself into this state, sweetheart? Heart failure at your age?" She slides a sideways look at Dad. "Has he been feeding you meat again?"

"Mum, you know I stopped being vegan when I was twelve."

"Yes, just after your father went over to the dark side. Well, no wonder your chakras are shot to pieces, not to mention your arteries. Perhaps you could revisit the idea, sweetheart? Isn't it quite trendy to go vegan these days? Meat-free Monday and all that? It's a shame you slept through your birthday because I made you a cake. Substitute the eggs and butter for beetroot juice and the recipe works just as well."

"Never mind." Dad gives me a wink. "I'm sure the nurses enjoyed it."

"I can't believe I slept through my entire birthday," I grumble.

15

"You were awake for some of it, love," says Dad. "You just weren't making a whole lot of sense. Going on about fairy dust and all sorts, you were. Here you go, then, better late than never." He hands me a gift bag with a slim box inside.

No way. It's the new phone I wanted. "Wow, Dad! I thought you said it was too expensive?"

"That was before." Dad gives me an awkward smile. "Your mum's got you something as well."

"Practical gifts." Mum dips into her hessian tote, producing various paper bags. "I've brought you some jade for healing and a lovely piece of rose quartz to warm your new heart centre. When they let you out, how about coming back to the commune with me for a little holiday? It's lovely in Wales just now and an organic, macrobiotic diet will do you a damn sight more good than these silly drips and drugs. You wouldn't believe what they put in some of those tablets."

The imaginary Tilly yawns, swinging slim legs over the edge of the bed. "Does she *ever* shut up?" she asks, rising gracefully to lean against the radiator. "*Don't* answer that. We need to convince them you're not losing the plot."

Figment, figment, figment, I tell myself but the temptation to answer her is too strong. "Am I losing the plot?"

The replies come from all sides.

"No, love. It's just side effects from the meds." (Dad)

"Of course not. It's just no one else can see me. Which is totally inconvenient." (Tilly)

16

"Maybe a little bit, darling, but they do say it runs in families. Think about poor Granny Ursula on Dad's side." (Guess)

I nod. Assuming this *isn't* drug related and I really am being haunted by the ghost of my heart donor, there's a good chance Granny Ursula is the only one who'd believe me.

"I'm so thirsty. Could you guys go get me a drink?" I croak, hoping Dad'll take the hint and take my mother with him. "I might go back to sleep for a bit."

Mum looks disappointed. "I thought we could do some karmic chanting together. Or a visualization of healing silvery light…"

"Maybe tomorrow," I say. "My throat's a bit sore for chanting."

Dad comes to my rescue. "We'll get you some juice. Want anything else?"

Only my mind back.

Tilly watches as Dad frogmarches my mother from the room. "He must have the patience of a saint."

"Oh, go away," I say. No one gets to slag off my mother except me.

"No can do."

I glare at her. "What do you mean, no can do? If I've imagined you being here, I can just as easily imagine you *pissing off again*."

"You think you've imagined me? Don't flatter yourself,

sweetie. I'm really here, *in the north* of all places." She leans forward to place a freezing cold hand over mine.

I flinch as the hairs on my forearm lift. "No way. It's the drugs messing with my head. You're just a figment of my imagination."

"I'm not a figment!" Her shrill voice rises as I turn away. "And stop ignoring me, it's totally rude."

"It can't be rude to ignore you if you're not. Even. Here." I start to hum, but it doesn't drown out the outraged squeals of fury.

"You all right there, love?" Dad stands in the doorway, a jug of orange juice in his hand.

"I'm fine," I say, averting my gaze from Tilly's furious face. "Where's Mum?"

"Trying to convince the ladies in the cafe to ditch their entire stock of freeze-dried Nescafé and substitute it with herbal tea."

"I bet that's going down well," I mutter.

Tilly glares, first at me and then Dad. "We need to make plans. Can't you get rid of him?"

"I'd rather get rid of you," I say rudely as Dad shoots me a worried glance.

"If you want to get rid of me, you'd better shut up and listen." The imaginary Tilly folds her arms. "The important thing is to convince them you're not totally unhinged. So don't let them hear you talking to yourself."

"Ha! You've just admitted it," I say, as Dad dumps the

18

OJ and rushes out of the room calling for help. "I was talking to myself, not you. Because *you* don't exist."

Tilly tuts and flicks her perfect hair. "Whatever, sweetie. You keep telling yourself that."

4

Next morning, they confiscate all the happy, floaty drugs and wheel in a psychologist called Celeste instead.

Mum approves. She recognizes a kindred spirit – she and Celeste obviously frequent the same sort of shops to buy their wafty, tie-dye skirts and crappy crystals.

"Let it all out, darling." Mum bends to kiss my forehead, nearly knocking me unconscious with a dangling tribal pendant made from solid silver and turquoise. "Come on, Jeff. Let's leave them to it."

Once my parents have gone, Celeste sits next to my bed, looking supportive as I ramble on.

"I think I'm going mental. The girl who died – I

feel like she's still here," I confess, wondering for the hundredth time if I really am losing it while Tilly dances around the bed, tearing at the roots of her shiny hair and shrieking: "God's sake, Jess, shut up!" at intermittent intervals.

The psychologist inclines her head in a sympathetic gesture. "That's understandable. We call it survivor guilt."

"You don't get it. I feel like she's really, *really* here." You'd think working in the Transplant Unit, Celeste might have had some previous experience with this kind of thing. Tilly seems too robust to be a ghost – she isn't even see-through. I've tried ignoring her, I really have, but it's not possible in a room this size. Unless I hide under the bedclothes, she's everywhere I look.

Celeste twiddles with the sparkly scarf holding back her afro. "It's OK to feel your donor's still here with you, sharing your life. In some ways, they are. A part of them always will be."

"I seriously hope not," I say, as Tilly glowers from her favourite spot near the radiator.

"Try not to worry. You'll adjust in time and there's lots of help available." Celeste pulls a pile of glossy leaflets from her folder. "Online and in-person support groups, for example. You're not the first one to feel like this, Jess."

"It's different for me," I say.

She gives me an indulgent smile. "I understand you might feel like that now. It's quite normal."

21

"It's not normal to see your heart donor everywhere you go." I narrow my eyes at Tilly.

"Well, no. But that's not happening, Jess. You don't actually *see* them!" Celeste glances around looking slightly alarmed.

Not as alarmed as Tilly. "Do you *ever* want to leave this hospital?" She springs up from her radiator and pushes past Celeste to grab me by both shoulders. "Or would you prefer to be carted straight off to the funny farm?"

I try hard to focus on the right person as two pairs of anxious eyes stare back, awaiting my response.

"No," I say. "I don't."

"Perhaps it would help to meet up with another transplant patient?" Celeste suggests. "There's an outpatient clinic this afternoon. I could introduce you to one or two of the younger ones."

"That's quite a good idea." Tilly approves. "There might be others there like me."

I can kind of see her logic. If all heart transplant patients are being stalked by the ghosts of their dead donors, I could pick up a few tips on how to cope with her ladyship. And get a better idea of how long this situation might last.

Because of my crappy immune system, the ward sister won't let me go down to the clinic, but Celeste offers to bring one of the patients up to the ward. Sister helps me into clean pyjamas and then walks me and my trusty drip stand down to the day room. From the brown sofa, I've got a clear view of Celeste approaching with a tall guy in his twenties.

"This isn't going to work," says Tilly, her eyes dull. "There's no one with him."

"Just because you can't see them, doesn't mean they're not there." I humour her/myself. "Maybe only the recipient can see them?"

"I'm totally deceased, sweetie. Don't tell me I can't spot another ghost when I see one."

"Could be a good thing," I whisper. "Maybe it means you won't be here forever."

"What, like I'm just part of the usual post-op regime? Seven days on ICU, biopsy at two weeks, discharge at three weeks if you've been good and four if you haven't?" Tilly's voice rises higher and higher. "How many weeks before the ghost of your unspeakably generous donor ascends the glittery escalator to heaven, Jess? Six weeks? Eight? Or maybe *never* unless you do something in return, like bloody well help her find out why she was murdered—"

"Jess, this is Ryan," Celeste interrupts. "He's here for his six-month check-up."

"I guess you're still pretty immunosuppressed so I won't shake hands," the tall guy says in an American accent. "Celeste tells me you're having a little trouble adjusting."

"Yeah," I say. "It's a bit weird but, since my transplant, I feel like there's someone with me all the time."

"Not weird at all." Ryan sinks into the chair opposite

23

and crosses his gangly legs. "After my surgery, I could feel a new presence close to me at all times."

Wow. Pay dirt. No *way*.

I widen my eyes at Tilly. She stands up, circles him slowly and then gets up close and personal with the whole jazz hands thing like some hyperactive drama kid from *High School Musical*. Ryan doesn't flinch.

"This presence," I say, peering round Tilly's denim backside which is right in my face, "who did you think it was?"

Ryan inclines his head reverently. "The Lord Jesus Christ. I made some poor choices before my surgery, but He taught me to be grateful for my second chance at life."

"Are you sure it was Jesus? Not just … somebody else?" Maybe Ryan's donor had a beard, sandals and a really sick sense of humour. "I mean, did you actually *see* him?"

"I felt him." He taps his chest with a beatific smile. "Here inside my new heart for always."

"What a giggle." Tilly returns to sit beside me. "Maybe I should have done that – told you I was the Virgin Mary or something."

"I don't think the Virgin Mary ever had a pair of Prada jeans," I say.

"I guess she didn't." Ryan flicks his eyes sideways at Celeste. "Anyway, I'm due to see the doc soon. Good luck with your new heart, Jess."

"Thank you, Ryan." Celeste sees him out with an

apologetic smile. "Jess, dear, is there anyone else you'd like to chat to?"

"Is there anyone more like me? I mean — somebody who's just had it done?"

Celeste's silent for a moment, clearly weighing up the disadvantages of exposing a newly recuperating patient to my obvious weirdness. "Yasmin had her surgery two weeks before you. She's due home today but we might still catch her. She's coping extremely well, but she did have the mental advantage of being better prepared. She was on the transplant list for nearly a year, bless her."

We wait while Celeste goes off to pre-warn the well-adjusted Yasmin. She returns twenty minutes later with a round-faced girl a few years older than me.

"I've just got to take this call," says Celeste, holding up her phone. "I'll leave you two to chat."

"Us three," says Tilly bleakly, as the door closes. "There's no one else here, Jess. It's just us this has happened to." She retreats to the far end of the sofa and cuddles her skinny knees.

Yasmin flashes me an awkward grin. She already has her denim jacket on ready to go home. "Did you wanna ask me something?"

"If you don't mind," I say. "I know it's a weird question, but do you know anything about your donor?"

"Nah, they're not supposed to tell you nothing, are they?" she says. "I did overhear one of the nurses say he

25

was an old guy – like in his thirties. Head injury. How about yours?"

"Car accident."

"Mur-der," corrects Tilly.

"I wish someone could help me," I plead. "I feel like my donor's still here. Like she's in the room *right now.*" I swallow hard, feeling seriously overwhelmed. *In for a penny, in for a pound*, Granny Ursula always says, so I might as well just go for it. "Sometimes, I think I actually see her. Have you had anything like that?"

I gaze at her, willing her to say yes.

Yasmin shakes her head. "Sorry, babes. I haven't seen or felt no one with me since my op. I've waited a long time for this and just feel amazingly lucky." She looks embarrassed as she gets up to leave.

Despite Tilly glowering in the background, I've never felt more alone. I trundle my drip back to my room and lie on the bed facing the wall. If I can't see her, I can pretend she's not here.

"You'll have to talk to me some time," she calls. "We need to make a plan."

"You're not here," I say. "I'm just going mental."

Even with my fingers stuck in my ears, I can't miss the scorn in her voice. "God's sake, Jess. You're not mental. Deluded, *incredibly* naive even, but definitely not mad. I'm here and you'd better get used to it."

I roll to face her. "What if I don't want to get used to it?"

"Then we'll never get out of here." She waves her arms in an all-encompassing manner around the small side room. "And I, for one, am beginning to find this grim green paint a bit bloody depressing."

5

Visiting time doesn't make me feel any better. Now I'm over the worst, Dad and Mum take turns like a tag team. My mother arrives first so Tilly lies low by the radiator, but when Dad rolls up, she moves to the end of my bed to listen in.

"You all right, love?" Dad says. "You seem a bit quiet."

"Sorry. Not sure I'm up to company tonight." I direct the comment over his shoulder to where Tilly's sitting.

"And I don't feel like being stuck in this nasty little room, but I don't appear to have a choice," she snaps. "If you made even the slightest attempt to appear normal, maybe they'd let us leave."

"I won't stay long then," Dad says. "What have you been up to today?"

"Making friends with all the other transplant patients."

"I hope you played nice." Dad rustles about in a bag for life and brings out bottled water, more grapes to add to my growing collection and one of those naff celebrity magazines with an interchangeable array of Fanta-faced footballers' wives on the front. "If you don't want to chat, how about something to read?"

How about a book, Dad? Does he not know me at all?

I skim the glossy cover. Yup. Chelsea striker's girlfriend shows off Burberry clad newborn. Disgraced former MP joins *Strictly*. Harry and Meghan invite us into their zillion-dollar holiday home. Blah, blah, blah.

Dad smiles expectantly so I flick over the page and that's when I see the photo.

No freaking way. I ignore the main headline about Hollywood superstar skydivers and focus on the column next to it. *Socialite Dies in Tragic Car Accident*. Above the text, a photo shows a familiar face smirking in an off-the-shoulder cocktail dress.

My new heart stutters and then goes into overdrive as the page zooms up to meet me.

"Hey, hey." Dad grabs my shoulders and steers me back against the pillows. "Are you OK? You've gone a horrible colour."

Tilly leans across to tap the photo with a perfectly

manicured fingernail. "There," she says triumphantly. "*Now* do you believe me?"

"I believe you," I whisper as the green walls buckle inwards and fade to black.

6

"Deep breaths, Jess, there's a good girl." The ward sister wheels in the ECG monitor and then sticks an oxygen mask over my face while Dad faffs around getting in the way.

In the background, Tilly scrutinizes the magazine article with a scornful expression. "Socialite?" she says. "God's sake, what century do they think this is? Can you believe they used that photo? The dress is totally last season."

"Bollocks. I didn't imagine you," I say, as the nurse unbuttons my pyjama top and starts sticking leads on to my chest. "You're really here, aren't you?"

"Of course I'm here." The nurse raises her eyebrows at Dad, who doesn't even tell me off for swearing. "On duty until nine."

Tilly ducks under the plastic oxygen tubing to perch beside me. "Look. You want to be rid of me and I want to go, I really do." She gives me a beseeching look, her lower lip trembling. "If you can help solve the mystery of what happened to me, maybe my tortured soul can move on."

She looks so mournful, I can't help it. I burst into giggles.

The nurse frowns. "I see what you mean, Jeff. She's not herself. I'll bleep Mr Khan's registrar."

"No, no." I turn the laugh into a cough, regretting it as the pain zings through my chest. "I just went dizzy for a sec but I'm fine now, honest. Just a bit of chest pain."

The nurse appraises the monitor with a critical eye. "Your heart rate's a bit high. That's to be expected after a transplant, but we need to keep an eye on this blood pressure. Stay there until the doctor's been round. I'll get you something for the pain."

"And I'll get you some fresh water." Dad grabs the empty jug on my bedside cabinet and follows the nurse to the door, obviously looking for an excuse to talk about me.

"OK, OK, that was over the top," Tilly admits as they move into the corridor conversing in terse whispers. "But god's sake, Jess, *please* don't let them give you any more drugs."

"It's only painkillers," I say, buttoning my pyjama top. "They won't give me the spacey stuff any more."

"I'm not surprised," says Tilly.

"Let's get this straight," I say. "You're really here, not just in my head?"

"I'm totally here."

"But it says you're *dead*." I push the magazine towards her and it slides off the sheet on to the floor. "Isn't there some tunnel with a white light you should be skipping towards?"

She shakes her glossy head. "No tunnel, no white light. Something's keeping me here and I think it's because you've got my heart."

"Well, I didn't ask for it and I can't give it back," I whisper, keeping a watchful eye on the door. Dad's probably in the nurses' office right now, stressing out over my bizarre behaviour.

"I have a theory," Tilly says. "I think I'm still here so you can help me find out why I was murdered."

"You *seriously* think you were murdered?"

"Yes."

"And you expect *me* to find out who did it?"

She narrows her eyes. "God, you never listen. I said *why* not *who*."

"No shit. You already know who it was?"

She nods. "This guy called Leo. He'd come to take me to lunch."

"You were on a *date?* And your boyfriend killed you? What a bummer. No wonder your soul's tortured."

Tilly rolls her eyes. "He wasn't my boyfriend, silly. He was my chauffeur."

"You had your *own* chauffeur?" I squeak. "How posh *were* you?"

"No one has their *own* chauffeur, Jess," Tilly says in a super patronising voice. "Chauffeurs are people you hire for the evening. If they work for you full time, then it's a *driver*. Only a complete pleb would make that mistake."

"Whatever." I'm in no mood to have a discussion on the correct etiquette of how to address one's servants with a posh dead girl no one else can see. "Maybe if you'd just got an Uber like everyone else, this would never have happened."

"Using a town car service is no different from getting an Uber," says Tilly. "Except the cars are nicer and the chauffeurs have better manners."

"Hello? You just said he was a murderer?"

"Well, yes. But, in fairness, he was new. We've been using that company for years and they usually send me either Ranjeet or Norman. Both total sweeties who wouldn't dream of killing anyone."

"Why can't you just go and find this guy on your own?" I pull off the oxygen mask and crane my neck to look for Dad. There he is, filling my jug from the tap and talking to the lady porter with the Man United tattoos.

34

"I can't." Tilly bites her lower lip. "I seem to be stuck here – if I move too far away from you, it feels like a rubber band pulling me back."

"What are you talking about, *stuck*?"

Tilly spreads out her hands, measuring. "I can go three metres, four max. I'll show you." She stands up and slowly backs away but, as she crosses the threshold of the doorway, a weird twangy sensation plucks at my chest, squeezing all the air out of me. I cringe back, terrified my chest is going to burst open like that dude in *Alien,* but this makes the tight feeling even worse. In the corridor, Tilly's face scrunches up like she's in pain too. She walks back in and the elastic band feeling slackens off, leaving behind a pinching, stinging feeling like I'm wearing a bra that's too tight.

"See?" Tilly rubs the place where her heart used to be. "Now do you believe me? I'm not getting out of this place until you do."

7

Tilly's little revelation means I'm stuck on bed rest until my blood pressure stabilizes. At next morning's ward round, Mr Khan looks almost offended as he scrolls down my chart with long fingers.

"I don't understand it. We had a great match, my surgery was textbook perfect, but this is not a happy heart." He turns to the junior doctors trying to hide behind each other. "Give me three common reasons for post-op heart failure."

"Ooh, me, me!" Tilly raises her arm with heavy sarcasm.

"Organ rejection?" suggests one of the doctors.

"Yeah, but her biopsy was fine—"

I wait until the discussion's in full swing before I mutter into my oxygen mask. "This is your fault for winding me up."

Tilly rolls her eyes. "Well, if you don't want to share, you know the solution, sweetie. Help me solve my little problem and you can have this heart all to yourself. God knows, it's no use to me any more."

Dad hovers awkwardly while Mr Khan grills the nursing staff on my medication regime and the physio on why my stamina is so rubbish. Finally, the ward sister draws him to one side, explaining something in a low voice. I strain to hear what she's saying, but I can pretty much guess because Dad's nodding.

The traitor.

Next minute, the door opens and Celeste the psychologist slides in, flashing me a quick, apologetic grin. I've never seen her rock up for the ward round before.

Mr Khan gets straight to the point. "What's all this business about her mental health?"

To my (and probably everyone else's) surprise, Celeste calmly disses the suggestion I'm *bonkers*.

"In view of Jess's acute illness and emergency admission, her distress and confusion is perhaps to be expected. Most of our transplant patients have months to prepare for major surgery – Jess had only days." Celeste gives me a warm smile. "I'm sure things will settle down once she accepts her situation and embraces it."

Mr Khan frowns down at me. "Jess, we'll adjust your medication and you can restart your physio today. But you need to calm down and work with us on this. Do you understand?"

"Do you, Jess?" Tilly pinches the skin of my upper arm and twists it hard. "Do you understand?"

I swallow and nod. "Yeah. I understand."

Ten days later, Dad gets the all clear to take me home. I'm not hugely optimistic but can't help secretly hoping that when I leave the hospital, I'll be able to leave Tilly behind too.

No such luck.

"I hope the decor at your place is a bit more tasteful than this hospital," she says sulkily, following us outside into the rain. As Dad's idea of cutting-edge interior design is using Blu-tack instead of Sellotape to hang his United posters, I sense she's doomed for disappointment.

In the car park, Tilly shivers, glaring up at the dark sky. "Bloody hell. Does it ever stop raining here?"

"It is Manchester," I murmur. We get into the car and wait while Dad goes off to pay the meter.

"Can you turn up the heater?" From the back seat, Tilly gives a dramatic little shudder. "If it's this cold in the north now, what on earth will it be like when winter comes?"

"Stop being so dramatic. It's only Manchester. You make it sound like something off *Game of Thrones*." I whack up the heating while she whines on.

"You have no idea what it's like for me. It was awful not knowing where I was when I first arrived. I couldn't get a word of sense out of you and to start with, I thought I was still in London. One of the scruffy areas, obviously, not the nice part where I live. Lived, I mean. I had a lovely flat in Chelsea." Tilly flaps her hand in front of her face like she's going to burst into tears. "How did I even get here?"

"Don't you remember?"

She shakes her head. "I remember the accident. Next thing I knew, I was in the Intensive Care Unit standing next to your bed. You looked awful," she adds, with unnecessary satisfaction.

"Yeah, well. I'd just had a heart transplant."

"Totally bizarre," Tilly says. "When I signed up for that donor card, I never considered my organs might go to a *northern* person."

"Shame you can't ask for your money back." I rub a circle in the condensation of the car window and stare out at the rain. An overweight man in a dressing gown, swollen feet stuffed into slippers, huddles under the bike shelter, trying to light a cigarette.

"Hey." Tilly taps me on the shoulder. "*You* don't smoke, do you?"

"Do I look like I'm daft?" I say. "Of course I don't smoke."

"You sound like you do. You sound like you smoke forty a day."

"Shut up." I'm still self-conscious about my croaky voice. Mr Khan says it's a hangover from having the breathing tube in for longer than usual and it'll get back to normal soon, but I'm sick of sounding like a wheezy old woman.

"And your ankles are all puffy like his."

"That's nothing to do with smoking," I say. "It's completely normal to have swollen ankles after heart surgery."

"If you say so." Tilly glares at the man shivering under the shelter. "Maybe we should lay down some ground rules. I heard your mum say you eat red meat."

"Sometimes."

"Like steak and kidney pies?" Tilly lowers her voice. "Ew. Please don't tell me you eat those."

"All the time," I say, even though it's not true. I'd rather eat my own kidney.

Tilly looks like she's going to puke. "With … chips?"

"Big, fat, greasy ones cooked in lard. With mushy peas and loads of gravy. Northern, see?" I revel in her grossed-out expression. "Anyway, you can't talk. Don't you southerners eat jellied eels or whelks or something?"

Tilly shudders. "I'd never eat food that's sold in the street. I'm extremely healthy if you must know."

"You're dead," I mouth as Dad opens the car door to get in.

8

Tilly looks around the living room of our terraced house as I stagger to the sofa, completely out of breath. "How cosy."

"If you mean small, why don't you just say so?" I hiss as Dad goes off to get my stuff from the car.

"No downstairs loo?" she enquires, peering through open doors as I line up packets of medication like dominoes on the coffee table. Painkillers, steroids, immunosuppressants.

I look up. "Why? Do you need a wee?"

"Hardly. There are some benefits to being dead," she says. "Don't need to go to the loo, pluck my eyebrows *or* shave my legs. How many bedrooms are there?"

"Two."

Her eyebrows shoot up, wrinkling her smooth forehead. "How do you manage without a spare?"

"Perfectly well." I grit my teeth. "If we did have a spare room, my mother would be staying in it right now instead of in the Wiccan hostel down the road."

"Good point." Tilly flops down on the sofa beside me. "Where am I going to sleep?"

"Didn't think you needed to sleep," I say in surprise.

"Well, I sort of snooze sometimes." She pokes my foot with the pointy toe of her boot. "It's not as if I can do anything else while you're out for the count. A nice armchair might do. Anything's better than those awful hospital chairs – that's why I kept getting on your bed."

"OK, love?" Dad comes in carrying my overnight bag. "Why don't you put your feet up? I'll bring you a glass of juice."

"I'm fed up with juice," I grumble. "Can't I have a can of Coke?"

Dad whips a familiar looking instruction booklet from his coat pocket. It's called something like "Ten Thousand Things You Are Not Allowed To Do After Your Heart Transplant".

"Avoid caffeine," reads Dad. "This leaflet sounds like it was written by your mother."

Tilly looks virtuous. "I hope you're paying attention, Jess. Remember, I have given you my heart – I expect you to look after it properly."

"Oh, give it a rest," I snap.

Dad looks hurt. "Only telling you what it says in the book, Jessie."

"Sorry." I flip a discreet V at Tilly. "If I can't have a can of Coke, how about a steak and kidney pie?"

Dad looks surprised but, before I can point out it was a joke, we're interrupted by the doorbell.

"Oh, god. Your mother's here," Dad and Tilly say in unison.

Mum bustles in, laden down with bags. "I've brought you some lunch. A woman from the South Manchester Coven kindly allowed me to borrow her kitchen," she says, handing Dad a huge casserole dish. "I told her all about you, darling, and she let me have the run of her spice rack!"

"Thanks, Mum, but I'm not hungry. Really tired."

"You're tired because that hospital kept feeding you E numbers, mash and bloody spam. I couldn't believe the stodge they were serving up."

"I need the extra calories – for healing or something."

"That's a matter of opinion." Mum flings open the kitchen window to let in fresh air but just gets horizontal rain. "My healthy stew will do you the world of good. Everyone at the commune compliments me on my cooking – even a carnivore like your father won't turn his nose up at this."

In keeping with the uneasy truce they have going, Dad

43

allows Mum to dish up for all of us while Tilly retreats to the arm of the sofa to watch daytime TV.

"Is this your own recipe, Angela?" says Dad, hiding leftover mung beans under a bit of wholemeal bread.

Mum preens. "I can write it down if you like."

Dad winks as he whips away my barely touched bowl. "Swap the beans for half a cow, it might be a goer." His voice is low but not quite low enough. Anyway, it's not true. It could have been the best fillet steak and we still couldn't have eaten it. I love Mum but seriously, she's the worst cook ever.

"We all know you prefer to feed your daughter processed white bread and bits of dead animal." Mum's mouth is like a cat's bum. "I knew it was a mistake letting Jess stay with you. She'd never have got sick if she'd come to the commune with me."

"She'd have got sick of you," says Dad. "You think chakras and chanting and bloody auras would have prevented this, do you? Anyway, it was Jess's choice. She wanted to live with me, remember?"

"And look what happened to her," shrieks Mum. "I've got just two words for you, Jeffrey. Saturated fat."

"I'm going to my room," I say. Tilly leaps up to follow me.

"Yes, go and have a nap, Jessie." Dad glares at Mum. "Angela, would you like a lift back to the hostel or can you make your own way?"

Mum bristles. "If you want me to leave, why don't you just say so?"

"I just did. Now, do you want a lift, or have you brought your broomstick with you?"

Truce well and truly over. I must be getting better. When I'd been properly ill, they were far too worried to bicker.

"Let me know if there's anything you want," Dad calls up the stairs as Mum slams the door. "I've told them at work not to expect me in all week."

"What?" Tilly looks outraged as she prowls around my bedroom, checking out my books and posters. "He's going to be here all week? Totally unacceptable. He doesn't leave us alone for two minutes and we need to make plans."

"He's my dad – he's just trying to look after me," I whisper. "Look, if you really are going to be sticking around, maybe it'd be easier if we told him."

She gives me a pitying look. "And I thought you had a modicum of common sense."

"He might … understand."

"Of course he won't!" Tilly grips my shoulders, her hands freezing. "He'll think you're out of your mind and we'll end up back in that decoratively challenged hospital room. Promise you won't tell him."

"OK, OK," I say, my heart racing. "I promise."

*

I sleep fitfully, tossing and turning all night. Maybe it's the strange dreams where I look into the mirror to see Tilly's blue eyes gazing back at me. Or maybe it's just her bony knees nudging my back as we top and tail in the narrow bed.

Next morning, I clear the books off the floor and ask Dad if I can have the old armchair that takes up too much space in the hall. "The physio said I should sit out rather than staying in bed."

He gives me a puzzled look. "Can't you sit in the living room?"

Tilly gives my bicep a vicious tweak.

"I want to read and, um, the light's much better in here," I say, rubbing my upper arm.

Dad looks unconvinced as my bedroom's north facing, but he promises to move the chair anyway. "Are you coming downstairs for breakfast? I've made porridge."

"What, no croissants?" Croissants are always the default breakfast when I'm ill.

"Porridge is better for you." Dad consults his dog-eared leaflet. "Says here we've got to watch your cholesterol. Those steroids can make you put on weight."

"Great, cheers, Dad." Clearly, me being ill has turned Dad into some sort of food fascist. Before my surgery, he enjoyed a Greggs pasty as much as the next man. Although not often at breakfast time.

Tilly nods in approval. "He's right, you know. We don't

46

want you to drop dead before we find out who ordered the hit on me."

She's becoming more and more dramatic by the day. Maybe it's time to embrace this conspiracy theory thing. At least then I might be able to get rid of her.

9

Tilly and I sit cross-legged on the striped duvet cover, facing one another. We're on our own. I lied to Dad and told him Mum was coming over and I lied to Mum and told her Dad was staying in. I'm relying on the fact that, as they're not talking to each other, they won't check. Now I've finally got her to myself, it's time to get some answers.

"So," I say, "you really think you were murdered?"

"I know I was murdered," she says.

"You said it was a car crash. Don't you think it might just have been an accident?"

"You could be right," Tilly concedes. "But that wouldn't explain why the bloody chauffeur drove downhill at top speed towards a dry-stone wall, opened his door and rolled out into the road like Jason bloody Statham. Would it?"

"Fair enough. Then what happened?"

"I hit my head on the glass partition and then I died." Her smooth forehead creases into a petulant frown. "I told you, I don't know what happened after that. Next thing I remember is being in the hospital with you. In *Manchester*."

"Why don't we google it?" I say before she starts going on again about the frozen north.

"Google what?"

"Your accident."

Her face brightens. "Genius! If the story was in that magazine, maybe it was on the news too."

Tilly hovers at my shoulder, muttering random phrases as I type into my new phone. "Sixteenth of September. Hertfordshire."

I look up. "I thought you lived in London?"

"Yes, but at the time of the accident I was weekending at a country estate."

I snigger. "Did you just say *weekending*?"

"Just get on with it. I'm sure the car was a green Jag. Type that in."

I tap *search* and we sit back to wait.

"That's it!" she shouts in excitement, pointing to a London newspaper article. I click on the image of a crumpled car which leads on to a studio portrait of Tilly wearing a school blazer and a familiar smirk.

Phew. I've already got my head around her *not* being a hallucination, but it's a relief to have it properly confirmed when I'm not off my face on post-op painkillers. I check the date of the newspaper article – just one day after my heart surgery.

"Heiress dies in tragic accident," I read out loud. "Blimey, Tilly. An actual heiress? That's unreal."

She shrugs. "Oh, that."

"So you had loads of money?"

"Well, I nearly did. If I hadn't died two weeks before my eighteenth birthday, sweetie. So frustrating – I was really looking forward to buying a round of cocktails in Bart's without having to use my fake ID."

I read on. "Matilda Spencer died at the scene. The driver survived the crash with cuts and bruises." I look up at her. "Is your name really Matilda?"

"Yes."

"And Spencer – any relation to Princess Diana?" I'm only winding her up, but she surprises me with a nod.

"On Daddy's side. Only very distant. Look at this bit: 'I asked her to wear her seat belt, but Miss Spencer refused,' said Mr Rossini in considerable distress." Tilly narrows her eyes. "The bloody little liar! He slowed down then asked me if I could lean forward to get a CD case which had gone under the front passenger seat."

"A CD?" I say. "Don't they have Spotify in London?"

"Classic car, sweetie. No Bluetooth, I guess. Anyway,

50

that's not even the worst thing. Guess which CD it was?"

I shrug.

"Michael Bublé," she says through gritted teeth.

No *way*. I look up at the posters on my bedroom walls. The Killers, Blossoms, Sam Fender. Jeez. Imagine a Bublé song being the last one you ever hear.

Tilly nods. "He waited until I'd unbuckled and then drove straight at the wall. I yelled at him to stop, but he just went faster. It was, like, so totally deliberate."

I check the newspaper report. "Says here that a deer hit the car causing him to swerve."

She shakes her head in disgust. "He'd already hit the deer when he came to pick me up. There was fur and yucky stuff all over the front bumper. When I asked him why he hadn't washed the car, he said he didn't want to make me late. The sneaky bastard must have planned the whole thing!"

I scroll down to find his name. Leo Rossini, Camberwell. "It doesn't make sense. Why would this Leo plan to kill you if he didn't even know you?"

Tilly looks thoughtful. "Maybe someone put him up to it – you know, paid him."

"But why would someone pay him to kill you?"

"I've really no idea. Jealousy, maybe?" Tilly drops her voice to a confidential whisper. "I was supposed to be a bridesmaid for Venetia Farquharson next month and the dresses have been specially designed by Marc Jacobs. I know plenty of girls who'd kill for a couture gown."

I've heard of Venetia Farquharson – a vacuous blonde influencer engaged to some famous rugby player. She's always on the front of *Hello* magazine, flashing an engagement ring with a rock the size of a Big Mac.

"You seriously think someone had you bumped off just to get their hands on your bridesmaid's frock?" Is she for real? "Don't be daft. It must have been something else."

"Well, that's what I need you to find out," Tilly says impatiently.

"And if I do, will you go away and leave me alone?"

She lifts her shoulders in a helpless shrug. "I can try."

"Better make a start then." I type "Leo Rossini, chauffeur" into the search engine.

The top results are an American actor, a lawyer and a drugs rep. I try adding "Camberwell" but no luck.

"Electoral roll?" suggests Tilly, supervising as I type.

"Nada. Hey, might he be listed on the chauffeur website?"

Tilly looks doubtful. "They're very old-fashioned and discreet. Daddy used them for years and my school always books them for social engagements. I bet they get most of their business from word of mouth so I'm not sure they'll have that sort of advertising, but you could look. They're called Jarvis and Woodhouse."

"Is this them?" The website's super basic. "Jarvis and

Woodhouse established 1952. It doesn't even have a price list."

"If you have to ask the price, you can't afford it," Tilly says haughtily.

"What about Leo's socials?" I type his name into Instagram. This time we're overrun with results. "Jeez. There are hundreds of Leo Rossinis. We'll be here all day."

"So sorry to inconvenience you, Jess. Did you have other plans?" says Tilly sarcastically. "If you want to get rid of me, you'd better start scrolling. We're looking for a man in his twenties – dark hair, quite good looking for a murderer."

"Yeah, a murderer." I've got goosebumps. "Even if we find him, what do you want me to do about it?"

"Do stop fussing. You're just like your father. He's a worrier too. Every time one of the alarms bleeped in that Intensive Care Unit, he was there hovering, checking you were still breathing." She leans over my shoulder to jab at the screen. "Look! That's him, I'm sure it is."

Leo J. Rossini.

I click on the image of a dark-eyed guy laughing into the camera. More images follow, nightclub or party scenes with Leo's arms around a succession of platinum blonde babes wearing minimal clothing. Leo leaning against the bonnet of a Rolls-Royce wearing a suit, his chauffeur cap at a jaunty angle. And a couple of moody close-ups with his arm in a sling and scratches down his face.

"Definitely him," Tilly says. "Let's see who he follows. Hmm, no one who follows me. Just a load of casinos and betting websites."

"So?"

Tilly rolls her eyes. "So, Jess, maybe this can help us track him down."

"I'm not eighteen. I'm not going to get into a casino, am I?" Just as well. I have no desire to play roulette with a murderer.

"We'll think about it while you look up my funeral." Tilly taps ineffectually at the search bar. "I want to see what everyone was wearing and what sort of flowers they put on my eco-friendly casket. I do hope they remembered sunflowers are my favourite."

10

This was a super bad idea. Once Tilly finds her obituary, there's no stopping her.

"Look!" she crows in delight, making me click on yet another link. "My school's having a memorial service for me."

"You were still at school? I thought you were supposed to be a *socialite*." I do the inverted commas thing with my fingers.

"Being upper sixth doesn't stop you going to parties, sweetie. Look, it's next Friday, can we go? Can we?"

It's like having an irritating little sister, asking for a lend of your new top and insisting you take her to a K-Pop concert.

"It's in Surrey," I object.

She rolls her eyes. "Hardly the moon."

"Might as well be. Dad's not going to let me go all that way on my own. Anyway, I've got a hospital appointment next Friday, I can't miss that."

"Your appointment's on Wednesday." Tilly consults Dad's hastily scribbled checklist on the dressing table. "Ooh, we could go on the train. I love the train, don't you?"

"I can't gate-crash a funeral," I say, flopping back on to the duvet. Even the thought of getting on a train exhausts me.

Tilly pouts. "It's not a funeral. It's a celebration of my life, see?" She taps her index finger on the screen. "All my school chums will be going – it would be so lovely to see them again. Please, Jess?"

"I can't just turn up," I hiss. "What do I say? I'm the girl who got Tilly's heart when she died?"

"We'll say you're my pen pal. My northern pen pal. We'll say my father arranged it to broaden my cultural education."

"What, so you could learn all about steel mills and outdoor lavvys?"

"Totally!" Tilly frowns. "Feasible, no?"

"No. Anyway, won't your mum and dad be there? They'll know you didn't have a pen pal."

She looks down at the duvet. "My parents are both dead. They died in a fire last year."

"Oh god, I'm so sorry, Tilly." I'm mortified. My parents might be pretty annoying (especially my mum), but at least they're still around. "What happened?"

"Our house was really old, lots of timber – it was an electrical fault."

"Were you there?" My heart speeds up uncomfortably.

A little shake of her head; her caramel curtain of hair shifts and falls neatly back into place. "I was away at boarding school. Everyone said how *lucky* I was."

"Have you got any brothers or sisters?"

"I was an only child. Mummy was nearly forty when I was born and she couldn't have any more babies after me." Tilly bites her trembling lip. "I know this sounds silly but when I first realized I was dead, I was almost happy because I thought at least I'd be with my mum and dad. It's been more than a month now, Jess, and I don't know if I'll ever see them again."

I place my hand on her shoulder – it feels chilly and weird, but I leave it there anyway. "This school thing. If you really want me to take you then I guess I'll see what I can do."

11

Dad takes my outpatient appointment seriously. "Wrap up warm, love," he insists, even though it's not cold for October.

"I'm fine," I say irritably as he drapes a cardigan around my shoulders. A pink one I don't even recognize. "What the hell is this?"

"Granny Ursula sent it. She said they were on offer: two for one in Primark. There's another one in the bag. Blue."

"Blue and pink? What does she think I am, newborn twins?"

Dad grins. "Put your fleece on, then. As long as you don't get cold, OK?"

Tilly peers out of the window at the buttery sunshine. "What a fusspot. I know we're in Grim-Up-North, but it isn't even raining. For once."

"I'll nip out and bring the car right up to the door." Dad inadvertently shoves Tilly out of the way as he picks up his keys. "I had to park miles down the road last night. Don't want you to have to walk too far."

"I'm supposed to walk," I say. "To build up my exercise tolerance or whatever."

Tilly steps aside to let Dad pass. "Is he always like this? Hovering over you?"

"No, he's pretty laid back usually. Once I'm better, he'll get back to normal and we're going to go on holiday. Swimming with dolphins," I add defensively.

We drive into the car park ten minutes before my appointment and Dad parks right next to the entrance in a disabled bay.

"You can't park here, Dad," I say as he belts round to open the car door for me. "You'll get a ticket."

"I'll move it once you're inside. There's no parking near the transplant clinic." He eyes a row of wheelchairs inside the entrance foyer.

"Don't even think about it," I say, as Tilly trails sniggering in my wake.

We wait two hours for the pleasure of precisely ten minutes with Mr Khan.

He's not impressed with my progress. "You shouldn't be

this breathless five weeks post-op. This heart is working twice as hard as it should. What have you been doing? Are you taking your tablets?" He looks sceptical as I nod, then hands me a little blue appointment card. "Call this number and make an appointment for cardiac rehab. And we'll see you back here in two weeks with a chest X-ray and ECG on arrival."

It's raining again so Dad insists on going off to collect the car.

Tilly shivers dramatically as we wait. "Thank goodness that's over. I thought we were going to be stuck in that bloody waiting room forever. Did you hear what he said about the heart working extra hard? Maybe it can't cope with both of us being here at once."

I hadn't thought about it like that. My new heart gives an unpleasant bump.

"Stop it," says Tilly, rubbing her chest. "I can feel it when you do that. To wear out one heart may be regarded as a misfortune; to wear out two looks like carelessness. Oscar Wilde said that, you know."

"I don't think Oscar Wilde said that."

"Well, maybe it was someone else." Her butterfly brain flits onwards. "Hey, have you ever heard that theory about us all having a certain number of heartbeats in our life?"

I shake my head.

"Well, you know little mice have really fast heart rates and don't live very long but big animals like elephants have slow heartbeats and they live until they're seventy or something? It's like the mice use up their lifetime supply of heartbeats quicker, get it?"

"Sounds like a load of pants to me."

"It's true, though," Tilly says. "Big mammals do live longer than smaller ones."

"Are you talking about the size of my bum again?" I start to laugh. "Hey, nothing wrong with a big booty, especially if it means I get to live longer. It's a win–win situation."

"Whatever. Make a joke. But if it's true that this heart can't cope with both of us, the sooner you get rid of me the better." She flicks her hair over her shoulder. "If you want to make it to your next birthday, Jess, you'd better start helping me."

She's annoying but she could be right.

"I've been looking up some stuff about transplants," I say to Dad once we're in the car with the heating turned up full blast. "There's a memorial service for this girl who died and donated her organs – I thought maybe I should go and show my support."

"That's a nice idea, love," he says. "I'll come with you. When is it?"

"The day after tomorrow."

He frowns. "That's my first full day back at work. Is it morning or afternoon? Maybe I could go in a bit late."

"Erm. It's in Surrey, actually, Dad."

61

"Surrey? Near *London*?" Dad looks shocked. "You can't go gallivanting off down there, Jess. You've just had major heart surgery – you could have died."

Tilly kicks the back of my seat. "Here we go again. There's only one person around here who actually died and that's me."

"This girl," I say, "her accident was the day of my transplant."

Dad stares at me. "You think she was your heart donor?"

"Maybe. Yeah. It all fits."

"Careful," urges Tilly. "Remember what we agreed; he won't understand if you tell him about me."

Dad starts the engine. "It's just a coincidence, Jess."

"It's bloody not!" I snap in frustration. "I told you – she was there in the hospital when I woke up."

He thumps his hand on the steering wheel. "Not this business again."

Tilly pinches my shoulder with chilly fingers. "Stop it, Jess! He thinks you've lost the plot."

I ignore her and turn back to Dad, desperate for him to understand. "I know you don't believe me, but it's her heart, honestly it is. I can tell."

"Calm down, love," he says. "You'll make yourself ill. You don't want to end up—"

"Back in hospital!" shrieks Tilly, leaning between the two front seats. "Shut up, Jess! Do you know what he's got in his wallet? Do you? The business card for that psychologist woman at the hospital – do you really want him to get on the phone to *her*?"

They're both talking at once and I cover my ears.

"Just worried about you, love," Dad says.

Now she's started, Tilly can't or won't stop. "He thinks you're *loopy*. Do you know what he told your mum the other day? That he'd heard you talking to yourself, just like you did when you were in hospital."

I glare at Dad. "Did you tell Mum I've been talking to myself?"

"How did you know that?" he says. "You were asleep."

"You wouldn't believe me if I told you," I say truthfully.

"Hallelujah!" says Tilly. "She finally sees the light. Like you said, he won't *believe* you."

"We're just trying to look after you, love. Last month, I really thought we were going to lose you." Dad looks worn out.

My anger shifts into guilt. "I've got to start doing normal things sooner or later."

"I get that. But you're not serious about this memorial thing, are you?"

I drop my eyes to my lap. "It was just an idea."

Tilly juts out her chin. "We'll see about that."

12

When we get home, Tilly drags me straight upstairs.

"What are you going to wear to my memorial party?" she demands, peering into my open wardrobe.

"Hadn't thought about it," I say, crawling on to the bed. All I want to do is sleep but Tilly's not having any of it. She links my arm and marches me over to the wardrobe.

"St Agatha's is super smart; we don't want you to stand out any more than necessary."

"Thanks a lot."

Tilly laughs gaily. "There's not a lot we can do about the fact that you'll be the only person there sounding like an extra from *Coronation Street*."

"If only we had time for elocution lessons," I say sarkily, flicking through hangers. "What about this?"

She frowns as I pull out the dress I wore for my great-aunt's funeral last year. "That won't do. Navy or dark green perhaps, but definitely not black."

"But it's a funeral."

"I told you, it's not a funeral, it's a celebration of my life," Tilly says, peering into the bottom of the wardrobe. "What about shoes? Everyone will know there's something dodgy about you if you're wearing the wrong shoes."

"What, they'll guess I'm being stalked by the vengeful ghost of a former pupil?" I pull an agonised face. "Or will they just think I'm poor?"

Tilly ignores me. "Where are the rest of your clothes?"

Usually on the floor, but the blue carpet's mostly visible. Dad must have put a wash on while I was in hospital.

"This is it." I sweep my arm across to encompass the IKEA wardrobe and chest of drawers. "That's your lot."

Tilly looks appalled. "But it's all leggings and trainers. Haven't you got anything else?"

"You can't talk," I say. "I haven't seen you out of those jeans and jacket once."

She looks down at herself. "This is what I was wearing the day I died. Smart but casual – I was on my way to a lovely lunch at Portia's Pantry with Aunt Lulu. I seem to be stuck with it for now. Could have been worse; the jacket's brand new and at least I wasn't wearing my fat jeans."

I start to laugh before I realize she's not kidding.

"Tilly, I've seen gerbils with bigger backsides than yours," I say. "In what parallel universe did you have a pair of fat jeans?"

"I *did*." She drops her voice to a confiding whisper. "Designer, of course, but with a stretch waistband. So comfy, sweetie. I used to wear them when I went out for afternoon tea."

"A stretch waistband?" I do my best *Home Alone* face. "No way!"

"It's true!"

She never gets when I'm taking the piss. "Anyway, no one's going to care what *I'm* wearing," says Tilly unironically, narrowing her eyes at my favourite trackie bottoms. "Are you sure you haven't got anything else tucked away – a lovely outfit off at the dry cleaner or somewhere?"

"Absolutely positive."

"Maybe we could go shopping. There's a Harvey Nicks and a Selfridges in Manchester, isn't there?" She's almost salivating. "I can pretend I'm back in London."

Just thinking about doing an epic trawl round the shops exhausts me. "I'm knackered. Anyway, there's no way Dad'll let me go shopping on my own."

"Can't you borrow something?"

"Who from? My mother?"

"The tie-dye queen?" Tilly shudders. "I think not.

What about your best friends? I always used to swap frocks with Bea and Tanika."

I shake my head. "My mates all live miles away. When Mum and Dad split up, we were living in Sheffield. Mum moved to Wales and Dad was offered a promotion back here. We only moved in August."

"So you haven't made any friends yet?"

"Nope. I'd only been at my new school a few days when I got ill. The kids were nice – two of the girls even came to see me in hospital, but we're not exactly at the clothes swapping stage."

"Hmm." Tilly points into the wardrobe. "Is that your uniform?"

"We don't wear uniform in sixth form." I pull out the hanger. "This was from my old school. Don't know why I even kept it."

"The skirt's pleated. That might do with this little lilac sweater, I suppose."

"Whatever. You're the boss," I say, flopping back on to the bed.

"Yes, I am." Tilly looks gratified. "It's good you've finally accepted it, sweetie. It'll make your life so much easier."

13

Tilly gazes out of the grimy window with a petulant expression. "I've never travelled second class before."

"Maybe you should get a life," I say. "Oops, sorry, you can't."

Luckily, we've had the train carriage to ourselves for most of the journey. I turn away from her sulky face to watch the scenery rushing past and then check my phone. Dad's sent me a GIF of two poodles having a pedicure. I'm guessing he believed my outrageous fib about spending the day at an organic spa in Cheshire with my mother.

Tilly fidgets in the opposite seat. "There are cigarette

burns in the upholstery. I thought all public transport was supposed to be no smoking."

"Stop whinging, Tilly. You wanted to go to this thing and we're going. Sorry it's not an air-conditioned limo or a private jet but funds are limited, yeah?" After paying for my return train ticket to Surrey, I've only got about sixty quid left.

"Please will you stop worrying about money. I'll see what I can do."

"How? You're dead, remember?" A well-dressed man comes to the sliding door of the carriage, sees me talking to myself and goes away again.

"You have no idea how resourceful I can be." Tilly bounces in her seat. "Oh, look, this is our stop."

We sway along the aisle to the carriage door and step down on to the picture postcard pretty platform.

"Where now?" I follow her through the barrier towards the cab rank outside the station.

"Taxi! Taxi!" Tilly's already pushing to the front of the orderly queue. She swings round as no one takes any notice. "Bloody hell! You'll have to do it."

I station myself wearily at the end of the line. I'm already knackered and we haven't even got there yet.

In the taxi, Tilly rattles off last minute instructions. "Thank goodness you have an acceptable Christian name, Jess. Just imagine if you were called Kylie or Leanne!" She laughs her nasty tinkly laugh. "We have to find someone suitable on the guest list that you can pretend to be, maybe someone who left last summer."

"Huh? I thought I was supposed to be your pen pal?"

"Try to keep up. This is the easiest way to get you inside; the security at these events is tremendous. I think there was a Jessica in upper school when I was in lower."

"Upper and lower? Did you actually go to school this century?" I take a swig of bottled water and cram my lunchtime tablets into my mouth. "God, I hope there'll be something to eat. These are supposed to be taken after food."

"There'll probably be canapés. And Mrs Braithwaite from the kitchen does the most gorgeous cakes." Tilly looks glum. "Not that I'll be able to have any."

The taxi drops us at the school gates and I negotiate the sweep of gravel driveway feeling self-conscious in the heels I hardly ever wear, especially as my ankles are still swollen. I've already changed out of my jeans in the cramped train toilet while Tilly hovered, complaining my black bra strap was showing and that I was wearing the wrong type of knickers.

We round the corner to see a large honey-coloured house covered in ivy.

"Isn't it gorgeous? Don't you just love the gardens?" Tilly surges towards the throng of well-dressed people milling about on the landscaped lawns. My heart strains as I hobble behind.

"I guess," I say, wondering if I'll ever feel this nostalgic about my own seventies built comprehensive. On balance, I decide not.

"See her at the door? That's Harriet Compton-Burnett, she's Head Girl." Tilly tows me towards a tall blonde wearing a velvet Alice band. "Pretend you recognize her, go on!"

"Yo, Harriet!" I wave as the blonde girl steps back in surprise.

Tilly shakes her head in despair. "You should have offered her your cheek, silly." She skips past me to skim read the clipboard Harriet holds. "There we are. Jessica Bingham-Jones. Two years above me but her cousin was in my dorm. Tell Harriet you're her; she won't have a clue. Too much inbreeding – all the Compton-Burnett girls have memories like sieves."

"Jess Bingham-Jones," I mutter as directed.

Harriet flicks cold blue eyes down the list and nods. "Oh, yah. Go straight down to the library."

My footsteps echo on the parquet flooring as we walk down a dark corridor dominated by oak panelling and enormous oil paintings of old women with disapproving expressions. It smells of furniture polish and beeswax, unlike my own school (school dinners, LYNX Africa and bubble-gum flavoured vapes behind the bike sheds).

Tilly turns left into a royal-blue carpeted foyer and leads me into an old-fashioned library with a huge fireplace and domed ceiling. Skinny teenage girls with sleek shampoo-commercial hair mingle with well-dressed

71

women in jewel-coloured dresses. Even the younger girls wear expensive-looking jewellery and some of the teachers have black university gowns over their knee-length dresses. I smooth down my old school skirt and follow as Tilly charges ahead, pausing to pick off a smoked salmon blini and a duck parcel along the way. The waitress looks stunned – no one else seems to be eating anything.

Tilly watches closely as I chew. "One advantage to being dead," she says, "is not being hungry all the time."

I pretend to speak into my mobile as we agreed. "How come you were hungry all the time? I thought you said the food here was fabulous."

"Just because food's fabulous, doesn't mean you should eat it." Tilly rolls her eyes.

"Dieting, you mean? No way, you're tiny."

"*The less there is of you, the more people think of you.*" She licks her lips as I select a miniature cheesecake.

"Is that a quote?" I mutter, my mouth full. "That's just sad."

Tilly cranes her neck to see past a crowd of people. "When I get to heaven, I expect I'll be able to eat whatever I like. Look, there are Bea and Tanika." She waves energetically at yet another skinny blonde, then drops her arm with a sigh as the girl stares straight past. "Can we go over?"

"It's your funeral." I follow her towards the two girls.

"Stand just here," instructs Tilly. "I expect they're talking about me and I want to listen."

Five minutes later though and the pair of them are still discussing what they're going to wear to some society wedding at Christmas.

"That's the one where I was supposed to be a bridesmaid," says Tilly dolefully. "I wonder who they've chosen to replace me – I bet it's that little bitch Jemima Montague. Same dress size as me but super short legs; they'll have to chop six inches off the bottom. How frustrating not knowing. You'd presume being dead, you'd get a direct line to all the gossip."

"Do you want me to try talking to them?" I say into my phone, hoping she'll say no. They look seriously intimidating.

"Would you, Jess?" Tilly gives me a trembly smile. "The Indian girl is Tanika and Bea's the blonde. You can say you've heard all about them from my letters."

I can't keep up. "So we're back on the pen friend thing?"

"Oh, yes. There's not much point in pretending to be Jess Bingham-Jones now you're in; Bea's known her since nursery. She dated Jess BJ's brother, Eddie, for, like, the whole of the winter season at Klosters last year."

Jeez. I grab a glass of buck's fizz from a passing waitress.

Tilly raises her eyebrows in disapproval. "You're not supposed to be drinking."

"Dutch courage," I say, without moving my lips. If I get through this situation in one piece, I could launch a sparkling new career as a ventriloquist.

14

I've never realized before how rude posh people can be. I spend at least ten minutes trying to join the conversation, but the two girls slowly turn their backs on me like I'm some pervy bloke at a festival.

Tilly looks anxious, her eyes darting between them as they move on from wedding outfits to the fundraiser Halloween ball for the leaking school chapel roof. No mention of the person whose memorial service this is supposed to be. Some mates. Even though I haven't seen Bex and Nisha for months, I know they'd never do that to me.

Feeling sorry for Tilly, I tap the nearest girl on the

shoulder. She turns to fix chilly navy-blue eyes on my hand. How many blue-eyed blondes are there around here? It's like walking into the House of Lannister.

"Can I help you?" she says.

"Hi, er …"

"Bea," hisses Tilly at my side.

"Bea," I say, with an inane grin. "I've heard about you. You were Tilly's friend."

Her eyes drop to my hand, which lingers on the sleeve of her expensive-looking silk dress. As I remove it, she raises her hostile gaze to my face.

"And you are?"

"I'm Jess Bing— " I correct myself as Tilly shakes her head ferociously. "Jess Bailey. I was mates with Tilly too."

Bea's eyebrows shoot up towards her high forehead. "Really? I don't remember her mentioning you."

"Probably because I live in Manchester."

"That explains a lot." She stares at my skirt as her friend stifles a giggle.

"We used to write to each other," I persist.

"Aah." The other girl, Tanika, widens her eyes. "Were you involved in one of her little charity things, then?"

Tilly gives an encouraging nod.

"Yeah, that's it," I say. "Did you get involved with Tilly's charity stuff too?"

"Now and again."

"Huh. Like, not ever," corrects Tilly.

Bea gives my outfit an appraising look, probably calculating exactly how much it didn't cost. "Your people must be in a bit of a spot now Tilly's dead. You'll have to find another source of funding, won't you?"

Cheeky cow.

"You've got it all wrong. I wasn't, like, part of the charity," I say. "Me and Tilly were mates."

"Of course you were," says Bea dismissively. "And I expect you're hoping for the opportunity to make some more *mates* today. Excuse us if we don't have the time or the inclination to introduce you."

Rude or what? I freeze, mortified, heat flooding my face.

"Oh, don't be a bitch all your life, Beatrice," says a bored voice from behind me.

I turn to see a glamorous redhead standing there, hands on curvy hips. She smiles at me and leans in conspiratorially but doesn't bother to lower her voice. "Ignore them, darling. They think they're channelling *Made in Chelsea*, but they're more like St Aggie's answer to *Mean Girls*."

I let out a squeak of laughter as the pair turn on their high heels and swish away through the crowd.

"Ciao," calls my rescuer, wiggling coral fingernails at their rigid backs. She turns to me with a mischievous eye roll. "Sorry about that."

"No need for *you* to apologize." I glance at Tilly beside

me but, for once, she seems lost for words. "I'm Jess, by the way."

The redhead turns to swipe two glasses from a passing waitress and hands one to me. "I'm Georgie Morley. I was Tilly's sort of …"

"God-sister," prompts Tilly, finding her voice at last.

"God-sister, I guess," finishes Georgie.

"God-sister?" I say. "How does that even work?"

Georgie smiles. "So, my ma was Tilly's godmother. Tilly used to call her Aunt Lulu."

"And my dad was Georgie's godfather," adds Tilly. "She called him Uncle Ollie."

"Our parents grew up together," they say in stereo. It's super distracting.

"I get it," I say. "So you and Tilly were at school together?"

"Not really." Georgie shakes her head, tossing long auburn locks over one shoulder. "I'm six years older – by the time Tilly started here I was upper sixth so we had our own sets of friends. I never understood what she saw in those two girls, but she wasn't always the best judge of character, poor darling – Tilly Billy, I always called her."

Seriously terrible nickname, but Tilly doesn't seem to mind. She's already snuggled up to Georgie's armpit, looking too rapturous to even notice I'm on to my second drink. She looks up with brimming eyes. "I never dreamed for a minute Georgie would be here. Thank you for bringing me, Jess."

Oblivious to the one-sided embrace going on, Georgie takes a sip of her drink and frowns before abandoning her half-full glass on a nearby bookshelf. "I see they're saving a few quid by being stingy with the champers again – this is all bloody bucks and hardly any fizz. So how about you? Were you a friend of Tilly's?"

"Yes," I begin cautiously, waiting for a nod of approval. Tilly's otherwise engaged: eyes closed and both arms wound around Georgie's waist, although this doesn't impair Georgie's ability to scoop a mini meringue from a passing waiter's tray. I'm impressed.

"She talked about your family," I say. "The last time was just before she died – I think she was meeting your mum for lunch?"

"That was the day of the accident. I was at the restaurant too, decided to join Ma and Tilly at the last minute, but of course she never arrived." Georgie's brown eyes fill with tears and she wipes them on the back of her hand. "God, I promised myself I wouldn't cry. Can we change the subject? I heard you mention the charity, is that how you knew her?"

"We were pen friends, actually. We've been writing to each other since we were little." I try to attract Tilly's attention, hoping Georgie doesn't think I'm perving on her chest.

Tilly looks up. "My dad met your dad, remember?"

Oh yeah. "Tilly's dad met mine at some work thing. He thought it would be good for Tilly to have a northern pen pal – you know, see another side of life."

Georgie smiles. "Typical Uncle Ollie. He was such a sweetheart – always reminding us there was a world outside London, with normal, less fortunate people existing in it." She puts her coral fingertips to her mouth. "Whoops, that sounded rude. Now you'll think I'm as bad as those two over there." She waves her half-eaten meringue towards Bea and Tanika with a peal of laughter.

Tilly gives a delighted squeal. "Jess, look! She's wearing my Tiffany ring!"

It's true – on the little finger of her left hand, Georgie is wearing a pretty silver ring made of interwoven leaves. It matches exactly the one Tilly wears on her right middle finger.

"Wow," I say, leaning in for a better look. "Your ring is just like the one Tilly had."

"Darling, it is the same ring." Georgie's bottom lip wobbles. "My mother had to go and identify the er ... body and afterwards, the hospital gave her a bag with the things Tilly had been wearing. I know I shouldn't have, but I took the ring out and slipped it on my finger – it's stayed there ever since. I guess I should hand it over to the solicitor, but it makes me feel closer to her wearing it." She smiles through her tears. "Gosh, you're not going to dob me in, are you?"

"No way," I say. "Anyway, I reckon Tilly would have wanted you to have it."

"You really think so?" Georgie twists her little finger, looking anxious.

"Positive," I say, as Tilly gives me a vigorous nod.

"Oh, balls! Here comes The Fox with her begging bowl." Georgie winces as a stocky lady in a tweedy skirt strides towards us. "Collecting for this term's worthy cause. Quick, zip up your handbag before she wheedles you out of your last tenner."

"The Fox?" I raise my eyebrows in question, but Tilly answers first.

"Miss Fox-Longley – the headmistress, you know. She can't stand Georgie." Tilly giggles. "She was deputy head when Georgie was in Lower Sixth. The girls played some totally hilarious tricks on her."

"So she was deputy head when you were here?" I say to Georgie, who seems surprised. "Tilly told me about the pranks you played when you were in sixth form."

"Gosh, it seems like yesterday." Georgie gives a nostalgic sigh. "I still think about that chilli powder on the staff loo seat. Ouch!" She and Tilly burst into simultaneous giggles.

"Georgina, how very nice to see you enjoying yourself." The headmistress glides to a majestic halt in front of us, a frosty smile flickering on her lips. "I thought I might see your mother here today."

80

"She's in Barbados," says Georgie.

"Of course she is." Miss Fox-Longley arches her eyebrows as she holds out an ornate silver bowl stuffed with twenties and maybe even fifty-pound notes – I'm not sure I've ever seen one in real life before. "We're collecting for a new hockey pavilion. Perhaps you'd like to contribute, Georgina, although I seem to recall you weren't much of a team player yourself."

"Bitch," says Tilly, cuddling Georgie's arm defensively. "And totally untrue. Georgie has amazing people skills; she works as an events organizer, you know. Does the most fabulous parties."

Georgie smiles politely. "I'd love to chip in, Miss F-L, but I'm afraid I never carry cash."

"We cater for all methods of payment." Miss Fox-Longley burrows into her cardigan pocket and produces a card machine which she thrusts under Georgie's nose.

"I'll donate later. On the website." Georgie waves an airy hand. "I'm afraid I have to dash now. Work, you know."

"Really?" The headmistress lengthens the word into at least four syllables. "I presumed you were a lady of leisure these days."

As Georgie's face falls and then swiftly recovers, Tilly meets my eye with a hiss of annoyance.

"Georgie's an events organiser actually," I say, surprised to find myself speaking up. "She does seriously amazing parties."

"How very nice. Well, I must mingle." Miss Fox-Longley adjusts her cardigan. "Send my regards to your mother, Georgina."

Georgie nudges me as the headmistress moves away. "Hey, thanks. You didn't have to stick up for me."

"No worries. Anyway, you stuck up for me earlier."

"I don't get it." Georgie's brown eyes are puzzled. "How did you know about my job?"

"Tilly mentioned it. I reckon she was really proud of you," I say as Tilly reaches over to give my hand a grateful squeeze. "She talked about you and your mum a lot."

"Sounds like you knew her pretty well. I can't understand why she never mentioned you." Georgie shakes her head and looks at her tiny diamond studded watch. "I really have got to go. I've got a charity auction tonight and I must nip to the dry cleaner on the way home. Hey, can I give you a lift anywhere?"

Tilly bounces at my side. "Say yes, say yes! Pleeease, Jess!"

"Won't we miss the speeches?" I say, for Tilly's benefit. "The headmistress might have some nice stuff to say."

Tilly looks dubious as she clings to Georgie's arm. "That dreary old bag? I doubt it — she never liked me anyway. Let's go with Georgie instead. She's got a gorgeous car; wait 'til you see it!"

Georgie smiles mischievously and, just for a second, I'm convinced she can hear what Tilly's saying. "Don't tell

82

me you want to stay? Fox–Longley will just be droning on about donations for the chapel roof or the hockey pavilion or whatever it is this week. And it's bloody freezing in here. I know the school's a bit strapped for cash, but I can't believe they've cut back on their heating bill." Georgie flings a cashmere scarf across her goose-bumped bosom, but this doesn't deter Tilly, who stays put.

"OK," I say. "If you're honestly sure, a lift to the train station would be great."

15

Wow. Georgie's car is one of those open top silver sporty numbers you only see in films with Hugh Grant in them.

"It's an old-style Porsche," Tilly says. "Isn't it totally gorgeous? Her last stepfather gave it to her for her twenty-first."

"Get in!" Georgie beckons from the driver's seat then delves into the glove box and produces a silk scarf. "Here, take this."

I stare down at the unexpected gift, checking out the designer label. Is Georgie so minted she goes around handing out Hermès scarves to people she's only just met?

Tilly sniggers. "Duh! It's for your hair, silly. Haven't you ever driven in an open top before? Well, it plays havoc with your hairdo. What are you waiting for, Jess? Put it on."

I shake out the silk square, fold it into a large triangle and await further instructions.

"God's sake. Under the nape, not under your chin," Tilly reprimands as I pull it over my hair. "Unless you want to look like the bloody Queen?"

Actually, I feel more like Grace Kelly as I slide into the passenger seat. The leather's soft as butter.

Georgie tucks long red hair beneath her own scarf and smiles across. "Ready? Seat belt on and let's go."

The engine gives a throaty roar as I snap the belt into place. I try not to wince but can't help it; it's still super sore across my breastbone.

Georgie's sharp eyes miss nothing. "All right there, darling? You look as if you're in pain."

"I'm OK. I've just had some surgery, that's all."

"What sort of surgery?"

"Erm, boob job," I improvise.

Tilly chortles from the bucket seat behind as Georgie looks surprised. I'm only a 34B.

"Reduction," I amend hastily. "They were huge before. Ginormous."

Georgie nods, keeping her eyes on the winding drive. "What a pain."

My phone vibrates on my lap as we veer out of the school gates and on to the open road. I fish it out – two missed calls from Dad. I'll just have to phone him from the train.

"Tell me about you and Tilly," shouts Georgie over the throbbing engine as we motor along, the wind streaming through my silk-scarfed hair. "Were you involved in all her charity stuff?"

That's the second time someone's mentioned Tilly's charity work today. She doesn't exactly strike me as the benevolent benefactress type. I look over my shoulder to see her nod.

"A bit," I say, hoping Georgie doesn't ask for details.

She looks sad. "I worry how they're going to manage now that Tilly's gone. I often think I should have done more to help. If you're involved, Jess, maybe you could keep me up to date?" Her face brightens. "We could meet for lunch one day and you could tell me all about it. And we could share Tilly stories. God, I miss her so much, but the only person who knew her like I did was my mother and she doesn't do emotion. As soon as the funeral was over, she buggered off to Barbados."

"Say yes," Tilly breathes into my ear. "Please, Jess!"

"I'm going back to Manchester today." I avoid Tilly's furious glare. "But maybe another time? I might be coming to London soon."

"Next time you're down, then, I'll take you out for lunch. Or afternoon tea, if you like. I know some gorgeous

86

places." Georgie pulls up near the train station and digs out an expensive-looking business card. "Here's my number, call any time. Ciao for now."

I wave as she roars off. Too late, I realize I'm still wearing the Hermès scarf.

Tilly sulks all the way to Manchester.

"Look, it's hardly a priority, is it?" I say, slumped against the window seat.

Tilly tilts her pointy chin. "What's that supposed to mean?"

"We've got a job to do – find out why you were murdered." The only other person in the carriage is a student wearing headphones and facing the other way, but I still lower my voice. "We're supposed to be tracking down this Leo. Georgie's not going to know anything about him, is she?"

"She went to my funeral. Maybe she saw someone there."

"What? Like a spivvy bloke with dark glasses and a violin case with a gun in it?"

"Fine, take the piss." Tilly's lower lip wobbles. "You've no idea what I'm going through."

"Likewise." I fold my arms and unfold them again, my chest still stinging from the bloody seat belt.

Tilly changes tack. "Please, Jess. I really want to see her again. So, when we're back in London, can we?"

"Maybe. If you stop whining. And only if we have time. I still haven't figured out how we're going to do this – it was bad enough making up an excuse for today. How the hell do we get away from my dad for long enough to track anybody down?"

"Light bulb moment!" Tilly squeaks. "Just use the same excuse as today. Your mum keeps inviting you to visit this bloody commune. This time, you say yes."

"I don't know about that, Tilly. They might not even have Wi-Fi. And I've got a hospital appointment the week after next."

"I don't mean actually go there, you pleb." Tilly makes an impatient noise. "Just tell your dad you're going to visit your mum and tell your mum you're staying with your dad. Simple. That gives us at least a week to go to London and solve the mystery."

"London's a big place. We don't even know where to look for this guy."

"We could hire a private detective."

"And ask him to do what? Find out why Leo murdered you?"

"No." Tilly gives me a scathing look. "Find Leo's address, obviously."

"How much is that going to cost? I've only got sixty quid. Maybe another two hundred in my savings account."

Tilly frowns. "That won't be enough. Haven't you got a credit card?"

"Nope. Just a debit card," I say. "I'm only seventeen, remember?"

"Well, it won't be a problem, sweetie. I've got pots of money."

"In case you've forgotten, you're dead. Won't your bank accounts have been frozen by the solicitor?"

"Only the ones they know about." Tilly gives a little cat-like smirk.

"What? You've got some secret bank account?" I snigger. "Yeah, right. Who do you think you are, a spy or something?"

"Not a spy, sweetie, just spoilt rotten." She shrugs. "I just really wanted one and so Daddy set it up for fun. You don't need a bank card, you just have to remember a special number. It's a little private bank, see?"

I nod doubtfully but I don't see, not really. Tilly waits, clearly sensing my scepticism.

"Look, I promise I can get the money." Her expression swaps from pleading to persuasive. "We can do this, Jess! We'll make a brilliant team – it'll be just like *Scooby-Doo*!"

"Hardly." I laugh. "Unless you reckon we're going to find this Leo in a haunted hotel or some spooky deserted fairground. Anyway, we already know who the ghost is."

"Yes and I'm not the baddie here." Tilly grits her teeth, emphasizing every word. "We know who did it, Jess. Between us, we just need to solve the mystery of *why*."

"You make it sound so easy," I say. "In *Scooby-Doo*, there were four meddling kids and a dog. We've only got two in our team, and one of them's dead."

"You're such a spoilsport." Tilly folds her arms and flops back against the seat. "If you're not going to help, then you'd better get used to the idea of me sticking around. Forever."

"Jeez, fine." I give in. "If you really can get the money then I guess I can give you a week, as long as I'm back home in time for my appointment. Does this fancy bank of yours have a branch in Manchester?"

"'Fraid not."

"London?"

Tilly pinches her finger and thumb together. "A smidgeon further than that."

"Further than *London*?"

"God's sake, Jess, stop sounding like the town mouse and the country mouse."

"Am I supposed to be the country mouse in this scenario just because I don't live in bloody London? Manchester's hardly the back of beyond, Tilly."

"You're totally right, sweetie." She gives me a patronising smile. "And the best thing about Manchester is it does have an airport. Quite a big one."

"So?"

"That's why I asked about the credit card. We need to book a plane ticket."

"A plane ticket? To where?"

Tilly doesn't meet my eye. "Geneva."

16

Dad completely swallows the story about me going to visit Mum.

"We had a really nice time at the spa and she asked me to come and stay for a bit," I say, avoiding his eye.

Dad looks anxious. "Is there proper electricity and central heating in this commune place? I don't want you getting cold."

"Mum showed me some photos. It looks really nice, Dad." I shake the rain off my hood and hang my coat on the radiator to dry. "And she says the weather's loads better than here."

"That's something, then." Dad gives me a reluctant nod. "How long were you thinking of staying, love?"

"A few days, maybe a week. I've got a hospital appointment the Wednesday after, so I have to be back for then anyway."

"I'll drive you to Wales in the morning. I can always go in to work late."

This is a complication we can do without. I ignore Tilly's throat-cutting gestures in the background. "No need, Dad, I can get the train. You've already taken a shedload of time off work because of me. Anyway, you know Mum drives you crackers. She'll only say something to wind you up."

Dad nods. "If you're sure, I'll drop you at the train station. Promise me you'll look after yourself. And if you're not happy, I'll come and get you any time you like."

Once Dad's gone to bed, we make plans.

"I don't get why we have to go all the way to Geneva just to go to a bank," I say.

"Because Swiss banks do tend to be in Switzerland, sweetie."

"You mean it's a proper Swiss bank account?" I yelp and then lower my voice in case Dad hears. "Like in films with international art thieves and Nazi war criminals?"

"Yes! Isn't it fun?" Tilly bounces on the bed, looking gleeful.

"I don't know, Tilly. I thought we were just going to London. On a *train*. I'm not supposed to go abroad for the first year."

"Oh, nobody takes any notice of that."

"Says you. I'm the one who's had major surgery." As if I didn't need reminding, my heart speeds up to double time. "What if the wires in my chest set off the airport alarms? What if I get a DVT on the plane?"

Tilly rolls her eyes. "What the hell is a DVT?"

"You know – a blood clot in my leg." Dad's not the only person to have read up on the scary stuff.

"Do stop fussing. It's only a two-hour flight. If we go early enough, we can even come back the same day. I'm good for the cash and once we get there, money will be no object," Tilly says grandly.

"That's all right, then," I say, sarkily. "I'm sure EasyJet will accept an I.O.U. saying 'Tilly Spencer is good for it'."

She ignores me. "Look, if we can just get the money, the rest will follow. Please, Jess?"

I hesitate, reluctant to encourage her. "I guess I could borrow one of Dad's credit cards to pay for the flight. As long as the ticket isn't mega-expensive, he might not notice."

Tilly swallows heroically. "We could always … fly budget."

"Slum it, you mean? Come on then, you poor little princess." She follows as I sneak downstairs and slide Dad's wallet out of his jacket pocket.

93

He's already gone to bed, but Tilly keeps watch while I shuffle through numerous credit cards using the torch on my phone. Mr J Bailey. Jeffrey Bailey. Mr Jeffrey Bailey. J Bailey. Bingo.

"That's the one!" Tilly reaches over to grab it, but her fingers swipe right through the plastic. "Will he notice it's missing?"

"Probably not, as long as we don't hang on to it for too long." I replace the wallet. "He only checks his cards when the bill comes at the end of the month."

"We'll pay it back before then," Tilly says confidently.

We creep back to my bedroom and close the door, Dad's credit card burning a hole in my dressing gown pocket.

"How handy, both your names beginning with a J," says Tilly. "You could even use that card in person if you knew his PIN."

"I do know it," I say, looking up budget airlines. "Dad uses the same number for everything. 1999 – the year Man United won the treble."

Tilly looks perplexed. "What does that even mean?"

"Just football stuff. Bollocks, there are no cheap flights over the weekend. The next one is on Tuesday morning. Seventy quid each way." My hands are sweating as I key in Dad's credit card details. "The return flight's seven forty-five p.m. Will that give us enough time?"

"Oh, I think so, sweetie." Tilly's cocky now she's got

her own way. "But look for return flights to London not Manchester. Once we've got the money, we can fly straight there to start our search. Leo Rossini had better watch himself. The *Scooby-Doo* girls are on the case!"

17

It feels super weird checking in at the airport on my own. My bag isn't heavy, but my sternum still feels like it might snap open as I juggle my rucksack containing a shedload of tablets and a pink holdall with a dodgy zip stuffed with enough underwear for a week. To my relief, we get through security without setting off any alarms, but I have to steer Tilly away from the VIP lounge to the normal waiting area.

"Why do poor people even bother to go on holiday when they have to sit on seats like this?" She indicates the rows of joined-up metal chairs. "How do you sleep if your flight's been delayed?"

I point to the floor. "Is that gold plated enough for you?"

"Ha, ha." Tilly scowls as I head towards the shops. "Where are we going now?"

"Pharmacy," I mutter into my phone. "I'm going to buy some flight socks."

"What on earth for?"

"I told you; I'm not supposed to fly anywhere for the first year. I might get a blood clot."

"Sorry, sweetie. Totally forgot you were ninety-four."

"Listen, mate, if I drop dead on the plane, you don't get to find out why you were murdered."

But Tilly's not paying attention. She's hovering at the doorway of the cosmetics hall, eyes closed and taking ecstatic and unnecessary deep breaths.

"God, I've missed this," she says. "Can we take a quick look at what's new in at Jo Malone?"

"Jo Malone? Seriously?" It seems a bit grown-up for Tilly. "Isn't that, like, for middle-aged posh women?"

"If you mean sophisticated, then yes." Tilly looks offended. "My godmother adores Jo Malone and all the royals shop there, you know. Please, Jess?"

"Go on, then." We're OK for time so I indulge her. As we approach the counter, I'm jolted by a familiar fragrance. "Weird. It smells just like you."

"You can *smell* me?" Tilly turns from a display of body lotion, looking tragic. "Ugh. What do I smell of? Hospitals? Dead people? Eau de bloody ectoplasm?"

I stifle a laugh and sniff experimentally. "You smell like this place. Satsumas or something. It's nice."

Her face clears as she takes a whiff from her own wrist. "Oh! It's my Orange Blossom cologne. I must have been wearing it the day I died. It was a present from Aunt Lulu." Her mouth crumples like a little girl's.

"What's the matter now?" I mutter, as she stops in the middle of the aisle.

"I miss her, Jess. And I just want to go *home*." There are real tears in her eyes.

"*Excuse* me." Two flight attendants trundle past, catching me on the back of the ankle with their little wheely suitcases.

I try to tow Tilly towards Bobbi Brown instead, but she digs her heels in. My heart stings as she strains against me.

"Please let's go back to Jo Malone," she begs, pointing at the rows of glass bottles. "I just want to smell them. It'll make me feel better, I know it will."

"Fine." I avoid the hovering saleswoman's neon smile as I spray samples for Tilly to sniff.

"Wild bluebell. Aunt Lulu's absolute favourite for daytime." She looks wistful. "Can we buy some? Please, Jess?"

I do a double take at the price list. "You're joking. It costs over a hundred quid."

"I'll pay for it," Tilly urges. "I'll buy you some as a present."

"You're dead and you haven't got any money."

The approaching saleswoman freezes and then slowly backs away.

Bollocks. Forgot I was supposed to be on the phone.

18

If it was weird getting on the plane without Dad, it's even weirder stepping out of the airport in Geneva. It's not remotely like I imagined.

"Hurry up." Tilly powers ahead and then twists round to look at me. "What are you staring at?"

"It's Switzerland," I mumble into my jacket collar. "I thought it would be more Christmas card-y. You know … powdery snow on the rooftops, twinkly lights, children wearing mittens and woolly hats with pompoms…"

Tilly gives me a look of utter condescension. "It's not even November."

"*I know.* It's just not how I imagined it."

"You're such a pleb." She sighs, pointing to a tidy line of commuters on the pavement. "Come on, let's get a cab."

"Where are we going?" I remember to talk into my phone this time.

"The financial district."

"I still don't get how I'm supposed to access your money without any ID," I murmur, moving up the queue. "Are you positive the account won't have been frozen?"

"I told you, my solicitor doesn't know about this one." Tilly puts her fingertip to her lips with a conspiratorial shush. "Daddy set it up for fun when I turned sixteen. He called it my holiday pocket money account. You can have whatever's left in there," she adds generously.

"I thought you had to deposit, like, megabucks to set up one of those?"

"Nooo," she says scornfully. "Only about a hundred thou."

My heart speeds up. "A *hundred thousand* pounds?"

"Calm down." Tilly rubs her own chest, giving me a long-suffering look. "It's only *euros*, sweetie. Not sterling."

"Let's get this straight. You call a hundred grand 'pocket money'?" I squeak. A businessman behind me makes a comment to his friend and Tilly joins in with the laughter.

"Don't you speak French?" She's mistaken my stunned expression for confusion over the language barrier. "Honestly! In London, even the sink schools teach *Francais*.

They all think you're bonkers. That man just called you a crazy Englishwoman."

"He's right," I agree, sticking out my arm as we reach the front of the line. "I've just dropped everything to go on holiday with a ghost who may or may not exist."

"Tuh! Of course I exist, silly. You're not going to start all that again, are you? Anyway, this isn't a holiday – it's a business trip for financial purposes."

Our taxi draws up and I climb in, relieved to get away from the amused commuters.

"If this is just pocket money," I whisper as Tilly slides into the back seat beside me. "How much did you have in your real bank account?"

"My trust fund, you mean?"

I nod, half frightened to hear the answer.

"All in all, with the shares and property, I guess it was about forty-two, maybe forty-two point five."

"Forty-two point five what?"

She rolls her eyes. "Million, of course. Look, the driver's waiting for you to tell him where we're going. The bank is called Stutz et Cie."

"You'd better tell me the address," I say faintly, trying to remember to breathe.

Tilly smiles. "Don't worry. He'll know where it is."

19

I freeze at the entrance to the bank, feeling like a master criminal. I've turned up the collar of my denim jacket and I'm wearing a huge pair of sunglasses hastily purchased from a shop across the road.

"Are you ready?" Tilly whispers. "Remember the number?"

I nod. "34-22-32. Sounds like the vital statistics of a very skinny woman."

"Mine actually." Tilly looks smug. "So we're agreed. We won't ask for too much cash this time. Just twenty grand or so."

Jeez. "Fine by me." If she can do deluded, so can I.

Tilly steers me in through the carved wooden doors. The marble foyer stretches ahead, customers in dark suits milling about. "That's Herve, the manager. He knew Daddy really well and he might remember my account so let's avoid him. Hmm, that one looks new. Let's go over there." She tows me towards a young male cashier.

"*Excusez-moi*," I begin, about to place my rucksack on the pristine counter before changing my mind.

"No! Act like you own the place," Tilly instructs. "They all speak English. Just tell him you want to make a withdrawal. He does this every day so just give him the number."

I do as I'm told. The cashier gives me a slip to write down my number and my hand shakes as I pencil in the figures. *Twenty grand*. No freaking way.

He takes the slip. "Can you give me the password on the account, please?"

Password? What password? I stare at Tilly, swallowing down panic. She looks equally shocked, her face bleached of colour as our heart flutters, making us both wince.

"The password, madam? You have not forgotten it?"

Has she? Has she forgotten it? I watch Tilly's complexion change from white to a delicate shell pink.

She swallows hard. "The password? It's er … Mrs Styles."

"*Mrs Styles?*" I repeat in delight.

"That's correct, madam." The cashier keeps a straight face as he taps into his computer.

"As in Harry's wife?" I say as Tilly gazes stonily ahead.

The cashier's mouth twitches. "You don't need to explain, madam."

"I *was* only sixteen." Tilly goes on the defensive. "And keep your voice down, Jess, it's supposed to be private. While you're here, ask him for a balance."

I'm tempted to milk the Styles situation further, but the whole thing's way too scary to piss about. "Can I get a balance on my account?"

The cashier nods politely. "Of course. Your account is in credit to one hundred and seventy-seven thousand, six hundred and forty-two euros. Not including the twenty thousand you already have debited today."

"OK." I squeeze my lips closed but a little squeak still escapes. *One hundred and eighty bloody grand?* You could buy a house with that.

Tilly looks unimpressed. "Hardly any interest since I was last here. Still, what can you expect in a global economic crisis?"

We exit the bank, Tilly striding ahead, me scuttling behind, acutely conscious of the wad of cash in my rucksack. I draw the bag closer, clamping my damp armpit over it as we cross the busy street.

"Chill out," says Tilly. "No one around here's going to mug you for a paltry twenty grand."

"So what do we do now?" I reluctantly release the muscles in my armpit. "It's hours before our flight."

Tilly dances along the street with a huge grin. "Now, we go shopping. Welcome to the Rue du Rhône, baby."

20

I've never seen so many designer shops on one small street. Tilly skips ahead like a kid in a sweet shop as she escorts me from one expensive boutique to another.

"I feel like Julia Roberts in *Pretty Woman*," I whisper, lugging an armful of clothes into yet another changing room.

"Big mistake. Big. Huge," Tilly quotes, casting a critical eye over the red dress I'm holding up to my chest. "No, I mean it, sweetie. That's too low cut. We don't need anybody asking any questions about your scar."

I slump down on the velvet chair opposite the mirror, tracing the puckered pink line with my finger.

Tilly perches beside me, drawing my hand away. "It'll fade. It already looks so much better than it did – in a few months' time, I bet you won't even be able to see it. Hey, I saw some gorgeous high-necked tops in a shop window down the street. How do you fancy trotting along to Dior?"

"I'm not sure I'm really a Dior person." All this dressing and undressing is knackering me out and I feel itchy about spending Tilly's money. "Are you going to tell me why we need all these clothes?"

"Look, if we're going to find out about my murder, we might have to mix in a few different circles. We need to be prepared for every eventuality. Try this one." She strokes her fingers down the sleeve of a silky jersey dress. "Do you like it in the green or the black? Or both? If you like, we could get both?"

Her enthusiasm is infectious. I kick off my jeans and slide into the dress, luxuriating in the soft fabric. Apart from the dark circles under her eyes, the stylish girl in the mirror is unrecognizable.

"Yes!" Tilly approves. "That's the one. Perfect."

I flip over the price tag. "Bloody hell. Four hundred Swiss francs? How much is that in pounds?"

"Three hundred and something? Maybe four." Tilly counts on her fingers and shrugs. "But it is a gorgeous dress."

"Jeez, Tilly. We'll spend all that money in one go at this rate."

"So? We'll just go back and get more."

"Erm, I'm not sure we should." I've been torn between giddiness and terror ever since we left the bank.

She looks at me curiously. "Why on earth not?"

"It's not right," I say, chewing my lip. "It's your money, Tilly, not mine."

"Don't be so noble. I'm totally deceased, remember? It's not as if I can use it and no one else even knows it's there. If you don't make good use of that money, it will just sit mouldering in that bank forever."

"Yeah, but if we do take it, how are we going to get it home? Presuming you don't spend the whole lot on clothes, I can't exactly walk through customs with a suitcase full of cash."

"You are *such* a worrier. You're going to give yourself another heart attack, the way you're going, sweetie."

"It wasn't a heart attack," I mutter through clenched teeth. "I had cardiomyopathy. Because of *parvovirus*."

"Oh, yes." Tilly laughs gaily. "Our school gamekeeper's Labrador had that. It died, poor thing. Hadn't been vaccinated properly. Anyway, it's easy peasy to make a deposit. There are millions of European banks in Geneva."

"I haven't got a bank, remember? I've only got a crappy building society account."

"Open a new account, then. You've got your passport, haven't you?"

"I'm under eighteen. Don't I need my parent's permission?"

"God's sake, Jess. If we can't bank it, we'll just stuff a load of cash into a registered envelope and post it to your house. OK?"

"But what if my dad opens it—"

"Stop!" Tilly commands, pressing her chilly palm over my mouth. "Just go with it. Stop being so difficult."

"OK," I say, as we leave the shop, laden down with posh carrier bags. "What time does the bank close?"

"Four-thirty."

I grab my phone. "But it's nearly ten past now."

"Is it?" Tilly's face is all innocence. "Ooh, we'd better hurry, hadn't we?"

We skitter around the corner and along the street to the bank, but when we get there, the ornate wooden doors are already closed.

Tilly nods at the brass doorbell. "For special customers, they do make an exception, sweetie," she says.

Yeah, right. We both know I'm not pressing that bloody bell.

"Never mind. Maybe we should just head for the airport." Tilly avoids my accusing stare. "On the other hand, you do look shattered, sweetie. If we find somewhere to stay overnight, we can come back in the morning and empty the account. It's not as if your dad's expecting you home."

Now I get it. "Oh my god. You planned this."

110

"Of course not." Tilly widens her eyes in protest. "But what a shame to leave all that money behind when we're already here. I know just the hotel overlooking the lake – we can get one of those cute little yellow ferries which stop right outside."

"I bet it's expensive."

"I prefer the term exclusive." Tilly sticks out her bottom lip. "Please, Jess. It's where we always stayed when I came here with Daddy. He did a lot of business in Geneva and if it was school holidays, he used to let me tag along. I'd love to see it one more time…"

"You are so manipulative. You just wanted a mini break in Switzerland, didn't you?"

"Now don't be paranoid," Tilly soothes. "Sometimes these things happen for the best. On the plus side, the shops are gorgeous and I know a little salon where you could get your highlights done – just near the Tiffany's where Daddy bought my silver ring. Tomorrow morning, we can buy you some new luggage, empty the bank account and then have lunch somewhere lovely before we fly home. What do you think?"

"I think I've been well and truly conned."

21

I'm feeling seriously underdressed as Tilly directs me into the opulent foyer of a massive hotel. Exclusive, my arse. The uniformed doorman steps back, raising one eyebrow at my scruffy rucksack as I scuttle past.

"I don't think Dad's credit card can handle this," I whisper as we cross the gleaming black-and-white chequered floor.

"Don't worry," Tilly says grandly. "We'll pay the bill in cash."

I gesture to the huge chandeliers and marble pillars. "Isn't there somewhere else a bit less ... *you know*?"

"Somewhere a bit less *you know* won't remind me of Daddy." Her lower lip wobbles again.

"Fine." Hitching my rucksack over one shoulder, I approach the floppy-haired man behind the reception desk.

Tilly perks up. "Oh, look, it's Patrice! He's worked here for years; I had a major crush on him when I was about fifteen. Tell him we'd like a lake view."

"Erm, *parlez vous Anglais*?" My French is so crap.

Tilly laughs her nasty, tinkly laugh. "Don't embarrass yourself, sweetie. It's just like the bank – they all speak perfectly good English."

Patrice seems amused as he looks me up and down. "'Ave you booked?"

I grit my teeth. "No, I 'aven't booked."

"I will check to see if we 'ave a cancellation." He taps the computer screen haughtily. "You are in luck, miss. A small delegation 'as cancelled. Would you like a deluxe, lake view or a junior suite?"

"Tell him you know me," suggests Tilly. "He's such a sweetheart, we might get an upgrade."

"Let's go with whichever's cheapest," I say with a defiant grimace.

Tilly fans herself in horror. "Strike that. Don't tell *anyone* here you know me. I'll never be able to hold my head up again."

You're dead, I mouth before turning back to the counter.

"Is that all the luggage?" Patrice sweeps his floppy fringe to one side, looking almost affronted as he peers

113

over the counter to check out my scruffy pink holdall surrounded by fancy shopping bags. "You 'ave ID? And means of payment?"

"I'll be paying cash." I'm terrified how much this place might cost. My idea of luxury is a Holiday Inn Express.

"I still need to take card details." Patrice sniffs at Dad's visa card and my passport before reluctantly handing over a key card. Legs shaking, I cross the checkerboard floor to the lift. A production line of bell boys take it in turns to try and rustle my luggage and then slink away smirking as I hang on to my bag with the bust zip. Imagine if my pants escaped when they were carrying it?

The room's way over the top: fancily furnished and bigger than our whole downstairs at home. Tilly dances over to bounce on the king size bed.

"A little pokier than I'm used to but still fabulous." She leaps up to squash her nose against the massive window. "I wish you'd asked for a lake view. We could have watched the fountain. It's called the Jet d'Eau, you know."

"It's bloody lucky they had a cancellation. I'd have killed you if we missed the flight and then couldn't find anywhere to stay." I dump the shopping bags on the floor and then tip the contents of my rucksack on to the crushed velvet coverlet of the massive bed. I've never seen so much money in real life. Hands trembling, I undo the paper strip of the first bundle and let the notes run through my fingers.

Tilly watches with a superior expression. "Are you going to throw it into the air and roll naked in it?"

"No," I say, even though that's the exact image I have in my head. I suppress a wild desire to sniff the cash as I stack it into a pile. "You've been watching too many heist movies, you have."

"Ooh, let's order room service." Tilly tries and fails to open the tasselled, leather-bound menu by the side of the bed. "They do gorgeous seafood here. Do you like oysters?"

"Are they the ones that taste like phlegm? Yummy."

Tilly sighs. "Couldn't you at least try being a tiny bit adventurous for once?"

"Sorry, doctor's orders. I'm not allowed to eat raw seafood." I open the menu, trying to avoid looking at the prices. Once I've ordered (a burger costing about ten times as much as a Big Mac), it's time to phone Dad and pretend I'm at Mum's and then Mum and pretend I'm at Dad's.

"God's sake." Tilly clutches her head as I finish the second call. "I thought your mother was never going to shut up about that bloody commune."

"She loves it there," I say defensively. "She feels really at home."

"In *Wales*?" From her tone, Tilly might as well be saying *in prison*. "Why? Is that where you grew up?"

"Nah, I'm Manchester born and bred but we moved all over the show when I was little. As Dad went more

115

mainstream and wanted to settle in one place, Mum got even more over the top. When they finally split up, she wanted us to move to this Welsh commune and he got offered a promotion back in Manchester. I chose to go with him."

"You went for the safe option. Well, I can understand that, sweetie, if it was a toss-up between Manchester and a commune in Wales." She chews her thumbnail thoughtfully. "Is that why you became so boring, do you think?"

"Excuse me?"

"You know. You have this hippy childhood being dragged from pillar to post and as soon as you get the chance to escape, you go to the other extreme. Look at you – staying in a five-star hotel with a Michelin-starred restaurant and what do you order? A well-done burger for God's sake. Boring, just like your father."

"My dad's not boring," I say.

"Oh, he is, sweetie. He's all cardigans and porridge and taking your tablets on time. Even the swimming with dolphins thing – he only said it because he thought you were going to *die*." She tilts her head. "You're seventeen! Try being spontaneous for a change."

"I am being spontaneous," I protest, pointing out of the window at the pretty city lights. "I'm here, aren't I?"

She looks smug. "And don't you feel totally alive for once?"

116

"No." I'm irritable now. "It's completely stressing me out."

"But Geneva's so beautiful! And we did the shopping and room service..." Tilly looks at the new clothes strewn across the bed and trails off, her smooth forehead scrunched into a puzzled frown. She doesn't mention giving me all that money and I know I'm being mean, but she's so entitled and annoying.

"It's OK for you to just jet off to Geneva when you haven't got school or parents on your back," I say.

"You're totally right. Both my parents are dead. And now I'm dead too." She folds her arms. "Lucky old me."

I feel my face flush. "I didn't mean that. But when this is over, I've got to go back to school, decide what I'm going to do with my life. That was the best thing about fainting in that career's lesson – at least I didn't have to make a decision about what I want to do when I leave school because I haven't got a bloody clue. You didn't have to worry about that, you could just drop everything and go shopping in Geneva or to lunch at the bloody Ivy whenever you fancied."

"I wasn't just some dippy *socialite*, you know," Tilly shouts. "I had charity commitments."

"Oh yeah, the wonderful charity work everyone keeps banging on about." I laugh nastily. "What did that entail? Arranging flowers? Selling raffle tickets to your rich mates?"

117

"My trust fund sponsors a children's charity in Battersea," she says quietly. "We support play areas and youth centres for children in deprived areas and arrange days out for kids whose parents can't afford it. And at Christmas, we make sure every single one of those children gets a present from Santa."

"Right." Now I feel bad. "You never said."

"You never asked."

"Sorry."

"I'm sorry too. You're not really boring, Jess," she says. "You're just a bit of a wuss."

A wave of exhaustion washes over me. "Time for my tablets."

Tilly watches me pop pills out of blister packs. "How come you're still taking all those painkillers?"

"They're not painkillers, they're immunosuppressants. I've got to take them forever, otherwise my body will reject your heart."

"Hmm. Like you want me to stick around anyway."

"We'll both be in trouble if I stop taking them," I say with my mouth full. "If I get sick or die, you don't get to find out what Leo was up to."

"I hadn't thought of that." Tilly looks alarmed. "If you died, what on earth would happen to *me*?"

"Nice to know you've got your priorities straight." Seriously though, it doesn't bear thinking about. Both of us dead and still stuck together, bickering forever as we float around Geneva like a pair of supernatural conjoined twins.

"At least you're alive," Tilly says, her lip wobbling. "At least you didn't die a tragic untimely death on a country lane in Hertfordshire."

I concede defeat. "OK, you win, Tilly. I can't possibly top getting murdered." I want to stay annoyed but my curiosity gets the better of me. "What did it actually feel like when you died?"

"Hmm." She looks thoughtful. "I remember feeling fuzzy and that total bastard Leo bending over me. Then everything just went black – like a light switching off." She shrugs. "Next thing, I'm with you in the Intensive Care Unit."

"So you missed the actual heart surgery bit?" I pull on pyjamas and head into the bathroom.

"Yes, thank god." Tilly looks like she might puke. "I've never been into that medical stuff. I saw someone having a hair transplant on *Embarrassing Bodies* once and that was bad enough. Ugh."

I pick up my toothbrush, feeling a bit queasy myself. "Do you reckon they harvested any of your other organs? Your liver and kidneys and stuff?"

She shudders. "Don't say *harvested*, sweetie, it sounds gross. But I suppose they might have. I ticked the box saying they could take anything they liked."

I grin through a mouthful of toothpaste. "So your bits and pieces could be spread right across the north west?"

119

"That's right." She looks modest. "Saving lives all over the place, I expect. Funny, it was only the missing heart I seemed to notice."

"Did you know straight away they'd given it to me?"

"Yes, of course." Tilly looks surprised. "The bond between us … you felt it too, didn't you?"

I nod. "Do you think it's still as strong? Hey, maybe we should do another test? See how far apart we get."

"Good idea. This room's quite long. I'll go to the far end."

I stand my ground in the doorway while Tilly pulls away, but she only gets past the bed before the dragging sensation starts up in my chest.

"No change from this side," I call. "Your turn to stay still."

She braces herself as I strain backwards into the ensuite, the tautness building uncomfortably. I try a quick tug and Tilly tumbles forward, holding her chest.

"You're stronger than me," she says sadly. "Because I'm dead."

I look at her skinny wrists and laugh. "Nothing to do with being dead, Tilly. I reckon I could take you in an arm wrestle even if you were alive."

"Oh, do piss off."

"Yeah, wish I could." I climb into bed and turn off the bedside light. "But it looks like we're still stuck together for now."

Tilly's muffled voice comes out of the darkness. "Just until we solve the mystery. And then we can go our separate ways."

I nod but I'm really not sure who she's trying to convince. Me or herself?

22

If the staff at Stutz et Cie suspect anything suspicious, they don't say anything when we return the next day to empty the account. It's not the same cashier on duty but he probably wouldn't recognize me anyway. My hair's been cut and highlighted in the hotel salon and I'm wearing an expensive new coat and boots. I'm hoping I remembered to take the tags off.

"Ask for high denomination notes," Tilly advises, "or it'll be too heavy for you to carry."

I nod, my fingers trembling as I fumble to unzip my new designer holdall (Louis Vuitton and seriously gross but she insisted).

"Chill." Tilly lays her hand over mine as I open the bag wide enough for them to stash the cash in. "They've no interest in us. Most of their clients are probably international crime lords with multi-million-dollar accounts. Look at him over there – he'll be in the Mafia or something." She points at a bald man in a grey suit who's wheeling a neat little airhostess suitcase towards the counter.

I try not to stare as we pass him on our way out.

"That's his deposit," she says knowledgeably. "He'll have thousands of euros in there."

"Either that or a horse's head," I mutter, as we step out on to the street. This is the scary bit where I keep expecting the security guard's hand on my shoulder, but it doesn't come. As we cross the road, two police officers whizz past us on rollerblades and I tighten my grip on the holdall, too terrified to even find it funny. The cash weighs less than I expected but my chest still strains with the effort.

"Where shall we go for lunch?" Tilly strides off purposefully now that I haven't been arrested for theft. "There are some lovely cafes near *Lac Léman* – that's Lake Geneva to you. Now we've got the money we can make proper plans to track down Leo."

"I'm not sitting in a cafe talking to myself," I say, horribly conscious that I'm carrying enough cash to buy a two-bedroomed terrace. "I got enough funny looks in the taxi queue yesterday."

"But you're on holiday," Tilly says logically. "No one has a clue who you are. If you want to sit around talking to yourself in a designer dress, where better?"

Patrice looks super suspicious when I pay my account in cash. He spreads out the stash of hundred-euro notes like a professional croupier before holding one up to the light. Finally satisfied, he gives me a haughty nod and hands over my invoice. Looking at the figure on the bottom gives me palpitations all over again.

"Make him book a limo to take us to the airport," Tilly suggests with a malicious smile. She's gone right off him since we spotted him having his hair blow-dried two seats away from me this morning. "That'll piss him off even more."

I shake my head. The last thing we need is to draw any more attention to ourselves.

"'Ave a nice trip," Patrice says insincerely as the porter trundles my brand-new luggage towards the glass doors. This time, I've got enough cash for a tip.

We post the money packages from the airport. Tilly told me to ask for most of it in sterling and, to be on the safe side, we've split it into a number of smaller parcels with the money wrapped inside new jeans and tops. I address the last package, care of courier, to some fancy hotel in Chelsea.

"We'll need it when we're there," Tilly says cryptically.

"Where is this hotel anyway?" I wince in discomfort as she steams ahead to the Business Class lounge.

"Pickwicks? It's off the King's Road, round the corner from where I live. Lived, I mean. It's a gorgeous little place – Victorian. I used to stay there all the time."

"Duh," I say into my mobile. "If it's round the corner from where you lived, how come you stayed there all the time?"

"Birthday parties and society weddings, of course! Sometimes we'd take over an entire floor," says Tilly. "Once, Tanika ordered a magnum of champagne from room service and when the waiter arrived, we got him to stay and play spin the bottle with us. It was hilarious!"

"I bet he thought so."

"Of course he did! He was a good sport, not a misery guts like you. Anyway, we gave him a mega tip the next morning, so it was fine."

"If you say so. Look, it's time to board."

After the extravagance of the hotel, I'm weirdly at home in the First-Class cabin. Tilly's treated me to some AirPods from duty free so we can talk without me having to hold up my mobile. I snuggle into my extra legroom seat and accept a glass of champagne from the air hostess who doesn't even ask my age.

"Try not to kill yourself before we get the job done." Tilly's monitoring my alcohol intake like a novice nun at a hen party.

125

"Oi! I haven't had a single steak and kidney pie this week," I remind her as she clambers over me into the empty space. "*And* I've let you have the window seat."

23

The hotel manager smiles up from his computer. "We hope you enjoy your stay with us, Miss Bailey. Would you mind showing me some ID?"

Tilly rolls her eyes as I flash my passport, keeping my thumb over the date of birth. "What is it with these people? He's almost as bad as Patrice. And let's face it, sweetie, you look much smarter than you did last time we checked in."

The manager hands me a gold key card. "Sorry about that, miss. A parcel has just arrived for you and you can't be too careful about security these days."

"A parcel?" I say. "From Geneva?"

Wow, that was quick.

"That's right." He unlocks the safe behind the check-in desk and passes over a heavy padded envelope. "If you could just sign for it?"

Tilly smirks as I scribble my name. "Told you it would work."

Our new hotel room is large and modern with a huge bed where I dump all our stuff.

"This is more like it," Tilly says, dancing over to the window.

"No lake view, Tilly." I slip off my shoes so that my feet sink ankle deep into thick gold carpet.

She points out of the window to the busy street below. "See that down there? That's Dolce and Gabbana. And Hobbs. And Rigby and Peller. Who needs a lake view, sweetie, when you're this close to the shops?"

"No more shopping," I say firmly. "We're here to find Leo, remember?"

"I haven't forgotten." Tilly turns away from the glass. "Seeing all those town cars waiting outside the airport gave me an idea. I think the quickest way to find Leo is to book him for a job."

"Book him? You mean go for a ride in his limo?" My forehead prickles with sweat as I sit down on the gold counterpane. "Are you actually kidding me? Look what happened last time you got in a car with him."

"That's different. He can't go around killing off all his clients, sweetie, he'd be sacked in no time."

"It's not funny, Tilly, and I'm not doing it." I stand up and start to unpack, deliberately laying out my cosy old pyjamas rather than the slinky new ones Tilly insisted I buy.

"Don't be such a coward."

Unbelievable. I stare at her, heat rising to my cheeks. "Trying to stop myself from getting murdered doesn't make me a coward, Tilly."

"Keep telling yourself that. I'd have thought you'd be a bit braver now you've got my heart, but no – you're just like that cowardly lion out of *The Wizard of Oz*."

"And you're like bloody Toto, following me round all the time. I wish you'd just piss off."

"And I wish I could," she shouts. "You seem to forget: it'll be much worse for me coming face to face with my murderer."

"How can it be worse? You're dead already. He can't kill you twice."

"After all I've done for you, giving you my heart, you won't do one tiny thing in return." Tilly flounces off as far as she can get, which isn't far at all. "If I hadn't been carrying a donor card that day, you'd probably be dead by now. But have it your way. If we don't solve the mystery, I'll be stuck here forever. With you. Is that what you want?"

We glare at each other for a long minute until I give in. As usual.

"Fine. We'll book the bloody car. But this had better work, Tilly."

"It will, I promise."

"Good," I hiss. "Because *I* promise, if I get murdered as well, I'll kill you myself."

24

It feels like only minutes have passed before Tilly shakes me awake with her chilly hands. I blink up at the floral wallpaper, disorientated and seriously out of breath, before she hurries me out of bed and into the shower. Downstairs in the breakfast room, I glance guiltily at the blue cardiac rehab appointment card in my bag as I wash down my morning tablets with the sort of hot chocolate that could give you a heart attack just by sniffing it.

"Continental, full English or porridge with honey?" enquires the breakfast waiter and I opt for porridge without even thinking about it.

Beside me, Tilly makes plans with military precision.

"Let's do this as safely as possible. We'll get Leo to pick us up from a different hotel so he won't know where we're staying. You know, my school use Jarvis and Woodhouse all the time. How about we book a car on the St Aggie's account? They often ask for the same driver. And if Leo thinks you're from my school, he won't be surprised when you start asking questions about me."

The waft of scrambled eggs from the next table is making me feel sick. Or maybe it's just the thought of getting in a car with a murderer.

Tilly's ultra-perky now she's got her own way. "You know, Jess, with that husky voice of yours, I think you could get away with pretending to be Mrs Chisholm over the phone."

I glance pointedly around the busy dining room and raise my eyebrows in question. I've forgotten the AirPods and there's no way I'm talking to myself in here.

Tilly correctly interprets my non-verbals. "Mrs Chisholm's our school secretary. Unlike you, sweetie, she really does smoke forty a day, ha, ha."

Back in the room, I practise trying to sound like Tilly.

"God's sake, are you really going to do it like that?" she says. "Don't forget to ask for Leo Rossini by name. And tell them to put it on the school account."

"I know, I know." I take deep breaths as I dial the number.

It's answered almost immediately. "Jarvis and Woodhouse, how may I help you?"

"Dorothy Chisholm here from St Agatha's," I honk. "I want to book a car for one of our gels."

Tilly rolls her eyes. "Don't say 'gels', Jess. It's not the 1930s."

"I'd like Mr Rossini, if he's available," I continue, turning my back. "He comes highly recommended."

"Oh, yes. Mr Rossini is one of our most popular drivers," says the clerk in a giggly voice. Jeez, there's no accounting for taste. "But he does have availability this afternoon and tomorrow morning."

Crap. This afternoon? I shake my head at Tilly who nods sternly in return. "OK, I mean yes. This afternoon. The young lady's name is ... er ... Pandora Inglewood." Pandora Inglewood was a stuck-up cow with two ponies who briefly attended my comprehensive in Sheffield after her dad's business went bust. I give the clerk details of the route Tilly's planned between two of the busiest parts of London.

"Much less chance of getting murdered on a street full of tourists with cameras than on a deserted country lane like me, sweetie," Tilly says. "Now, we just need to make sure you look the part."

Near to the hotel where Leo's due to collect "Pandora", there's an expensive school outfitters.

"Come on." Tilly guides me inside. "Let's get you kitted out."

"I don't want to wear a uniform," I whisper. "I'm in sixth form, remember?"

"Look, it's safer this way. If you're wearing a school hat and blazer, that's all he'll remember. We don't want him to recognize you if he sees you again, do we?"

I've no intention of bumping into this guy more than once, but she has a point. "Fine," I mutter, heading towards the saleswoman.

I try on the straw boater which is OK – kind of retro cool actually – but the largest blazer they have in stock is so tight across my back, I can't even get my left arm into it.

"I think you need a twelve. There isn't much call for the larger sizes," whispers the scrawny sales lady apologetically. "I can put one on order if you like?"

"Buy it anyway," suggests Tilly. "If you hang it over your arm, he'll still notice it."

He can hardly miss it. The St Agatha's blazer is burgundy with shocking pink piping around the lapel and pockets. How come rich people have such bad taste?

I turn to the saleswoman. "Do you take cash?"

25

Tilly paces as we wait in the lobby of a huge hotel nearby. I've already been for a wee three times and I think I need to go again.

"That's one thing I don't miss," she says. "Going to the loo, such a bore."

In the mirror, my face is sweaty and scarlet. I bend to splash water on my burning cheeks. "I'm seriously not sure about this. What am I supposed to say to him?"

"We'll play it by ear," says Tilly. "Try mentioning my name – see how he reacts. You'll have to say something about me, otherwise this whole thing is a waste of time."

"If I say too much, he might shut me up for good."

"We've talked about this." Tilly fusses ineffectually with my straw boater. "The route's too busy for him to try anything."

"Yeah, but what if he just drives me out of London to somewhere secluded?"

"Oh, sweetie, he'd have to get past the M25 to do that. At this time of day, you'd die of old age before he got you far enough away to kill you." She pats my cheek. "Just engage him in conversation and we'll wait until the car stops at the other end. You can have the door open and one foot on the pavement before we put the frighteners on."

Put the frighteners on? Who does she think she is? Liam Neeson?

Tilly taps her watch. "It's time."

I lag behind as she leads me through the lobby and down the steps of the hotel into the busy street.

"Oh, god, that's him. That's really him." Tilly stares at a dark-haired guy in a suit leaning against a maroon Mercedes. She stops in the middle of the pavement and takes a series of rapid stuttering breaths like she's having a baby. "He's here, Jess."

"He's supposed to be here," I mutter. "Come on. Let's get this over with." It all seems horribly real as I tilt the straw hat over my eyes and walk towards Leo on leaden legs. It gets harder to move forward, like walking through treacle, until I realize Tilly's the one holding us back. I turn to look at her.

Her bottom lip wobbles. "Do you know, Jess, I'm not totally sure about this."

"We're here now. It's a bit bloody late to change your mind," I say into the back of my hand as I strain against her.

Tilly shakes her head and digs her heels in like Granny Ursula's Alsatian when it's going to the vets, but it's too late. Leo's clocked my burgundy blazer. He straightens up with a smile, very white teeth against smooth olive skin, as he moves towards me.

"Leo Rossini," he says. He might look Italian, but his accent is straight off the set of *EastEnders*. "You must be Miss Inglewood. St Agatha's, yeah? I hear you asked for me specially?" He doffs his cap with a cheeky wink.

Ew. I was seriously wrong – he's more cocky than Cockney. Tilly clenches her fists and I feel her fury as our heart races.

"I don't *think* so," I say haughtily in my poshest accent. "In fact, I was expecting Ranjeet. Are you new? Perhaps I could see some ID."

"Genius," breathes Tilly as Leo opens his wallet. "Total genius. His driving license will have his address on it. How clever of you, Jess."

I nod, pretending that was the idea all along. Leo holds out his ID, but his fingertips are covering the address. I lean past Tilly to inspect it, but I can only see the postcode on the bottom. Bollocks.

"All right now?" He moves to slot the card back into his wallet.

"Stop him!" Tilly rushes forward and grabs his wrist. Leo drops the card, Bambi eyelashes blinking in surprise.

"Did you see that?" Tilly's mouth is a perfect O. "He felt me, I'm sure he did. Let me try again." She reaches forward and prods him in the jaw. Leo looks around, stroking his cheek absently.

While he's distracted, I pick up the driving licence, surreptitiously tilting it towards Tilly so she can check out the address before I hand it back.

"Thanks, miss." Leo turns on a megawatt smile. "It's a bit chilly out here. Shall we get going?"

As he opens the rear door for me, Tilly takes the opportunity to give him a vicious kick up the backside. She's really going for it, but there's no way he's felt anything like the full force. He rubs the back of his trousers, expression puzzled more than pained, as he glances behind him.

In the back of the car, I wipe my damp hands on the leather seats while Tilly searches the interior like a sniffer dog. I don't know what she thinks she's looking for — it's not even the same car.

"Make conversation with him," she hisses, squashing her nose against the glass to peer into the front seat.

Reluctantly, I knock on the partition and Leo slides it back. "Yes, miss?"

"How long before we get there?" My voice wavers as Tilly wriggles her arm through the gap, reaching for the papers on the passenger seat.

"Probably about fifteen minutes in this traffic. Have you got an appointment you need to get to?"

I meet his eyes in the rear-view mirror and nod, all the while thinking *murderer, murderer, murderer.*

"Keep him talking!" Tilly's armpit deep between the front and back seats, swiping impotently through the paperwork, as Leo moves to push the partition closed.

"Dentist," I squeak, improvising.

"Aha, that's why you look so stressed." Leo smiles in the mirror as he starts the engine. "Don't worry, you'll be OK."

"Is this what you do all day?" I try to sound posh and aloof. "Drive schoolgirls around?"

Leo shakes his head. "Nah, I go all over. Tomorrow I'm ferrying B-listers for a celebrity baby shower and Saturday I've got an all dayer, driving a load of Japanese billionaires to and from this function at West Ham's ground."

"I'm not really interested in football," I lie, leaning to one side to avoid Tilly's denim bottom. I can't see what she's doing but, from her huffing and puffing, I guess it's not working. To give her more time, I nod along while Leo mansplains the pros and cons of VAR.

"Nothing useful as far as I can see," Tilly says, smoothing her hair into place as she eventually returns to the seat beside me. "Ask about me now."

139

"Not yet," I mutter.

Leo glances over his shoulder. "Sorry?"

"I said, we're not there yet."

"Nearly." He swings the car into a right turn. "Don't worry, I won't make you late."

"Bastard." Tilly's cheeks are flaming, but her eyes are chips of blue ice. "That's exactly what he said to me. About five minutes before he murdered me. Total bastard." She launches herself forward, her fingers around Leo's neck, squeezing hard.

He flinches, twisting the wheel to the right and narrowly missing a black cab.

"For god's sake, Tilly!" I hiss, grabbing her by the back of the jacket and hauling her back on to the seat beside me.

Leo pulls over to the side of the road, running a trembling finger around the inside of his white collar. In the mirror, his wide eyes meet mine. "Did you just say Tilly?"

We gaze at each other, the seconds ticking away. In the end, I bluff it out. "No, I didn't."

"I could have sworn you said Tilly." His eyes dart away and then back to mine in the mirror. "She was at your school. Did you know her?"

"Tilly Spencer, you mean?" I swallow, pretending to look thoughtful as my fingers creep to the door handle. "Not really. She was upper sixth and I'm only Year Eleven. You can let me out here."

"You've got him rattled, Jess. Keep going, he might let something slip." Tilly contains her anger long enough to point at the CD sitting on the dashboard. "Ask him about Michael Bublé."

What the hell? It's hardly the time to start questioning Leo about his dodgy musical taste. I give Tilly a *get lost* look as I ease open the car door, my forehead prickling in relief as I find it unlocked.

"Michael Bublé – don't you get it?" Tilly hisses. "The CD case he asked me to pick up from the floor just before the crash."

Leo stares ahead, jaw rigid as I exit the car. Once I'm safely on the busy pavement, I'm brave enough to lean towards his open window. "I hear you're a big fan of Michael Bublé. Weren't you playing that in the car the day Tilly died?"

26

As Leo roars off, I stand on the crowded street, legs shaking and heart racing like a train.

"Jess, that closing line was total genius!" Tilly gives me a high five and does a victory dance on the pavement. "Did you see his face? How spooked he was?"

"It hasn't got us anywhere, Tilly," I whisper into a convenient lamp post. "We still don't know anything."

"Yes, we do. We know Leo's address and we know he's going to be out of the house all day Saturday at West Ham's ground."

"Where's that?"

"At least half an hour's drive from Camberwell."

"Camberwell?" I can't keep up.

"Where Leo lives, remember?" Tilly's face is pink with excitement. "We can go round to his flat when he's not home."

"And do what? It's not like we can get in."

"You might not be able to." She gives me a superior smirk. "But I can. Totally deceased, remember?"

"And? I haven't seen much sign of you walking through walls so far."

"How hard can it be, sweetie? Look." She wafts her hand towards the lamp post and grimaces as her fingertips graze the metal and briefly disappear. "Anyway, it's not until Saturday. Plenty of time to practise. You can keep watch outside while I nip in and look for clues."

"What sort of clues?"

"Well, I don't know. Bank statements? A gun? A note written in green ink instructing him to kill me?"

"He didn't kill you with a bloody gun in the first place. Why would he have one now?" I can't even go there about Leo having a gun. What if it was stashed in the glovebox of his car? I slump against the lamp post, arms and legs like jelly. In the distance, a black cab with its light on approaches and I feel a rush of relief. "Can we go back to the hotel now?"

"Ye-es," Tilly says. "But my charity office happens to be only around the corner. Totally convenient. Couldn't we just pop in and see how things are going? Please, Jess?"

143

"Seriously? Totally convenient? You're the one who planned the bloody route."

"It's honestly just round that corner and you do look as if you could do with a sit down." Her concern looks genuine. "Kayla will give you a cup of tea and you can find out how the charity's doing. It's a win–win!"

"Who's Kayla?" I give in, stumbling behind on heavy legs, as Tilly sets off down a side street.

"She's my friend. She runs the office for me."

I'm surprised when we stop at a row of scruffy shops. "It's not very posh."

"Duh! It's not supposed to be," Tilly explains patiently. "They operate on a tiny budget and every spare penny goes towards the kids. If this was a smart area, the rental would sky rocket."

"I get it. I just can't see any of your snooty mates working in a place like this."

Tilly smiles. "Kayla's not snooty. You'll like her. Come on, the office is just above the launderette there."

She leads me through an alleyway that stinks of wee and we climb one flight of stairs to a half open door with a sign saying "Battersea Kidscope". I knock tentatively on the frosted glass and peer round.

A boy with curly dreads and a cool fade looks up from behind an ancient desktop. "Yeah, can I help you?"

"Not sure," I say from the doorway. "I was actually looking for Kayla?"

"She's gone to the bank. I'm just manning the phone 'til she gets back." He unfolds long legs and stands up with a grin. "I'm Wes."

"I'm Jess – a friend of Tilly's."

"Oh, sorry, man. What happened, that was *rough*. Come on in; she'll be back any second."

My legs are still wobbling as I step into the tiny office. I blink, trying to remember when I last ate, as the cracked lino blurs and then zooms up to meet me. "Is it OK if I sit down for a minute?"

"You all right?" Looking alarmed, Wes sweeps some papers off a chair and steers me towards it.

I lower myself down, suddenly having to swallow back tears. The stress of being in Leo's car must have hit way harder than I expected.

"Hey, hey." Wes squats in front of me as I hyperventilate. "Come on, you'll be OK in a minute."

He smells gorgeous, lemongrass or something else citrussy. I'm struggling to get my breath anyway but his nearness makes it worse somehow.

He leans in closer. "Do you want a cup of tea?"

"What?"

"Always worth a try, yeah?" Wes stands up again. "Cup of builder's tea and two sugars – it's my mum's solution to everything." He switches on the kettle and clanks assorted mugs on to a tray while I try to get a grip.

"Wesley bloody Lawrence." Tilly rolls her eyes.

"Bloody useless. Look, he's even giving you my favourite mug. What a waste of time – if I'd known Kayla was going to be out, I wouldn't have bothered bringing you here."

Wesley presses a glittery unicorn mug into my hands and wraps my fingers around it. "Get that down you. Man, your hands are freezing."

I take a sip of tea. It's too hot and disgustingly sweet, but it feels nice to be looked after instead of being bossed around.

Tilly looks up as the door bangs open. "Kayla," she squeaks in delight as a tall woman inches through the gap, carrying a bag for life full of A4 folders.

"Get the kettle on, Wes, I'm gasping for a cuppa," she says.

Kayla's nothing like I expected. Her accent's pure *EastEnders* and her braided hair's tied into a messy top knot with an orange Batik scarf which clashes violently with her pink cardie – a dead ringer for the one Granny Ursula got me from Primark. I wonder if Tilly used to give her a hard time over her wardrobe choices too.

Tilly clocks my expression with delight. "Surprise! Not all my friends go to private schools, you know."

Wes crosses the room in two strides to relieve Kayla of her shopping bag. "Mum, this is Jess. She's a friend of Tilly's."

"Oh! Didn't see you there, hon, but any friend of Tilly's is welcome here." She gives me a warm smile which swaps to a shiver when Tilly swoops in to give her a hug.

146

"She's feeling a bit dodgy." Wes nods at me as he puts down the bag.

"Oh, hon." Kayla leans across to rub my shoulder, her angular face full of sympathy. "I expect coming here brought it all back about Tilly. What a senseless waste. I bet you miss her as much as I do."

I bet I bloody don't.

"Thanks." I pass the half-drunk tea back to Wes. "I feel a bit better now."

"So, what can we do for you?" Kayla says, parking herself behind the desk. "Have you come to update us about the funding?"

Tilly and I exchange mystified looks. "The funding?"

"Yeah." Her smiling face falls. "Oh, bum. You haven't, have you, hon?"

"Sorry, no. I'm down from Manchester, just visiting."

Wes frowns and I realize I've got a St Agatha's blazer lying across my lap. I press on anyway. "So, before she died, erm, Tilly was thinking she might set up something similar there."

Tilly nods in approval. "Quick thinking, Jess."

"That's great," says Kayla, but her smile falters. "I run the Battersea project ... well, I do for the moment."

"She's not thinking of leaving, is she?" Tilly prods me. "Find out."

"What do you mean, for the moment?" I ask.

"Tilly was our biggest donor. She gave us the best part

147

of a hundred grand a year towards the programme, has done for the last two years, god rest her."

"Wow." I glance at Tilly who's looking well modest over by the photocopier. "I didn't know it was that much."

Kayla nods. "Tilly set the whole thing up. God knows what'll happen now she's passed. The standing order for this month was cancelled; if it don't get sorted soon, I won't be able to pay the staff."

Tilly's expression turns from modesty to outrage.

"How many staff are there?" I ask.

"There's me, Maria and Tariq. Those two are part-time and the rest are all volunteers. I'm the only full-timer; I look after the office and the budget and do some hands-on stuff with the kids. Maria runs the breakfast club and the free crèche five mornings a week and Tariq drives the minibus." She puts her head in her hands. "It failed its MOT yesterday. Brake pads and two new tyres before we can get it back on the road and we got a trip to the bloody zoo booked this Sunday."

Tilly shakes her head. "There must be some mistake, Jess. Probably due to probate; they'll have frozen all my regular payments or something. Tell her to call my solicitor."

I nod, only half listening because I've already thought of that. "Have you tried phoning Tilly's solicitor?"

"Mr Standish? I just come from there. Patronising git, 'scuse my language, hon. Couldn't have been less helpful if he tried."

Tilly gazes at Kayla in confusion. "But Mr Standish is such a darling old thing. He's looked after my money since I was a baby. I'm sure there must be some mistake."

"What did he say?" I direct the question to Kayla.

She exhales into her cupped hands. "No money won't be forthcoming until the trustees make a decision regarding Tilly's finances. Said it wasn't just his decision to make."

"But Mr Standish *is* one of my trustees!" Tilly explodes. "This is ridiculous. Tell her we'll deal with it, Jess."

"Hey, don't worry. I'll see what I can sort out," I say. "I'm a family friend; maybe I can find out what's going on."

"God, that would be amazing." Kayla looks up. "No lie, I been worried sick. If you can get this month's payment reinstated, I could get the minibus fixed."

"How much will it cost?"

"Six hundred and fifty, give or take a few quid."

"Hang on," I say. Tilly nods vigorously as I delve into my smart Pandora-disguise handbag and surreptitiously count notes. "Seven hundred. Will that be enough?"

"Are you for real?" Wes looks stunned as I hand over the cash.

"You're a bloody star, girl, and no mistake." Kayla looks almost tearful as she takes the money. "Let me give you a receipt."

"No, it's fine, honest."

"Gotta make sure everything's above board." Kayla tears out the slip and hands it to me. "Thanks, babe. I bet our Tilly thought a lot of you."

"Yeah, not so sure about that." I stash the receipt in my bag. "I hope you get the bus fixed in time."

"Hey, if you're still around Sunday, come along," Kayla calls as I head to the stairwell. "Ten thirty. We can always use a spare pair of hands."

"That was the right thing to do, yeah?" I whisper anxiously to Tilly as we make our way down the poky staircase and through the smelly alleyway to the street outside.

"Totally," she assures me. "We can spare it. I just don't understand why the funding was stopped."

"The solicitor said it 'wasn't just his decision'. So who else gets a say?"

"The trustees. There were five originally." Tilly ticks off her fingers. "Daddy, but they never replaced him; Mr Standish from the solicitors' office; my bank manager – Mr Chen – has an advisory role but isn't a proper trustee. Daddy said it was a conflict of interest. My headmistress, Miss Fox-Longley, is one, and Aunt Lulu, although she never really gets involved unless they need her to sign something. She's hopeless with money, but Daddy wanted someone who'd be on my side. You know, after my parents died, the trustees thought I should sell the London flat Dad used when he was in town. Mr Standish and the bank manager both advised me to look for something a 'little more modest' when I finished school, but Aunt Lu waded in and said it was my money and if I wanted to keep the flat in Chelsea, I should bloody well be able to."

"So if your Aunt Lulu is a trustee, doesn't she have a say in all this?" I say as we walk to the bus stop. No one notices. It's super liberating being in London. I'm not the only person talking to myself in the street by a long shot.

"Jess, you're a genius!" squeals Tilly. "We can phone Georgie!"

"Georgie? But you said your auntie was the trustee?"

"She's in Barbados, remember, but Georgie can get hold of her for us." Tilly looks super smug. "I've been looking for a good excuse for us to meet up with Georgie again and now you've provided it."

27

The double whammy of meeting Leo, coupled with the trip to Battersea, has wiped me out. All I want to do is get into my trackies, order a pizza from room service and binge on box sets.

"Not *Stranger Things* again," begs Tilly as I scroll through Netflix. "It totally gives me the creeps."

"And you have the nerve to call me a wuss? Tilly, you are literally a ghost."

"You don't need to rub it in." She wanders away to the window overlooking the busy street.

"It's a good job I had that money on me," I say, as she

stares down longingly to the shops below. "I don't know how we'd have got it to Kayla otherwise."

"Easy. The hotel would have ordered a courier to take it for us."

"I didn't know they did stuff like that."

Tilly yawns. "People will do almost anything as long as you've got the money to pay for it."

"What, like having someone bumped off?"

"Yes, Jess. Even that." She glances down at her paper-thin Cartier wristwatch. "I'm so glad I was wearing this when I died. Imagine being dead and never knowing what time it is. Are you going to phone Georgie soon? She's usually home by now."

"I'd better order my tea first. I need to take my tablets."

"You're in London now, sweetie. We don't say tea. We say dinner. Or supper."

"I don't care what you call it as long as I get a pizza before I faint." I ring room service and then rummage through my bag for the business card Georgie gave me last week.

Tilly hovers in excitement. "You don't need that. I know the number off by heart. Are you going to let me listen?"

I hold the phone to my ear, well away from Tilly's chilly meddling fingers, but it goes straight to voicemail. She gestures at me to leave a message.

"Hi, Georgie. It's Jess Bailey – we met last week at

Tilly's memorial thing. I'm in London for a few days and I wondered if you fancied lunch? You can get me on this number."

My mobile rings almost immediately. Tilly pulls a sullen face as she sees my mother's face flash up on the screen.

Mum's in good form. "When are you coming to visit, Jess? The weather's lovely in Wales for this time of year. You've still got a few more weeks before you have to go back to that school – are you sure you're doing the right thing with those A Levels? Never too late to change your mind. How about an apprenticeship as a reiki instructor; I always said you had a real aptitude for it…"

"Can't you get rid of her?" Tilly interrupts. "Someone more important, like my god-sister, might be trying to get through."

"… best thing of all, you could have a nice break from the carnivore's cooking," Mum continues. "You wouldn't have to smell bacon ever again if you came to live here. Anyway, I was just telling our new reflexologist, Running River, about your transplant."

"Running River?" I say, as Tilly makes throat-cutting gestures in the background.

"Well, she's called Rhonda really, but she's one quarter North American Indian," says Mum. "She says it's a marvellous opportunity, spiritually speaking, to embrace someone else's heart and possibly share their spirit too!"

"Sounds gross," I say, as Tilly stamps her pointy boot in highly spirited frustration.

"Think of the possibilities," Mum says. "You could have anyone's heart in there! The original owner might have been a hospice nurse, a human rights lawyer..."

"A spoiled princess?" I suggest as Tilly flops down next to me.

"Get. Off. The. Phone," she hisses, rolling over on to her front. "This is important."

"I must tell you who else has joined us," says Mum. "Joaquim! You know, Wayne and Tracey's eldest. He always held a torch for you. He's a trainee Tai Chi instructor and does a bit of weaving too; makes lovely alpaca wool rugs in the colour of your aura. I've asked him to do one for you in a nice bluey-lilac. If you decide to stay at your father's, you could take it back with you. Goodness knows that house could do with a bit of brightening up..."

"Sounds great," I say to drown out the room service knock at the door. "Got to go, Mum, my tea's ready."

I eat two slices of Hawaiian ("Gross," says Tilly) and then make a quick call to Dad while Tilly stands over me, tapping her watch. I'm so tired I can hardly finish my pizza. Next thing I know, I'm waking up with my face on my half-empty plate and Tilly's cold breath up my nostrils.

"Wake up, Jess!" she says. "Your phone is ringing!"

I brush a chunk of squashed pineapple from my cheek

155

and reach for the mobile vibrating on the bedside table. Number unknown. "Hello?"

"Ciao, darling. It's Georgie." Her velvety tone takes on a note of anxiety. "Gosh, didn't wake you, did I?"

"No," I say, blinking at my phone screen. Crap. It's nearly half nine in the morning and I've slept twelve hours straight. No wonder I'm so stiff.

"If you still want to meet for lunch, I'm free today?"

"That would be brilliant. I can catch you up on all that charity stuff." I stifle a yawn and press speaker so Tilly can listen in.

"That sounds perfect. Where shall we meet?"

"You say. I don't really know anywhere in London, but I'm staying in a hotel Tilly recommended, just off the King's Road."

"I know it. Better still, let's do afternoon tea. There's a gorgeous little patisserie down the road where Tilly and I used to go all the time. How does that sound?"

I look to Tilly for approval before answering. "Yeah, great. What's the address?"

"Duh! I know where it is," interrupts Tilly.

I press mute. "Shut up. You might know but I'm not supposed to, am I?"

"Sorry."

I pretend to take down the address and arrange to meet Georgie at two thirty.

Tilly becomes business-like. "I'm glad you've had a nice

long sleep. It'll do wonders for those bags under your eyes, but if we've time, let's nip along to Harrods and pick up some decent concealer for you. I've never seen such a sorry state of affairs as your make-up bag."

"You've led a sheltered life." I stumble off the bed towards the shower.

"Ring down to room service first," she instructs. "By the time you come out, your porridge will be here." I'm beginning to see how she'd be an asset on some posh fundraising committee.

I eat breakfast while Tilly chooses my outfit.

"The cafe is cute but reasonably informal, so jeans and a nice top will do. Georgie and I used to go there when we were slobbing out and didn't want to dress up. She's probably chosen it to make you feel more comfortable," she says kindly.

"Cheers."

"They do gorgeous cakes. I really wouldn't worry about it."

"I'm not," I mumble, spooning porridge into my mouth.

"You can wear those new black jeans we got at the airport and either one of these." She reaches for the new tops spilling out of the suitcase we bought in Geneva, but her hands slither uselessly through the fabric. "Tuh, I wish I could pick them up. Which do you prefer?"

They're Tilly's new clothes not mine, but it's easier to

pretend I care. I point with my spoon to a dark green silky top with an asymmetrical neckline.

"Good choice," she says. "Perhaps you could hang it up for an hour? No point in having nice things if you don't look after them, Jess. If you hurry up with that breakfast, we can go out to the shops; I saw a dear little jacket yesterday that would go perfectly with this outfit."

"Look, if I'm going to have tea and cakes with Georgie then you'd better get me up to speed with the family set up," I say. "She was your dad's goddaughter, yeah, and she does events?"

"That's right. Her mum, my Aunt Lulu, is an old family friend of my dad's. She's the one in Barbados. She's between husbands right now – doesn't have much luck with men, poor thing. I hardly remember her first husband, he died by suicide when I was little."

"Was he Georgie's dad?" I put down my spoon. "No way, that's awful."

"Financial ruin." Tilly lowers her voice. "Bad investments, not to mention that recession fiasco."

"Uh-huh." I have absolutely no clue what she's on about.

"But then Lulu married this lovely friend of Dad's bank manager. Pots of money. It only lasted three years, but she got a very comfortable divorce settlement. A couple of years ago, she got married again."

"That's nice."

"Not really. It was over within six months." Tilly pulls a face. "He was awful – not much older than Georgie and a terrible bum pincher. I think Georgie was pretty relieved when he did a runner."

"What about Georgie? Does she have a boyfriend? Or a girlfriend?" I don't give a toss but when Tilly's distracted, it's easier to dress without being told I'm wearing the wrong colour knickers.

"I'm pretty sure there's someone on the scene, but she's always secretive about her love life. Georgie likes older guys – any shrink could tell you she's compensating for not having a proper father around. On the other hand, Aunt Lulu's boyfriends are getting younger and younger. One of these days, they'll meet in the middle over some man and then there'll be trouble." Tilly frowns and points at my pants. "Not those, Jess. You don't want to have a VPL for Georgie, do you?"

28

The cafe's in Belgravia, twee but expensive looking. I'm on time but Georgie's already there, waving from a table for two in the bow-fronted window.

"That was *our* favourite table," says Tilly sadly. "And now she'll be sitting at it with you."

"So?" I'm trying to keep my verbal communication to a minimum in front of people who matter.

"What if you become her new best friend and she forgets all about me?" Tilly's lower lip wobbles.

"Get a life." I cover my mouth as I push the heavy glass door to go inside. "I'm going back to Manchester as soon as this is over. I've no desire to nick your favourite god-sister as my BFF."

"Jess!" Georgie gets up to kiss me on both cheeks. "How lovely, I never expected you'd call so soon."

"I wanted to give you this." I produce the silk scarf from my new handbag.

"Oh, keep it!" Georgie pushes my hand away. "Anyway, you might need it if you come for another spin."

"See?" Tilly parks herself on the purple velvet banquette and folds her arms. "I *knew* you were going to steal her."

"I haven't brought the Porsche today," says Georgie. "It's grim driving through London. Anyway, I thought we'd have a proper glass of bubbly to toast my darling Tilly Billy's memory." She indicates a silver bucket containing a bottle of orange-labelled Veuve Clicquot. "This was her favourite."

Tilly sticks out her bottom lip. "So unfair! Why can't I have some?"

Georgie pours champagne into two flutes. "Cheers! Here's to our gorgeous Tilly. If only she could be with us now."

"Maybe she is…" I say, as Tilly watches with an envious expression, "… erm, looking down on us and all that."

"You're probably right," agrees Georgie. "If Tilly was going to haunt anywhere it wouldn't be some mouldy old graveyard. It would be the make-up counter at Harvey Nicks or somewhere like here with lovely memories.

Mind you, I don't know why she loved this place so much – the cakes are beyond gorgeous, but she hardly ate *anything*. Unlike me – macarons are my absolute nemesis, unfortunately." She chokes back wine, somewhere between laughing and crying. Tilly looks on fondly, wriggling along the banquette so she can wind both arms around Georgie's shapely shoulders.

"Bloody chilly, though." Georgie flings a rose-pink cashmere scarf over one shoulder, catching Tilly squarely in the left eye. "Talking of graveyards, darling, I don't recall seeing you at the funeral."

"I was … erm … in hospital," I say truthfully, taking a cautious sip of champagne.

"Oh, yes, I remember now." Georgie wafts her hand towards my chest. "Your boob job?"

It sounds super callous, missing your mate's funeral because you're having a breast reduction, but I can't exactly tell her the truth.

Tilly grins across the table. "Georgie is officially the nosiest girl in London. She won't be satisfied until she knows everything. You should ask her about the royal family stuff later; she hears all the scandal."

"I hope you don't mind but I've already ordered the special high tea. I was starving and everything's so good here," Georgie says, as the waitress sets down a silver cake stand. It looks seriously amazing. There are tiny sandwiches on the bottom tier, fluffy scones piled up in the

162

middle and the top tier overflows with miniature desserts, macarons and strawberries dipped in chocolate.

Georgie smiles as my tummy betrays me with a low-pitched rumble. "Help yourself, Jess, and then I want you to tell me all about the charity. When we met at St Aggie's you said Tilly had wanted to do some of her charity stuff in Manchester?"

I reach for a scone. "Yeah, we talked about it when she came up for the weekend."

"Tilly went to Manchester?" Georgie pauses, a mini eclair halfway to her lips. "She actually set foot north of the border? When on earth was that?"

"Erm…" I try to look vague as I busy myself with jam and cream. "Some time over the summer holidays."

"God's sake, Jess," says Tilly. "Don't just make things up. If you put your fat foot in it now, she won't believe a single word you say."

Delaying tactics, I take a mouthful of scone and glare at Tilly. A bit of assistance would be good.

"I know!" Tilly flaps her hand in excitement. "Say it was the last weekend in August – there was some art gallery opening Georgie wanted me to go to and I said I couldn't because I was going to a health spa with Bea and Tanika. Not that I did; I went somewhere entirely different, but she doesn't know that."

What a gossip tease. Where's she been that she doesn't want Georgie to know? I'll have to pin her down later.

"I remember now," I say to Georgie. "August bank holiday."

She pauses mid chew. "How weird. Is there a health spa in your neck of the woods? I wanted Tilly to be my plus one at some dire fundraiser that weekend but she was away – off to some awful colonic irrigation place with those two bitchy schoolfriends. I have to say I was surprised because it wasn't her kind of thing at all. My ma tried it once when she was desperate to lose weight. You know, drop a dress size in a day and all that. All that happened was she spent three days glued to the loo and gained half a pound." She shrieks with laughter.

"I never knew Tilly was such a little fibber." I'm starting to enjoy myself. "Like, when she came back, did she *look* like she'd lost any weight?"

Georgie selects a macaron, still giggling. "She'd have been better putting some on. She was like a stick insect."

Tilly raises her eyes to the ceiling. "You two have got a nerve going on about my weight. I suppose I should be pleased you're bonding – if I get stuck with you forever, at least I can have a civilised lunch with my god-sister now and again."

Georgie looks thoughtful. "I'm surprised Tilly didn't say she was coming to visit you. After her parents died, Ma was sort of in *loco parentis* and Tilly spent most of her school holidays with us. There was stuff she didn't want Ma to know about, but me and her were like *that*." She crosses her fingers and gives me a conspiratorial grin. "I guess all us girls keep secrets from our mothers, don't we? I bet there are a few things your mum doesn't know about you."

"Just a few," I say, desperate to change the subject. "Hey, did you know Tilly fancied setting up another branch of Kidscope in the north? She thought her dad would have liked the idea."

"I didn't know, but Uncle Ollie would definitely have approved." Georgie nods. "He was a huge fan of worthy causes. Ma says he was always chronically skint as a child because he gave so much away. Once gave all his pocket money to some dubious wildlife organization called *Save the Earwigs* or something."

"Your mum knew him as a little boy?"

"God, yes. They grew up together – childhood sweethearts and all that."

Tilly nods in confirmation. "So cute, they used to snog each other at teenage parties."

"I loved Uncle Ollie; he was like a surrogate dad after mine died." Georgie tops up my glass. "I never got on with any of my stepfathers, but Uncle Ollie was always there if I needed him. And Tilly was the little sister I never had." She blinks hard before giving me an apologetic smile. "Sorry, Jess, you didn't come to hear me bleating on and feeling sorry for myself. Tell me more about her ideas for the charity."

The champagne is making me a bit fuzzy. I nod, trying

to remember which line of the script I've got up to. "Tilly invited me to London to show me how it worked here, but she died before we could sort out a date. I wanted to keep my promise, so I went to see Kayla yesterday, just like we planned."

"You went to the charity office?" Georgie looks alarmed. "Gosh, I hope you had your riot shield with you, darling. I used to worry about Tilly walking through that neighbourhood on her own. Some of those teenagers she helped were a bit rough."

"She actually met with the kids?" Wow. If Tilly was as patronising to them as she is to me, we'd better start exploring the possibility it was one of them who ordered the hit on her.

"God, yes. Tilly was very hands on, especially if they were short-staffed on those days out. Some of the delinquents were scary to begin with, but even the bad boys came round in the end. And the younger ones simply adored her. They never had enough volunteers. She even persuaded me and Ma to help out once or twice and my ex-stepfather did a stint as Santa at the Christmas party the year before last." Georgie giggles. "It was just before he left Ma and I've often wondered if the two things were connected."

"Do you know that they're struggling for money? The charity, I mean."

Georgie puts down her empty glass. "No, I didn't know that. What on earth do you mean?"

"Their monthly direct debit was cancelled when Tilly died. Kayla's really worried about all the stuff they've got planned."

"But that's awful, Jess! I'd no idea the money had stopped. I presume the accounts are pending because there's still some confusion about where Tilly's money will ultimately go, but that's just not on."

"Tilly said your mum is one of the trustees?"

Georgie nods. "Absolutely. Ma's cruising in the Caribbean just now, but I'll see if I can get hold of her when I get home." She eyes her wine glass. "Oops, if I'm sober enough. She should have been consulted before they did something like this."

"Who do you reckon stopped the money?" I ask. "Someone at the bank, maybe?"

Georgie frowns. "Possibly. Or it could have been Mr Standish from the solicitors. Nasty little man."

Tilly looks baffled. "But Mr Standish is such a darling old thing."

I select a sandwich. "Tilly always said he was a 'darling old thing'." Tilly winces as I mimic her upper-class drawl.

"Oh, you mean old Mr Standish. He's not at all well, poor darling; he went into hospital just before Tilly died. His grandson Sebastian is dealing with everything now. It's a family firm, you see."

"So he's standing in for his granddad?" I raise my eyebrows at Tilly.

"Unfortunately." Georgie nods and lowers her voice. "He isn't a very nice man. Perhaps it was him who stopped the money. I'll get on to my mother right away, darling, and if I can't reach her, I'll ring the solicitors myself. I have Ma's power of attorney when she's out of the country – I often stand in for her at meetings and things."

"Can this Sebastian dude make decisions like that without involving the other trustees?"

"I suppose he can in these sorts of circumstances. Whether he *should* is a different matter. Don't worry, Jess, if my mother's not in agreement, he'll have to stand down. Unless he's already got the other trustee to agree, of course."

I feign ignorance. "Oh? Who's that?"

"Estelle Fox-Longley, you know, the headmistress from St Aggie's? As long as she still gets her admin fee for being on board, I can't see her rocking the boat. I heard more than one rumour that the school's in a precarious position financially. Secretly, I think The Fox has got her eye on a Tilly Spencer Endowment Fund to rebuild her crumbling hockey pavilion." She splutters into her champagne as both she and Tilly dissolve into laughter. "Honestly, though, none of the trustees have had much to do of late. As Tilly was nearly eighteen, Mr Standish liked to involve her with decision-making – Ma and the others rarely needed to intervene. Apart from that ridiculous business with the flat in Chelsea. Did you hear about that?"

"Yeah, I remember Tilly telling me," I say.

"Well, she was still at boarding school and she spent most of her holidays with us, so she didn't really need the flat, per se, but she had such happy memories of the place. Over the summer holidays, she had a few girly weekends there, sometimes with me and sometimes with those awful schoolfriends you met at the memorial. She wanted to move in full-time once she left school, but Mr Standish thought she should sell. Bloody Fox-Longley agreed with him, but Ma managed to talk them both round in the end." Georgie breaks open a fruit scone and helps herself to jam. "Gorgeous flat, did you ever visit?"

"No. She invited me to stay but then…"

"It's all locked up now. Ma has a key at home. I'd show it to you, darling, but I can't face setting foot in there. Seeing Tilly's things scattered about would just set me off again." Georgie sets down her scone and twists the silver ring on her little finger. "I can't bear it. We had a surprise eighteenth birthday party planned and she never knew. We'd even arranged to bring her granddad down for an hour. Poor old man. I popped in to see him the other day and he's just heartbroken." She sniffs hard and burrows in her handbag for a tissue. "I'll have to bully Ma into going round to the flat with me sooner or later. All the plants will be half dead by now and there's no one else to sort out Tilly's personal bits and bobs."

I glance across the table, unsurprised to see Tilly in

169

floods of tears against Georgie's cleavage. I give her a couple of minutes to recover and then stand up.

"I'm just going to the toilet."

Tilly clings on to Georgie's arm, giving me a baleful, red-rimmed stare. "Don't you dare take me away now. I don't want *you*. I want Georgie."

"Just for a minute," I insist.

Georgie looks up from wiping her eyes. "Take as long as you like, darling. The loos are down the corridor to your left."

I head off, Tilly lagging so far behind that my chest burns.

"Are you OK?" I ask, once we're safely in the super posh ladies' toilet.

"It's all gone wrong," she sobs. "They were going to have a surprise eighteenth birthday party for me! With Aunt Lulu and Granddad! And now poor old Mr Standish is in hospital and his horrible grandson's in charge of all my money! Mine!"

I nod. I'd be devastated too if I was in her position.

"And I hate seeing poor Georgie so upset. I wish we could tell her I'm still here."

"Well, we can't," I say. "You were the one who said we couldn't tell anyone, not even my dad."

"This is different. Georgie *knows* me." Her bottom lip wobbles. "We could convince her."

"We can't risk it," I say, hardening my heart. "She'll just

think I'm a basket case and it'll ruin everything. Now, is there anything else I should ask before we go?"

Tilly lifts her chin. "Yes. I want to know *all* about that party. Where it was going to be held, what we were going to eat, who was invited…"

"I mean the other stuff with the money?"

"No, silly. Once Aunt Lulu's on the case, the charity payments will be sorted out like *that*." Tilly snaps her fingers, looking puzzled by the lack of noise. "While she takes care of the money, we can get on with our own detective work. The next thing on our list is to search Leo's flat, but we can't do that until tomorrow."

"Can't wait," I say, trying to lick strawberry jam off the sleeve of my posh top before Tilly notices. "Will I be allowed to wear my own clothes this time?"

29

"I've been thinking about my apartment," says Tilly, once we're back at the hotel. "It seems ridiculous to be staying here when I have a perfectly lovely flat just down the road."

"Georgie said it's all locked up." I'm having a food coma lie down with my ankles elevated on a tasselly cushion.

"I know where there's a key. And like she said, they won't do anything with my bank accounts or any of my furniture until they decide who gets it all. And that's going to take some time as I haven't left a will."

"You haven't made a will?" I say. "Are you serious? Why the hell not?"

"Because I didn't think I was going to die yet," she says stroppily. "Have *you* made a will?"

"Hello? Slight difference, Tilly; I've got nothing to leave. And you've got like forty-five million quid?"

"Duh. It's only forty-two point five, actually." She frowns. "I suppose the trust fund is a *sort* of will, but that was written by the solicitors not me."

"So, if your mum and dad are dead, who will it go to?"

"My granddad, I suppose. He's old and a bit doolally. He lives in a nursing home in South Ken. I haven't got anyone else. I wanted some of my money to go to charity and Mr Standish said we'd have to sit down for a proper talk after my birthday. Don't forget, I hadn't got my hands on it yet – I had a monthly allowance, but anything else was agreed through the trustees."

"What about the money for the kids' thing?"

"Before he died, Dad and I set up some charity payments. He liked me to have a social conscience and he allocated one hundred thousand a year until I was eighteen. He said once I was old enough to decide for myself, I could donate as much or as little as I liked."

"I nearly fainted when Kayla said how much you'd given them."

Tilly smiles. "Kidscope was my favourite, but I did donate to other things: little local projects as well as national charities like the NSPCC. I bet those payments have been stopped too."

"Maybe it's standard practice? They freeze your accounts until they know what to do with it."

"Your theory makes perfect sense until you remember that I was *murdered*. Something's not right, Jess, and I'm sure it's all linked." She peers out of the window. "One more sleep until we can go to Leo's flat. He called it an all-day job, but we'd better wait until after lunch to be sure he's definitely gone."

I sink back against the mound of freshly laundered pillows and flick through the room service menu even though I'm stuffed. "I still don't know what you think you're going to find in Leo's flat. It's not as if you can start opening the cupboards and drawers."

"Don't be so negative. There might be papers lying about, bank statements and so on."

"Are you positive you'll even be able to get inside?" I turn to the drinks page.

"I told you, I've been practising. Look." Tilly pushes her hand right through the menu and wiggles her fingers in my face. I slam the menu closed and she withdraws, looking pale but triumphant. The slight increase in our heart rate is the only giveaway of the effort she's expended.

"Don't forget to phone your parents," she says bossily. "And where on earth's your new jacket?"

I look around. "Dunno. Crap, I must have left it in the restaurant."

"I've told you a thousand times there's no point having

nice things if you don't look after them." My mobile rings and Tilly nods stiffly towards the bedside table. "I bet that's Georgie telling you she's got your coat."

It's not. It's Mum, updating me on the progress of my aura rug.

30

All through breakfast, Tilly goes on and on about her flat. She won't give it a rest.

"It's not breaking and entering if it belongs to me."

"When they catch you, you can tell them that," I say, spooning up porridge with a twinge of homesickness. They've sprinkled raspberries on top and it reminds me of Dad offering to do the same. "But hang on – they won't catch you, will they, Tilly? It'll be me getting arrested."

"We don't need to break in, silly – I told you I have a spare key. It's wrapped in a John Lewis bag and stuffed into the bottom of one of the ground floor window boxes."

"That sounds super secure."

"Totally," agrees Tilly. She never gets when I'm being sarcastic. "I hid it there as a precaution after I locked myself out one night. You know, a few too many apple martinis with the girls and I had to sleep in Tanika's spare room. Totally gross having to go home in last night's clothes. After that, I made sure I had a back-up plan."

"Does your Aunt Lulu know where you kept the spare key?" I ask, tipping tablets into my palm.

"Absolutely not!" Tilly looks horrified. "She'd have given me hell, especially after her arguing with the other trustees and telling them how sensible and mature I was."

"What about Georgie?"

Tilly shakes her head. "I never told a soul, not Georgie, not even Bea and Tans."

"OK, so even if we can get in, what if someone comes when we're there?"

"Like who? Aunt Lulu's in Barbados and Georgie hasn't been round to the flat. Like she said – it upsets her too much." Her bottom lip trembles.

"Yeah, right before she said she'd have to come round and sort your stuff because there's no one else to do it."

"That's all talk. Georgie's the worst procrastinator on the planet, just like her mum. It'll be months before those two turn up. Pretty please, Jess?" Tilly wheedles. "There are a few things I'd like you to shred for me."

Now I'm intrigued. "Like what?"

"Diaries and so on detailing one or two boys Aunt

177

Lulu wouldn't have approved of. And you could delete a few photos off my laptop – I wouldn't want to tarnish her perfect memories of me."

"Go on, then." I dump my empty bowl and roll off the bed. "We'll just go and see if the key's still there."

"Why not take your lovely new overnight bag?" Tilly dances over to the horrible holdall we bought in Geneva. "We can always come back for the rest of your things later."

"Fine." I fling pants, socks and a shedload of tablets inside. "But I'm not checking out of this place until we know we can definitely get into your flat."

"No offence, sweetie, but I think we should get a cab," Tilly suggests as we ride down in the lift. "It's only down the road but you do look rather out of puff again."

"I'm just stressed about going to Leo's house later," I say, wondering for the millionth time how I've ended up in this situation. "Anyway, I'm supposed to be improving my exercise tolerance. If it really is so close, maybe we should walk."

Tilly's right, it's not far at all. Within minutes, we turn into an old-fashioned square with a gorgeous gated garden in the centre. The square's surrounded by terraced houses nothing like the ones I'm used to. These are like a row of massive white wedding cakes, each house three or four storeys high.

"Here we are." Tilly bounces on her toes in excitement.

"Wow. This is really where you lived?"

"Isn't it totally gorgeous? It's Queen Anne, you know. That's my flat over there." Tilly points to the house second from the end of the row. There are colourful window boxes all along the bottom row of sashes just like she described. "Mrs Huntington–Creavey lives in the middle flat and the next floor up is a *pied-à-terre* for some Tory MP who lives in deepest Dorset the rest of the week."

"Right." I've no idea what a *pied-à-terre* is but I'm not giving her the satisfaction of asking. "Which window box is the key in?"

"The third one along. Just stop, you know, pretend you're on your phone and slide your hand in. The bag's rolled up underneath a tray of pansies."

I do a quick recce of the street, which is all quiet apart from a few mums with small kids playing inside the square. I lean against the window box and dig down under the flowers. I retrieve the plastic bag without difficulty and move away to cross the street.

"Let's go and sit in there for a minute." My legs are super achy and my new heart thumps like I've run a race. I'm seriously not cut out for this covert ops stuff.

We sit on a bench facing the play area while I get my breath back. The women I thought were mums are actually uniformed nannies.

Uniformed.

I look at Tilly in disbelief. "Are those nannies wearing uniforms?"

"Showy, isn't it?" she says. "Probably *nouveau riche*, even the wealthiest people just have au pairs from Eastern Europe these days. Or mannies – they're terribly fashionable, but of course you can't put the male nannies in uniform because they look like dentists. Ha, ha, ha!"

It's like some sort of parallel universe. I brush dirt from the John Lewis bag and unwrap a silver Tiffany fob bearing two keys.

Tilly's already on her feet, bouncing with excitement. "Hurray! I can't *wait* to go in."

31

"Why is it so quiet?" I whisper as we cross the empty road to the flat.

Tilly shrugs. "Saturday morning. Everyone's probably having a lie in as they're not at work."

"People who live here actually work, do they?"

"Shut up and open the door; it's the small gold key."

I unlock the dark green door and sidle into a high-ceilinged lobby, tastefully decorated in period colours: sage and ivory.

"This way." Tilly crosses the parquet floor to another door and indicates the large silver key. "When we get inside there's a keypad for the alarm. I hope no one's changed the code number."

Is she for real? "Now you tell me!"

"Stop fussing. If it goes off, we'll just have to make a run for it. Try 34-22."

"Again, Tilly? Anyone who's ever felt you up could get into every single one of your properties or bank accounts."

I unlock the second door and we step into an airy entrance hall with a vaulted ceiling and a number of panelled doors leading off it. There's a muted beep beep beep from the entry keypad. I type in the digits, holding my breath until the red flashy light turns green. I dump my bag on the polished oak floor and slump into a pink suede armchair, heart hammering so hard the neighbours can probably hear it.

"Come on, you lazy thing," says Tilly. "I want to show you around. It feels like forever since I've been here."

I get up wearily and toe off my trainers, conscious of making too much noise on the wooden floors, but Tilly dismisses me with a glance.

"The lady upstairs is about ninety; she never hears a thing. Anyway, it's all been insulated." She's almost vibrating with excitement as she leads me across the hall. "Hurry *up*, Jess."

I push open the double doors and we step into a beautiful high-ceilinged room with arched French windows at the far end. The duck egg blue walls are covered with splashy watercolours and there are books everywhere, on shelves either side of the period fireplace and scattered across the wide velvet sofa. I'm drawn to the far end of the room, pulling aside heavy tapestry curtains to look out on to a small walled lawn. It's like something out of *The Secret Garden* – ivy and wisteria climbing the weathered brick and the lawn covered with autumn leaves from a huge old oak tree.

"Oh, wow! Is that a treehouse?" I point up at a yellow hobbit-hole door, partially obscured by foliage. Lower down, a wooden ladder rests against the tree trunk.

"Isn't it sweet?" Tilly presses her nose against the glass. "Daddy had it built for my ninth birthday. In the summer, I used to sleep up there sometimes."

"Didn't the other people in the building mind your dad customizing the tree?" I laugh. "I bet you can see right into the upstairs flat from that little house."

Tilly shrugs. "It's a garden flat so the garden and the tree in it belong to us. No one else is allowed in there. Now come and see my proper bedroom."

She pulls me into the room next door where my socks sink into fluffy lilac carpet. "Look up, Jess!"

The corniced ceiling's scattered with luminescent stars above a huge canopied bed, swathed in violet tulle and festooned with strings of fairy lights.

"And you said you weren't a spoiled princess," I say as Tilly tunnels under the frothy fabric to fling herself on to

183

the embroidered duvet. "This is exactly like the Barbie playhouse I wanted when I was about six."

"Me too!" Tilly's rosy face re-emerges from under a pile of purple gauze. "Isn't it heaven? You should have seen the interior designer. His face was like a smacked bottom, but Daddy gave him such a huge advance he couldn't say no."

"Has anyone ever said no to you, Tilly?"

She crawls out to seat herself on a heart-shaped stool in front of the dressing table. "Apart from you? Not really." She stares down at the stool in dismay, her face crumpled like a little girl's. "Oh. I can't make it spin round like I used to."

"Hold on then." I indulge her, spinning the seat faster and faster as she twirls around, arms arced above her head like a prima ballerina.

"Hooray! I love being home. Come and see my clothes."

There's no wardrobe but another door leads to a walk-in closet. A rainbow array of silky dresses hangs above row upon row of doll-like shoes. Tilly kneels, alighting like a butterfly on one pair after another. "Aren't they gorgeous? You can borrow any you like. What shoe size are you?"

"Six," I say, feeling like one of the ugly sisters. "I don't think they'd fit."

Tilly shakes her head regretfully. "I'm only a four."

She stands up again, pouncing on a primrose yellow T-shirt with gold writing across the front.

"'Though she be but little she is fierce'," she quotes,

beaming. "Mummy bought me this in Stratford-upon-Avon because it reminded her of me. It's Shakespeare, you know. *Romeo and Juliet*."

I unfold the T-shirt. "*A Midsummer Night's Dream*, Act 3, Scene 2," I read aloud but Tilly's already moved on. I follow, obliged to admire her rainfall shower and high-spec kitchen in turn.

In the hall, I open another door to find a flight of stairs, this time carpeted in funky burnt orange. "Where does this go?"

"Upstairs, of course. There's Mummy and Daddy's room, another bathroom and Daddy's office." She dances up the stairs in front of me.

"But I thought it was a flat." I'm completely confused when we reach another landing.

"Duh, it's a duplex. That means over two floors."

Either side of the landing are two huge rooms, one with a king-size bed and the other scattered with squashy sofas and coloured beanbags.

Tilly points into the peacock-blue bedroom. "This was my parents'. I don't like to come in here much. Daddy's office was next door, but I've redecorated that."

"This closet has got all my suitcases in, look!" She makes me open a huge cupboard to find a pyramid of zebra-striped matching luggage, the largest suitcase the size of a bloody tumble dryer.

"And this is my den." She's already halfway across the

landing to the room opposite. It has the same cinnamon carpet as the staircase and above the fireplace is a framed picture of Marilyn Monroe in jazzy colours.

Even I recognize an Andy Warhol. "Cool. Is this a print?"

"They're all prints, sweetie, but this one's from the original run. It's signed, see?" Tilly runs her fingers across the glass. "Daddy got it for his twenty-first. I wish I could find some way of leaving it to Georgie, she always loved it."

As I gaze around in awe, Tilly looks shy for once. "Do you like how I've had it done up? Cosy, isn't it?"

I nod. Despite the massive rooms, the flat's really welcoming. I'm seriously tempted to give in to Tilly's idea about making it our base.

"Look, if we're going to even *think* about staying here, we have to be super careful going in and out," I say. "And we can't leave stuff lying about in case somebody comes."

"How many times do I have to tell you? No one's going to come."

"OK, but if they do, it has to look like this. We keep everything packed and ready to go in case we have to scarper."

"If you like. Everyone will just think your lovely new luggage belongs to me. We can put it in the cupboard on the landing. Ooh, look." Her butterfly brain's moved on. "My computer. Let's check my emails."

"Go on, then." I open the silver laptop. "Password?"

Tilly looks sheepish.

"Jeez, Tilly. Not Mrs Styles again?"

"Of course not. I'm not a baby any more, Jess." She lifts her chin. "It's 'Mrs Harington'."

"Harington?"

"You know, as in Kit?"

"The guy from *Game of Thrones*?" I try not to giggle. "Isn't he a bit northern for you?"

"Oh no, sweetie, that's just acting. He comes from down the road. I met him once at a red-carpet thing – too gorgeous in the flesh." She supervises as I type. "All lower case, one R not two."

"Only four hundred and seventy-three?" Tilly peers at her emails. "I thought there'd be more people wanting to offer their condolences."

"They'd hardly email you, would they?" I point out. "Not when they know you're dead."

"There's no need to be mean."

The most recent messages are all mail shots for expensive stuff but clicking back to September, we start to hit the personal ones. There's an invitation to a charity auction and a saga from one of her friends going into excessive gory detail about snogging some Oxbridge student called Tarquin. I skim quickly past that one before hitting an invoice for a vintage cocktail dress.

"Vintage?" I say. "Isn't that just a posh way of saying second-hand?"

Tilly gives my scar a meaningful look. "Nothing wrong with second-hand, sweetie. I seem to remember you weren't complaining. Anyway, I prefer the term pre-loved." She sighs, stroking her index finger down the image on the screen. "Totally gorgeous. 1950s midnight-blue velvet with a cowl neck, see? I was going to wear it for the St Aggie's harvest festival dinner. There was a cute matching jacket actually, but I said no to that because the collar was real fur. Yuck."

"There's one from your school here," I say, spotting St Agatha's in the sender line.

Tilly dismisses it with a glance. "Just my school fees. The solicitor sorted the payments, but Mr Standish had me copied into everything so I knew where my money was going."

"But this is dated a week after you died," I say. "That's a bit off."

Tilly shrugs. "I think you have to give six weeks' notice to cancel."

"You were dead! They can't expect you to give six weeks' notice if you're dead," I say. "Jeez, eighteen grand! Fancy charging you for the whole year."

"Oh no, sweetie, that's just the autumn term. Gives them breathing space to find another boarder. So weird to think of a new girl sharing my rooms with Bea. I hope they get on."

Unlikely, if Bea's as mean to her as she was to me, but I smile and say nothing as Tilly gestures at me to scroll down.

"Next, Jess."

"I'm not your secretary," I complain but do it anyway. There are a few promotions from cosmetic companies and then two messages from Georgie.

> Hi, Tilly Billy. Where are you? Don't say
> you've forgotten our lunch. Kiss, kiss. G x

Crap. I click on to the next one.

> T, you're not answering your phone and Ma's
> starting to get a tiny bit worried. Ring if you
> can. G x

Tilly shivers. "Ugh. I can't bear to think of her and Aunt Lulu waiting in that restaurant for me. They must have been *so* upset when they heard. I hope Rupert was on duty to break the news."

I move swiftly to the next message.

> Hello Tilly,
>
> I couldn't reach you on your mobile, but I
> wanted to tell you Mr Linwood's not very well
> this morning. We've had the doctor out, but
> he's asking for you. Can you come?
>
> Helen Carty from Greendale

Tilly stares at the screen, her face draining of colour.

"Who's Mr Linwood?" My heart bumps uncomfortably. "And what's Greendale?"

"He's my granddad," she whispers. "He lives in a nursing home called Greendale just a couple of miles from here. When was that email sent, Jess?"

"The sixteenth."

"The day I died. And I never knew." Her eyes fill with tears. "He's all I've got, Jess. Can we go, please? Right now?"

32

I call for a cab while Tilly strains at me, already halfway down the stairs.

"It was weeks ago, remember?" I remind her, pressing my fist against the burning sensation in my chest. "He's probably loads better by now."

"What if he's not? What if I never got the chance to see him again? What if he's dead? I'd know if he'd died, wouldn't I, Jess?"

She goes quiet once we're in the cab, but my erratic heart rate is a barometer of how upset she is. Every time we slow for a red light, it speeds up. I hold Tilly's chilly hand until the cab swings into a leafy street and pulls over to the kerb.

Greendale is a gorgeous ivy-covered Victorian villa at the bottom of a short gravelled drive. All the cars in the visitors' spaces are expensive ones: a Porsche, a BMW, two Teslas.

"It's so lovely here," says Tilly as we hurry up the stone steps. "Granddad chose it himself a few years back. He was already beginning to get forgetful, so he said he'd find somewhere himself rather than become institutionalized by Mummy once he'd completely lost the plot." She gives me a fleeting grin. "He liked the name Greendale because it's where Postman Pat lives. You know, the little kids' programme? Granddad thought this was a fabulous joke because he was a postman before he retired."

"Your granddad was a postman? But I thought—"

"What? That he had money?" Tilly shakes her head as we wait for someone to answer the bell. "Mummy's family are from Yorkshire originally and didn't have a bean. Dad was the rich one and when he met Mummy, his family pretty much disowned him. He was an only child, you see. Supposed to marry someone with the *right background*."

"What about your other grandparents? Your dad's mum and dad?"

"I've never met them. They didn't want to meet Mummy and me in the beginning and by the time they changed their minds, I'd already decided I didn't want to meet them either. My parents were getting on a bit when I was born – Mummy had to have a lot of IVF. Now my parents are dead too." Her face crumples. "Granddad is all I've got."

I squeeze her hand as the door's opened by a pleasant-faced woman dressed in a green nursing tunic.

"Can I help you?"

"I've come to see Mr Linwood, if that's OK? His granddaughter was a friend of mine, but she died last month."

The woman's face creases into a sympathetic smile. "Come on in, dear. We were all so upset to hear about Tilly, God rest her soul. Such a good girl and devoted to her granddad. She visited every week in the school holidays."

Even the compliments don't put a dent in Tilly's anxiety. "Ask how he is," she hisses into my ear.

"I heard Mr Linwood had been poorly," I say.

"Let me see." Her round face is thoughtful. "Stanley did have a very bad do a couple of months back. There's the funny thing – it was the same day Tilly died. Makes you think, doesn't it?"

"Weird." I'm prompted by a chilly prod in the upper arm. "But he's OK now?"

"Much better, bless him."

Tilly exhales and our heart slows to a steady thud.

"He's been very down since he heard the news about Tilly," the lady continues. "I'm sure it'll cheer him up to meet a nice young lady who can chat to him about his granddaughter. He's outside in the garden. Even when it's breezy like today, Stanley enjoys the fresh air."

She leads me through the house into a large lounge full of well-dressed older people and then through tall French windows into a lawned garden. The sunflowers by the back door are almost as tall as me. It's so quiet, you'd never guess we were in London.

"Heaven, isn't it? So peaceful," says Tilly as we follow the nurse across a neat lawn to a large sycamore.

"This is Stanley's favourite tree," says the woman. "As long as he's tucked up snug and warm, he likes to have a little snooze before lunch."

A tall elderly man sits in a wheelchair under the tree, eyes closed and knobbly hands resting on a tartan rug.

"Stanley, there's a young lady here to see you." The lady speaks clearly into his right ear and then straightens up to smile at me. "It'll be nice for him to have a bit of company – he hasn't had any visitors since Tilly died." She lowers her voice as she turns to go back into the house. "Take no notice if he seems a bit confused."

The old man opens his eyes, his wrinkled face creasing into a smile. "Tilly, love! I knew you'd be back."

"No," I begin. "My name's Jess. I'm a friend of Tilly's—"

"Shut up," whispers Tilly fiercely, as she drags me closer to the chair. "He's not talking to you. He's talking to me. Hello, Granddad."

33

I look from the old, wrinkled face to the young, smooth one. What the hell is going on here? Tilly's right – Stanley's not looking at me, he's smiling directly at her.

How cool is that?

"I'm so pleased you're OK, Granddad," Tilly says, her voice tender. "How are you feeling now?"

"All the better for seeing you, flower. It does my heart good." He raises tufty eyebrows at me. "And who's your friend here?"

"This is Jess." She pushes me forward. "She's been helping me."

195

"Does he know about you being … erm…" I'm not sure how to say it.

"Yes, of course," says Tilly, leaning forward to stroke his cheek. "You know I'm dead, don't you, Granddad?"

"I'll tell you what I don't know," he grumbles, placing his knotted hand on top of hers. "I don't know what you're doing buggering about down here when you should be with your mam and dad."

"Exactly." Tilly looks at me with a sigh. "We're working on that, aren't we, Jess?"

"Anyway, I'm right glad to see you, Tilly, love." Stanley's eyes are bright with tears. "Come and give your old granddad a hug."

Tilly kneels next to the wheelchair and presses her rosy cheek against his papery one. She looks up at me. "Is it OK if we stay for a bit?"

"'Course it is." I feel like I'm intruding so I retreat as far as I can without pulling her away and sit on the damp grass, my back against the trunk of the tree.

They stay like that for almost an hour, talking, but for the most part, just sitting very close, cheeks touching and Stanley stroking Tilly's shiny hair back from her face. She looks more content than I've ever seen her – a genuine smile instead of a smirk on her face, which glows brighter than the sunflowers by the door.

Eventually, I check my phone. "Sorry, Tilly, but if we are going to Leo's, we'd better make a move."

"Can we come back another time?"

"Definitely." I stand, brushing damp grass from my bum. "Nice to meet you, Stanley."

He peers up, shielding his eyes from the low autumn sun. "See you, love. Thanks for bringing her to see me." He sounds cheerful but his eyes cloud as he watches us leave.

Outside, we hail a black cab on the street and I give the driver the address in Camberwell.

"Thank you, Jess." Tilly's unusually humble as we climb into the back seat. "I feel much better about going to Leo's now."

I'm glad someone does because, now it's time, I'm bricking it. To distract myself, I make a list. "I need to take my tablets before we get there. We'd better stop on the way and get a sandwich," I say, putting in my AirPods. "Your fancy kitchen cupboards were like Old Mother Hubbard's."

"Even when I was alive, I never cooked. Just ate out or had food delivered. For Granddad's birthday in August, I ordered afternoon tea for three from Cutter & Squidge and we ate in the garden with Aunt Lulu." Tilly's bottom lip wobbles. "It was so beautiful and now everything's spoiled."

"At least you got to see him today – look how pleased he was." I give her a nudge. "Mind you, even I'd be pleased to see you if I'd had no visitors for nearly two months."

"That can't be right." Tilly frowns. "I've just remembered – didn't Georgie say she'd been to visit?"

"Shame you didn't bloody remember that earlier," I say grumpily. There would have been a lot less stressing about Stanley being dead already. "But maybe that nurse wasn't on duty when she came. It was super weird, wasn't it? I can't believe he could actually see you."

"You can see me," says Tilly, logically.

"That's different." I rub my chest. "Nobody else has ever been able to see you except me."

"That's true." Tilly shrugs. "Maybe it only works for people who are losing their marbles."

34

"This is it, Jess." Tilly points to a red door at the bottom of a flight of stone steps flanked by rusted railings. "The basement flat on the left."

I nod, watching the taxi drive away and wishing we were still in the back of it. My heart races, but now we're here, we're both so stressed it could be either of us.

"Don't just stand there," Tilly says, as I hover uncertainly on the top step. "You need to get closer to the door so I can go inside. Pretend you're collecting for charity or something."

"Are we sure he's definitely out?" I clasp my hands together to stop them shaking as I descend the steps.

"He said he was working all day at that football thing." She lets out a nervous giggle. "You could always ring the doorbell and run away if he answers."

I glance around. There's no one on the street but that's not necessarily a good thing. I ring the doorbell and then, at Tilly's insistence, ring again but there's no answer. The flap on the letter box is missing, so I squat down and peer through the slot into an untidy living room.

"He definitely out. Let's do this." Tilly places her palm against the door and presses lightly. Nothing happens. She exhales slowly, pops her neck from side to side and shrugs her shoulders like a boxer going into the ring. She lifts her hand again, brow furrowed in concentration.

I watch in fascination as her fingertips shimmer and disappear until she's armpit deep up against the peeling paint. "Cool."

"Not cool." Tilly withdraws her arm and slumps against the railing, looking faint and sweaty.

"Why have you stopped?" Our heart's thudding again, but this time I'm pretty sure it's not down to me.

"I'm not entirely sure I can do it." Tilly looks like she's going to puke. "It feels all wrong. Like I'm doing myself some serious damage."

"It's not like you can get any deader than you already are," I whisper. "You *said* you'd been practising."

"I have but it feels completely different going into the flat of the man who murdered me." Her jaw sets in

200

a stubborn line. "I'm sorry, OK? I thought I could do it, but I can't."

Bollocks. Now what are we going to do?

"Don't be such a wuss," I hiss, playing her at her own game. "This was your idea, Tilly, so get your shit together and *try again*."

Unbelievably, my pep talk works. Tilly glares at me and then extends her shaking hand towards the frosted glass in the door. My heart bumps in time with her measured breaths as she focuses on pushing her arm through the door until her forehead is almost touching the wood. It's super weird to watch, like she's been CGI'd out of a movie. Eyes screwed up tight and keeping up a constant low-grade whimper, she tilts her head forward until her nose and the rest of her face disappear too, leaving only her heaving shoulders behind.

"Aaaarggh!" The whimper ramps up to a full-on shriek, Tilly's head and shoulders suddenly re-materializing as the door is pulled inwards. She stumbles backwards, wide-eyed in panic, as Leo appears in the open doorway, sweaty and unshaven.

"You?" he says, lunging forward to grab the collar of my jacket. "What the hell are you doing here?"

My heart stutters as he yanks me inside and slams the door behind me. Now I'm on the inside and Tilly's on the outside. That wasn't in the plan.

201

35

Shit. I'm trapped inside a dark basement flat face to face with an unconvicted killer. How the hell did I let Tilly talk me into this? Dad thinks I'm in Wales, Mum thinks I'm in Manchester. If Leo kills me now, no one's ever going to find my body.

He blinks down at me but says nothing as he releases my jacket. I turn, scrabbling to open the door, but he braces his hand against it, armpit level with my nose. My legs wobble as I recoil from the smell of sour sweat and alcohol. The room's a complete tip, glasses and dirty plates piled on every surface. The curtains are closed, the air stale, and suddenly, I'm desperate for the loo.

On the other side of the door, Tilly's fists pound silently against the glass. "Jess? *Jess?* What's happening in there? Are you OK?" Her fingers inch through the open letter box to squeeze mine and, although they're freezing cold as usual, it's a comfort.

Leo staggers slightly, not taking his bleary eyes from my face. "It's you from that job the other day. What the hell are you doing here?"

"Bluff it out!" urges Tilly through the letter box. "Pretend you were reading the electricity meter."

"Reading the meter?" I don't know why I'm bothering to whisper. It doesn't matter if Leo thinks I'm lying. He killed Tilly and now he's going to kill me. I look around for something I can use to protect myself. On a nearby shelf, just out of reach, is a huge can of hairspray and a super-sized bottle of aftershave. Aramis, yuck.

"You're from that posh school." Leo runs a finger round the neck of his crumpled shirt. "Why are you following me?" I swallow and try to control my breathing as he leans into my face, shouting this time. "I said – why are you *following* me?"

"I'm not following you," I say, trying to avoid eye contact. "You weren't supposed to be here." I sidle towards the can of hairspray, flattening myself against the wall.

"Wait, Jess." Through the open letter box, Tilly's voice is puzzled. "Look at his face. He's not angry – he's terrified."

I make myself look up. She's right, Leo looks scared. If anything, more scared than me.

"He's frightened," she says. "Totally shitting himself. But why?"

"Who sent you?" Leo lurches forward and I sidestep, making a successful grab for the hairspray.

"He thinks you know something," says Tilly. "Say something, Jess. Quick, *anything*."

Like what? I direct the can towards him and try to sound cryptic. "Back off. We know … everything."

"Yeah, right," says Leo, but he moves away to leave a space between us.

"Tell him about the car!" hisses Tilly. "Tell him we know about the murder!"

I take a deep breath. "We know about Tilly's murder."

"You're talking crap," Leo says, but his voice breaks.

"We know about…" I swallow hard. "The *deer.*"

"The deer what caused the accident?"

"The deer didn't cause the accident." Anger overrides my anxiety. "You did."

Leo's hands shake as he reaches for a half empty bottle of vodka on the coffee table. I flinch, thinking he's going to hit me with it, but instead he unscrews the cap and takes a mouthful. "Look, a deer hit my motor, all right?"

"Yeah, like two hours earlier," I point out. "You told Tilly you hadn't cleaned it off because you didn't want to make her late for lunch."

"How the hell do you know that?"

"We've got a witness."

"No." He shakes his head. "No one else was there."

"I beg to differ," says Tilly. "Remind him about the CD."

"You got Tilly to unbuckle her seat belt so she could get a CD case from under the front seat."

Leo's olive skin blanches almost white. "I didn't!"

"Liar!" Tilly hisses in outrage.

"Yeah, you did. Michael Bublé, remember?" I force myself to meet his eye. "Then you drove her into a stone wall while she yelled at you to stop. Did you really think you'd got away with it?"

"Oh, Christ!" Leo's face crumples. "I knew something weren't right. The bleeding car was bugged, weren't it?"

"Good one, Jess!" Tilly says. "We should have thought of that. Keep going!"

"Yeah, it was bugged," I say. "So we know *everything*."

"Who are you? Old Bill?" That's weird. He sounds almost relieved.

Weirder still, he thinks *I'm* from the police? Seriously? How old does he think I am? I lift my chin, fixing him with my best *Line of Duty* impression.

"Don't say you're the police or we've nothing to bargain with," Tilly points out. "If you had any evidence, you'd have arrested him already. I know! Pretend we're going to blackmail him."

"We're not Old Bill," I say, channelling *EastEnders* instead. "We're loads worse."

Leo looks defeated. "You've come from him. This ain't right – if I did this one job, we'd be straight, Mr Barker said. He promised me."

"I bloody knew it!" says Tilly. "He was paid to kill me."

"And you believed him, did you?" I say to Leo, fishing for info.

"I'm not a murderer." Leo's voice cracks. "Just 'cause I've done a bit of stunt driving don't mean I'm qualified to take people out. And she was only a kid. I feel like shit, you know? I can't sleep, can't eat nothing."

"Well, boohoo," says Tilly. "Pissed and sorry for himself, more like. Be more bossy, Jess. Pretend we're back in the Swiss bank."

Leo's well clear of the door now, but I reach behind for the handle just in case. "Tell me about the arrangement."

Leo looks suspicious. "If you work for Mr Barker, you should know about the arrangement."

I brandish the can of hairspray with menace. "Maybe I'm working for someone a bit higher up the food chain."

The effect on Leo is instantaneous. "Christ. Are you here from Big Den?"

Big Den? Is that a person or a place? From the limited letter box view, Tilly looks as puzzled as me, but Leo's not finished.

"I get it. You're his daughter, yeah? Now you're not wearing that stupid hat, I see the resemblance."

"Ha! Apparently you look like a gangster called Big Den, sweetie," Tilly says, safe on the other side of the door. "That's what happens when you eat too many Jaffa Cakes."

"Shut up," I say fiercely, but it's Leo who shrinks away, reversing towards the kitchen.

"Don't let him escape," Tilly squeaks, her nails gripping the edge of the letter box.

"Don't think about running. I got back-up outside," I say, trying to sound like a gangster's daughter. "Front and rear. And we've got the recording from the car so you'd better tell me the rest."

Leo breaks down completely. Between self-pitying sobs and slugs of vodka, he admits owing money to a shedload of dodgy people, including a local businessman, Mr Barker, who promised to wipe Leo's gambling debt of one hundred and fifteen grand. In return, Leo had to arrange Tilly's murder.

"Find out why," Tilly instructs, but Leo doesn't know.

"Mr Barker's one of my regulars. A lot of business deals go on in the back of my car and he pays well for inside information," he says, his tongue maybe loosened by the vodka. "On Tuesdays, I pick him up from the Dog and Duck in Camden and tell him what I've heard while I drive him to some fancy office block in Canary Wharf."

"Every Tuesday?"

Leo nods. "He does a lot of business outside the office,

207

but he's cagey – uses different drivers, see? I just work for him Tuesdays."

"What time?" I say. "Write down the address."

Leo scrawls something on the back of a cigarette packet and hands it over. "A few months back, he says he wants more than just info and he's not the sort of bloke you can say no to. He said it'd be an easy job for someone with my skills, but it had to look like an accident."

"Everyone knows it wasn't an accident." I've no idea where this is coming from. "Us, the police. You messed up, didn't you, Leo?"

"Well, maybe Mr Barker should have got Charlie to do it." Leo's face contorts with anger. "It's not as if it was the first time. But Charlie's a bit of a one trick pony and Mr Barker said they couldn't use arson again. Not after last time."

Through the letter box, Tilly's blue eyes dart from him to me. "Find out what he means!"

"Mind you," Leo continues, running a shaking hand through his lank hair, "Charlie didn't do such a great job, did he? He was only supposed to kill the woman. Not both of them."

"What woman?" I whisper.

"Some rich cow in Surrey. Her husband got back early from his business trip, so he was in the house when it got torched – old Charlie got some aggro over that. Probably why they didn't trust him to do the job this time and got

208

muggins here to do it instead." Leo shakes his head. "I must have been mental. I'd never have got in so deep if I'd known Mr Barker was running the debt."

The last trickle of fear turns to fury as I understand what he's just said. Tilly's face has disappeared from the letter box, but I can hear her sobbing behind the door. I need to get her away from here.

I want to punch Leo's sweaty, self-pitying face but instead I wrench open the door into the fading light. "If you know what's good for you, you'll keep your mouth shut," I say. "Don't forget we've got the recording. We'll be in touch."

I grab Tilly's arm and hurry her up the steps, my heart hammering so hard it feels like it's going to burst out of my chest.

"Just a bit further," I murmur, as we step out into the street. "Not far now, Tilly."

We reach the sanctuary of a side street and duck into the dank doorway of an empty cab rank. Tilly lifts her tear-stained face to mine.

"They killed them," she sobs. "My parents. They killed them both."

36

Watching Tilly cry is the weirdest thing. The tears look real enough as they drip down her pink nose, but they disappear long before they fall on to the sparkly duvet cover. She can't stop shivering, arms clasped around her knees, as she rocks back and forth in the middle of the huge canopied bed.

It's getting dark but I don't dare put on the light – instead we sit in the violet glow of the twinkling fairy lights.

"I can't believe they killed my mum and dad," Tilly sobs. "This feels almost as bad as when it first happened. How could someone do that on purpose – set fire to the house while they were sleeping and let them burn?"

"Bastards," I say, pulling her against me.

"It was always a sort of comfort to know they died in their sleep, next to each other and they never knew anything about it, but I can't bear this," she says. "Why, Jess? Why them and why me? What have I done to deserve this?"

"Nothing, Tilly. You haven't done anything." I stroke her hair as she gulps and swallows so hard I think she's going to be sick.

"I just want to be with them, Jess." Her voice breaks. "Why can't I be with them?"

My heart aches for her – or maybe it's Tilly's heart aching for her mum and dad. Either way, I need to get a grip on myself because the last thing she needs right now is me breaking down too.

"We can't let those people get away with this." She clenches my hand with frozen fingers. "We've got to find out what's going on, Jess."

"We will," I promise over and over again. "Why don't you lie down and rest for a bit?"

Eventually, she curls up on her side, presses her streaky face into a battered old teddy bear and sleeps.

We spend the night in the claustrophobic confines of the purple bed. I don't sleep much either, waking every few minutes, my heart racing like a train, as Tilly weeps into the pillow beside me.

In the first light of morning, I open my eyes to find an

empty space beside me. *Where the hell is she?* A faint scent of orange blossom lingers on the pillow, reassuring me she can't be gone, not yet, because we need to finish this together.

I lift the gauzy curtains, almost relieved to see her sitting on the heart-shaped dressing stool. She's dry-eyed, hugging her knees to her chest.

"Are you OK, Til?"

She lifts her chin. "Oh good, you're awake. I feel better now."

I'm glad she does because I'm exhausted. Maybe once you're already dead, nothing fazes you for too long. I crawl off the bed to join her. "Really?"

"Yes, much better. I've been thinking while you were asleep. At least we know for sure my death wasn't an accident. And we know about … Mummy and Daddy." She swallows. "Something must have been going on for quite a while."

"It must be to do with the money, Tilly," I say. "Why else would someone want you out of the way? Especially now we know your parents' deaths weren't an accident either."

"You're right, it must be linked to the money, but I don't see how. The only person who benefits from my death is Granddad and there's no way he's involved."

"No way. But maybe your solicitor will know something."

"His grandson, you mean. Bloody Sebastian bloody Standish. I bet he's in it up to his neck. We already know he's been stopping money from leaving my account. The other thing we need to do is to track down this Mr Barker. And find out why he's going round paying people to *off* me."

She's channelling Liam Neeson again, but this time I can only think it's a good thing.

"We know where he'll be on Tuesday," I say, searching in my back pocket for the torn off bit of cardboard I took from Leo. "And we definitely know where to find Sebastian Standish. We could ring up, make an appointment – you know, say it's something to do with your charity?"

"Damnit, the solicitors isn't open on the weekend. We'll have to leave it until first thing tomorrow," says Tilly. She stands up and puts her arm around my shoulder. "You know, Jess, I feel awful about making you stay here. I'm being the worst hostess. You didn't have dinner last night and there isn't a thing to eat in the flat. Shall we go out and find you some breakfast? I don't want you to get sick."

"OK." After no dinner last night, I'm super hungry. "I'll just hide my stuff first."

"Leave it, Jess. I've told you, no one's going to come. Anyway, you left my laptop out yesterday."

"No, I didn't. I put everything away before we went out." I don't know why Tilly's in such a rush. She hovers while I change my T-shirt, clean my teeth and shove my holdall under the bed. "Ready."

"There's a gorgeous little French bakery just down the road, they do *the best* continental breakfast," she says, glancing at her watch. "You looked after me so well last night, I think you deserve a morning off from porridge."

I know Tilly well enough by now to guess she's up to something, but the cafe looks super nice so I just go with it. I stuff down two pains au chocolat and a custard Danish while she devises various methods of torture for Leo and the unknown Mr Barker.

"All finished?" she says, standing up. "Let's go. We can have a stroll over the river and see the shops."

I follow as she moves briskly through the streets. "Slow down a bit," I pant. "Where are we going?"

"Surprise. You'll see in a minute."

The streets get scruffier as we head south. I recognize a corner shop and a launderette. "Tilly, are we going to the charity office?" I say but she doesn't answer.

We round a corner and there it is — a smart yellow minibus with the sliding door open and half a dozen kids jumping up and down on the pavement. A tall woman with long braids down her back bends over a little boy sitting in a wheelchair. She talks into a mobile tucked between ear and shoulder as she wrestles with the brakes.

Tilly looks guilty. "Please, Jess? It's my last chance to see them all."

The penny drops. "Is this the trip? The sodding safari park?"

"It's not a safari park. It's a tiny zoo with a play area and pets' corner. And the sweetest little otters." Tilly bites her bottom lip and glances up through glistening lashes. "Please, Jess? I've had such a crappy week and it would really cheer me up to see the kids enjoying themselves one last time—"

"No. No way, Tilly," I hiss, turning to make my escape. It's a bloody good job she's already dead.

"Jess? Whoa, this is so cool!" Wes appears from the far side of the bus and lopes over to me, white Air Force Ones flashing as he crosses the road in long strides.

"Wes." My heart bumps as he bounces to a stop in front of me, a huge grin on his face. "I didn't know you'd be here."

"Yeah, I'm chief kid wrangler and wheelchair pusher today."

"Don't forget to tell him you're not staying, Jess." Tilly sounds innocent, but her expression borders on smugness as Wes takes my hand and pulls me over to the bus.

"Hey, Mum, look who I found."

Kayla looks up from her struggle with the red wheelchair. "Jess? Oh my god, brilliant timing, hon. One of our volunteers phoned in sick and we always need an extra pair of hands when we've got Tyrone with us." She smiles at the little lad in the chair who's clapping his hands in excitement. "Poor little love, I thought we were gonna have to call his mum and tell her to come back. Tariq can only do drop off and pick up today – there's no way me and Wes would have coped on our own. Thank god you turned up."

"You can't back out now." Tilly looks virtuous. "Look at his little *face*."

"You owe me big time," I mutter, keeping up the pretence as I heave myself up into the bus.

"Honestly, you'll love it." Tilly beams at the scruffy, undersized occupants. "Those two at the back, Ayesha and Rihanna are real cuties, but keep an eye on Darius there – he picks his nose and wipes it on your bum when you're not looking."

I can't answer because Kayla's right behind me. "Bless you, hon, first you sort the money for the bus repairs then you rock up to give us a hand today."

"No worries." There's a warm glow around my heart that probably belongs to Tilly rather than me. "Hey, I spoke to the daughter of one of Tilly's trustees on Friday. She's going to ask her mum to get your bank payments reinstated."

Kayla gives me a fist bump. "You're a bloody star, girl. You know who you remind me of? Our Tilly, that's who."

The warm glow subsides slightly as I glance sideways to see Tilly's full-on smirk. I look around for somewhere to sit as Kayla does the rounds buckling seat belts.

"Hey, plenty of room up front with me." Wes pats the wide front seat and then nods at the driver. "Take it away, Tariq!"

There's a resounding cheer from the children as the bus rolls away from the kerb.

"Who knows the words to 'The Wheels on the Bus'?" yells Kayla behind me.

"I do! I do!" shrieks Tilly, drowning out the kids.

Over the noise, my mobile warbles with a notification from Dad.

> What are you up to today, Jessie? Goat yoga
> or wind chime appreciation, LOL?

Oh, crap. With all the stress of last night, I completely forgot to phone him.

On way to Battersea Zoo in minibus, I'm tempted to reply before thinking better of it.

37

I've never seen Tilly so smiley. She skips as she tows me from one pen to another, showing me the emus, the ring-tailed lemurs and the Tamarin monkeys with their daft moustaches. And I guess it's kind of nice to have a day off from all the drama. Kayla hands out homemade veggie samosas and apples for everyone to eat as we go. The zoo's only little so I don't get too knackered – I even manage to keep up with Tyrone as he does impressive but terrifying wheelies around the adventure playground in his red wheelchair.

Afterwards, I sit on the wall getting my breath back while I watch Aleesha and Rihanna on the slide.

"Budge up," says Wes, handing me a ninety-nine.

218

"Ooh, thanks." It's not exactly ice-cream weather, but Mr Whippy's my favourite.

"You seem to be a hit with Wesley." Tilly watches enviously as I nibble my flake. "He never once bought me an ice cream."

"Maybe he thought you could afford your own," I mutter as Wes dashes off to retrieve Darius, who's stuck at the top of the climbing frame.

"You gave him seven hundred pounds on Wednesday," Tilly points out maliciously. "He probably thinks you can afford your own ice cream."

"Don't remind me. God knows how I'm going to explain that."

"You don't owe anyone an explanation, sweetie." Tilly scowls at Wes as he returns to sit on the other side of me. "Especially not Wesley Lawrence."

"I don't get you." Wes jostles against me as he takes a lick of his ice cream. "Last week, you're there flashing the cash in your fancy gear, this week, you seem … normal, man."

"I am normal, you cheeky sod," I say, relieved I'm wearing my own clothes for once.

"You're not like any of Tilly's other mates."

"Definitely not," I say, thinking about that Bea and Tanika. "Look, that money wasn't mine, you know."

"Whoa." Wes raises his eyebrows. "Whose was it, then?"

"Digging yourself into a hole there, sweetie," says Tilly, examining her fingernails.

I try again. "It wasn't nicked, if that's what you're thinking. Tilly, erm, lent it to me before she died and I never got the chance to give it back. Now I have."

Wes shrugs. "You don't have to explain nothing to me. Not my business, anyway. Mum's happy, the kids are happy." He gives me a sideways grin. "I'm pretty happy right now."

I feel myself flush under Tilly's hard stare.

"God's sake. He *fancies* you. And you fancy him back, don't you?" Tilly flattens her palm over her chest looking outraged. "I can *feel* it, Jess."

Busted. As I try to control my treacherous heart rate, Wes tips back his head to finish his cone in one gulp.

"That reminds me." Tilly glares at him as she stands up, brushing imaginary dirt from her immaculate jeans. "Two o'clock. Time to feed the pigs."

After the rare breed piglets, it's tea time for the short-clawed otters. They are *super* cute – their demanding little high-pitched cries remind me of Tilly, but I don't tell her because she's too busy sulking. The afternoon goes so fast, I'm surprised when it's time to get back on the bus. This time, I sit on the back seat between Ayesha and Rihanna, who teach me the words to Taylor Swift and Lizzo songs (clean versions only) and won't let go of my hands, even when it's time to get off.

While Kayla's busy distributing kids to grateful parents, Wes turns to me with a grin.

"Thanks, Jess. You've been amazing today." He pulls me into a one-armed hug and I wince. His face fills with concern. "Sorry, man. Mum always says I don't know my own strength."

"It wasn't you," I say, catching my breath as Tilly and I rub our chests in unison. "I had, erm, heart surgery recently and it's still a bit sore."

"Shit." Wes steers me over to the minibus and sits me down on the step. "Are you OK? Do we need to get you into bed or something?"

"What?"

"Aw, man." He ducks his head in embarrassment. "I mean, like, shouldn't you be resting?"

"God's sake." Tilly rolls her eyes. "Get a room."

I ignore her. "I'm OK, honest," I say to Wes. "It just catches me out sometimes. But I'm good. Better than good. I really enjoyed today."

"Maybe we could do it again sometime?" Wes brushes a blob of something sticky from his back pocket as he takes out his phone to exchange numbers. "Urgh. Next time, maybe without snot nose Darius, yeah?"

38

"Not that jacket, Jess." Tilly screws up her face. "Definitely not those jeans. This dress might do, I suppose." We've collected the rest of my new clothes from the hotel so that she can choose what I'm wearing to the solicitor's office.

"Where is this place anyway?" I stand in my bra and knickers, waiting for her to decide.

"Chancery Lane, near the Law Courts."

"Is that near here?"

She rolls her eyes. "It's near the Strand, of course. Surely you know where the Strand is?"

"Sure I do. *On a Monopoly board*." I'm trying to cut Tilly some slack after the crap week she's had, but she's being a total pain. "What is with you today?"

"Nothing."

"Jeez, Tilly. Just tell me."

She hesitates, looking hurt. "I can't believe you told Wesley Lawrence about our heart surgery."

"Is that all? I had to say something."

"You told Georgie you'd had a boob job."

I feel myself flush scarlet. "Well, I wasn't going to say that to Wes, was I?"

"Why? Because you fancy him?"

"I don't fancy him," I lie. "I just think he's a nice guy. I don't see what you've got against him."

"I don't have anything against him." Tilly looks surprised. "I'm just not sure he's right for you, Jess."

"Why? Because he's not rich like your other mates?"

"Pur-lease. You of all people know I don't care about the money. He's OK, I suppose. He's just all a bit *whoa* and *chill* and *yeah, man*." Tilly does some weird street hand gestures, making me giggle. "If I'm forced to listen in, it'd be nice to have a bit of intellectual conversation at least. He's just not very deep, is he, sweetie?"

"Actually, he's going to uni next year to study politics," I say. "Says he wants to make a difference like his mum. I thought you'd approve."

"Well, good for him," Tilly says. "Anyway, if our plan works out, I'll finally be able to move on and Wesley Lawrence will be your problem not mine."

"What *is* the plan when we get to the solicitor's?" I

say. "What do you think I should say to this Standish guy?"

"I like your idea of saying you're a volunteer with the charity. You wouldn't even have to fib," says Tilly slyly. "Definitely ask about the payments being stopped."

"I'm seventeen, Tilly, we'll be lucky if he tells me anything. How do we find out the stuff we need to know?"

"I don't know, sweetie. You distract him while I take a look at the paperwork. I'm bound to come across some clues."

"Clues? What do you think this is? *Miss Marple*? *Murder She Wrote*?"

"I've told you – we're Team *Scooby-Doo*," says Tilly impatiently. "I'm Daphne, obviously, and you can be the other one. Ooh, what's she called? You know, the nerdy, sturdy girl."

"Velma's not sturdy!" I say. "She's just *normal*. Not everyone's got to have a size zero backside, Tilly. Anyway, I'd much rather be Velma. She's clever and she gets on with it instead of just poncing around looking pretty."

"You do you and I'll do me." Tilly turns her attention to the shoes under the bed. "I'm not sure any of these are suitable for visiting a solicitor's office. Such a shame your feet are too big to borrow a pair of mine. Have we got time to trot along to the King's Road and pick out a new pair?"

"Gosh, are you sure they'd have anything in my size?"

Two hours later, we're waiting in the outer office at

224

Standish and Sons, Corporate Solicitors. I'm wearing the green dress we bought in Geneva and uncomfortable new heels.

"This doesn't bode well." Tilly strides about the drab beige room. "This is the outer sanctum. Mr Standish's secretary always made the peasants wait out here. There's a much nicer waiting room for important clients."

I nod towards the reception area where an efficient looking secretary types at a computer. "Who's she?"

"Miss Bryant. She's been here donkeys' years. Complete bag but devoted to old Mr Standish." Tilly looks at her watch and huffs. "God's sake, I wouldn't have been kept waiting like this in the old days. They never keep you hanging around in the *nice* waiting room."

"Welcome to the real world," I mutter, fidgeting on the scratchy hessian sofa.

The telephone in the secretary's office buzzes and she beckons me through. "Mr Standish will see you now," she says sternly. "You were very lucky to get an appointment at such short notice."

We follow her past the posh waiting room (where two women with dogs in their handbags are discussing divorce settlements) and down a short corridor to another office.

"Wait here, please." Miss Bryant shifts a pile of paper folders to her other arm as she knocks on the door.

"Come in," calls a young man's voice from the other side.

The secretary opens the door and Tilly slides through the gap alongside her just before the door closes again.

Genius! I lean against the wall wondering what she's hearing that I can't. It's a good five minutes before Miss Bryant flings open the door to admit me to an old-fashioned office with overflowing bookcases and paper files on every surface.

"This is Mr Standish junior." She gestures towards a short blonde man who gives my hand an unenthusiastic shake.

In the background, Tilly pulls a face. "You didn't miss much. They were just bickering about the state of the office. *She says* he's too untidy and *he says* he wants everything on paper transferred to computer. *She says* his grandfather preferred everything on paper and *he says* it's no longer the Dark Ages..."

I zone out from her as the blonde man invites me to sit.

"You're here from the Kidscope charitable organization?" He sifts through the papers on the desk and pulls a thick folder towards him.

"Yes." I take a deep breath. "There's a problem with the monthly donation from Tilly Spencer's trust."

Standish looks annoyed. "Can't you damned people synchronize watches? I've already spoken to someone about reinstatement of the payment."

"Yessss! Good old Aunt Lulu!" Tilly punches the air behind him.

226

I motion her to get on with it. "So the money will get paid as usual?"

He opens the folder and skims the top document as Tilly peers over his shoulder. "That's what I just said. Perhaps you could check your facts before you come down here wasting my time. I'm extremely busy."

"Can I ask why the payment was stopped in the first place?" I say, as Tilly tries unsuccessfully to turn the page.

"No, you may not," he says, standing up again. "How Miss Spencer's trustees make their decisions is none of your concern. Just be grateful they've allowed the payments to continue for now, because I can't guarantee how long this will carry on. The division of Miss Spencer's assets is pending."

"This is no good," Tilly says. "These are the minutes from the last trustee meeting, but I can't see the page underneath. Maybe you should go on ahead, Jess, but try and leave the door open. I'll see if he looks through it after you've gone."

"OK. Thanks, anyway." As Standish escorts me to the door, Tilly stays behind the desk, huffing and puffing like the big bad wolf. One sheet of paper floats to the floor and then another. She scowls as he starts to close the door. "Wait, I'm nearly there. Keep him talking, Jess; *don't* let him shut me in."

I pause in the doorway to smile up at him. "It was really kind of you to see me. I'm sorry I've taken up so much of your time."

227

"Then don't waste any more of it."

I only just remove my fingers from the frame before he shuts the door in my face. Bollocks. Now what are we going to do?

There's a muffled wail from the other side of the door. "Jess! God's sake, don't leave me."

I bend down and pretend to tie my shoelace, realizing too late I'm not wearing my trainers but the ridiculous girly shoes Tilly insisted on buying (in the sale and half a size too small, but she completely fell in love with them).

Miss Bryant comes around the corner with a stack of folders. "Miss Bailey. What are you doing down there?"

I abandon my imaginary trainers and clap one hand over my left eye instead. "I've dropped my contact lens."

"Let me assist you." She kneels down to examine the beige carpet as Tilly's mournful voice floats under the door.

"Jess, I can't get out!"

"Try harder," I mutter.

Miss Bryant glares at me. "I'm doing my best, young lady."

One-eyed, I stare at the office door as Tilly's manicured fingertips appear, only to twitch and disappear again.

"Ugh, I feel *sick*. I can't do it, not after last time. You have to open it, Jess."

I give the secretary a sheepish smile. "I'm really sorry, but I think I might have dropped it in there."

228

She sighs and raps on the door. "Mr Standish junior? May I come in?"

"If you must. And stop damn well calling me Standish junior, will you? I'm not at prep school."

She opens the door and Tilly skids through the gap, looking nauseous but relieved.

"Found it, thanks!" I call, as we set off down the corridor.

"That was horrible," Tilly says as we pass the nice waiting room and then the beige one. "I thought you were just going to walk off and leave me."

I roll my eyes. "Tilly, in case you've forgotten, I can't go anywhere without you."

"No, but you could have totally forced me to come through that closed door. Even the thought of it makes me feel ill."

"I know. I wouldn't do that to you."

"Oh." She looks surprised. "Thanks."

"So did you see anything?" I whisper as we spill out into the busy street.

"Some of it. There was a list of my investments. And underneath were the minutes for the last trustee meeting, the week before I died. I was reading the top half when he started to shut the door and I'm afraid I panicked. Sorry." She hangs her head.

"Never mind. What about the investments list?"

"There were a lot of companies – some I recognized, some I didn't." She shrugs her shoulders. "That's nothing

229

new. They've always divided my money up into different investment opportunities. Less risk, get it?"

"Not really." *Not at all.* "Explain."

"Well, they move money from one company to another depending on how the shares are performing. Mr Standish sent me an email at the start of the financial year. Maybe we should look at that, see if there's anything different to the list I've just seen."

When we get back to the flat, I open Tilly's silver laptop.

"Look in my emails," says Tilly. "Mr Standish used to send me quarterly updates. Not that I ever read them."

I find the attachment and Tilly scans down the contents. "Does anything look familiar from the list you saw today?"

"Hmm." She taps at the screen. "These are all property: two houses and an area of land in north London. I've had those forever – Daddy inherited them from his grandparents."

"Jeez. I get why they gave you a hard time about keeping this place if you owned two other houses," I say.

"Duh! They're in north London. As if I'd want to live there. Daddy wanted me to keep hold of those and the land too, said it would increase in value."

"OK, so nothing dodgy there." I run my finger down a list of company names. "What about these?"

"Stocks and shares. My trust invests in these companies

and they pay me dividends. They're all property companies – Daddy always said that was safest."

"Do you know all the names?"

"Not really. I never paid much attention to them."

"God, Tilly. Millions of pounds of your money and you weren't interested?"

"Of course I was interested! That's why I was due to meet old Mr Standish after my birthday. He knew I wanted to move my money out of property and into ethical companies. You know, socially-responsible with green and fair trade policies. I sent him a list of the ones I liked, so he could discuss them with Mr Chen. You know, decide which were most financially sound."

I'm impressed. "So, after your birthday they were going to rejig your whole investment portfolio? Put your money with these green companies instead?"

"That's right. Daddy always said it was like that line from Spider-Man: with great money comes great responsibility."

"I don't think Spider-Man actually said that."

"Oh, shut up – you know what I mean. And I *want* to be responsible with my money. I'm not just interested in shoes and handbags, you know."

I nod faintly. I'm beginning to realize that.

Tilly laughs. "Well to be fair, I totally love shoes and handbags. I just don't buy them from designers who use child labour."

231

39

We spend the evening finalizing our plans for the stake out at Canary Wharf.

"Leo said he usually drops Mr Barker off at half one," I say, examining the address on the bit of card he gave me.

"Then we'd better get there early," says Tilly. "If we miss Leo's car, we have no idea what this Barker man looks like."

"We don't know *anything* about him," I point out. "What he looks like, who he works for. Why the hell he arranged the hit on you—"

"With luck, it'll all fall into place tomorrow, sweetie."

Tilly's optimistic as she busies herself checking over my new clothes. "There are lots of smart offices at Canary Wharf. If we're going to meet him, you need to fit in."

"Hell-o? We're not meeting anyone," I say. "We're just going to watch some dude get out of Leo's car and see where he goes. Who cares what I wear?"

"If we follow him into the office building, you'll need to look the part. Maybe we should have another little word with Leo too."

"Leo the hired assassin? Cool. Great idea."

"Leo the bargain basement Bublé, more like," Tilly says with a sneer. "With his shiny shoes and his cheesy grin, pathetic. Anyway, you saw the state of him on Saturday – I doubt he's capable of killing anyone at the moment unless you count drinking himself to death. And don't forget, he thinks we have the recording from the car."

I shrug sulkily.

"Please," she wheedles. "The sooner we find out, the sooner you'll be rid of me."

"Yay," I say, half meaning it. No more Tilly.

But then … no more Tilly. I don't even want to think about that. She might be a massive pain, but she's kind of grown on me.

"Good riddance," I add, trying to sound convincing, but Tilly's not fooled.

She squeezes my hand. "We can work out the details tomorrow. Now, why don't you hang up this jacket and have supper while we watch TV? You choose, Jess. *Derry Girls* or season one of *Game of Thrones*?"

Next morning, Tilly supervises while I dress and then gives me elaborate instructions for putting my hair up in a chignon. "You really do look the part. If only your face weren't so round."

"It's the *steroids*," I say, through a mouthful of hairgrips.

"Tuh! You blame those tablets for everything. With luck, we can get into the office block without anyone challenging you. If they ask, just pretend you're there for a meeting. Team *Scooby-Doo*, remember?"

Twirling in front of Tilly's mirror on the heart-shaped stool, dressed in a horrible khaki skirt and matching jacket, I feel more like *Safari Barbie* than Velma.

"There are more clips in that glass bowl," Tilly says as I fiddle with strands of loose hair which keep escaping. "Open that top drawer, Jess, it's where I keep my make-up. Help yourself to anything you like."

I gaze at the unopened packets ranging from Christian Dior and Clarins to Bobbi Brown. "Wow. Thanks."

"That suits you," says Tilly, as I try out a brand-new coffee-coloured lipstick. "Keep it. What a shame my life was snuffed out so prematurely. I would have made a brilliant personal shopper. You look perfect – totally unrecognizable!"

I ignore the backhanded compliment and put the torn

off cigarette packet with the address, along with Tilly's laptop, into a huge handbag she's lent me. "Are we getting a taxi to Canary Wharf?"

"No. Tube then DLR, sweetie," she says as we head out into the street.

"Hold up," I say, my feet already killing me. How can she walk so fast in those high-heeled boots? "What's a DLR?"

"Docklands Light Railway. Overground rather than underground." Tilly slows to keep pace with me. "It goes to the *Cutty Sark* – you know, that boring old boat? Daddy used to take me when I was little."

"Whatever," I say, hobbling behind in the same impractical shoes from yesterday. "I don't care as long as I get a seat. I'm absolutely knackered."

An hour and a half later, we're loitering in front of a large glass-fronted office block.

"I don't think they're coming. Do you reckon he gave us the wrong address?" I squint at Leo's serial killer-esque handwriting. "Or maybe he was too pissed to come into work again."

Tilly shakes her head. "It's one thing blowing off a load of businessmen on a jolly, but I bet Leo's too scared of Mr Barker to skip work today. Look, isn't that his car?"

Even though it's not sunny, I slip on my shades as the maroon Mercedes draws alongside. Leo has his window wound down, looking composed but hungover. I don't think he's clocked me, but I crouch behind a handy litter bin anyway, peering round as he opens the back door for a man to get out.

Tilly and I exchange puzzled glances. *This* is Mr Barker? I'd imagined a cross between Quentin Tarantino and the Kray twins, but this guy looks more like a bank manager than anything else. Maybe early forties, with an unobtrusive grey suit, rimless glasses and light brown hair slicked back, probably to cover the fact that he's thinning on top.

Tilly nudges me as he walks into the office building. "Come on, let's follow him."

"And then what?" I whisper into my jacket collar.

"I don't know, sweetie, we'll just have to wing it."

I glare at her. "We can't just wing it, Tilly, we need a plan. The man is dangerous."

"It's an office block in the middle of the day," she says. "He can't do anything to you and he doesn't know where we live."

"Easy for you to say." Tilly's got a lot less to lose than me, vital organs wise. I shake my head as I push open the glass revolving door to follow him into a small, marbled foyer. It doesn't look much like the lair of a criminal mastermind.

A middle-aged receptionist sits behind a high desk. "Can I help you?"

Tilly ignores her, pointing at Barker who's still talking on his mobile. There's no indication he's noticed me. "Quick, he's getting into that lift!"

The back of his balding head disappears as the doors close and numbers start to light up above the elevator.

"I said, can I *help* you?" The receptionist gives me a frosty look.

"No, thanks," I say as Tilly tows me towards another lift. I press the button, but it refuses to light up.

"You can't access that elevator without a swipe card." The receptionist sounds smug.

"I see," I drawl, trying to sound like Tilly. "Can you tell me which floor Mr Barker works on?"

"Mr Barker? I don't believe we have anyone of that name here."

"Hell-o?" I say before correcting my slipping accent. "I mean, I've just seen him getting into that lift."

"Young lady, I've already told you we don't have a Mr Barker working here."

"Are you absolutely sure?"

"I'm positive, dear." The receptionist puffs out her ruffled lace chest like a pigeon. "May I ask the nature of your business?"

"Erm…" Mind blank, I look at Tilly for inspiration, but she's wandered off to look at a row of brass plates in the doorway. "Forget it. It doesn't matter."

Bloody hell, what a waste of time. We've lost him and

now we'll have to wait a whole week I haven't got for Leo to do this trip again. I can't believe we've come all the way here for nothing.

"Never mind, Jess." Tilly swings round, her eyes wide. "I've found it! I've got the information we're looking for!"

40

Tilly grabs my hand, gesturing at me to push open the glass door so we can leave.

"What did you see?" I mutter once we're both squeezed into the same section of the revolving door.

"Tell you in a minute."

I follow as she heads over to a cafe on the opposite side of the road and steers me into a booth with a good view of the office entrance.

"Sit here, Jess. They've got Wi-Fi – can you bring up that email with my investment portfolio? I need to check something." She glares up at the super prompt waitress who's come to take my order. "Not now, sweetie. Can't you see we're busy?"

Bursting with impatience, I order a drink and a sandwich. Once the waitress has gone, I open the silver laptop and stick in my AirPods so I can talk while I open the attachment.

"What the hell did you see, Tilly?"

"There!" Tilly extends her index finger triumphantly at one of the companies on the list. "I *knew* I'd seen it before. Broughton-Marley Ltd – the same name as on that brass plate I just saw. They're based on the third floor of that office block. It can't be a coincidence, can it? Barker must work for them."

"That receptionist said they didn't have a Mr Barker."

"So? Maybe she's in on it too," says Tilly.

"Or maybe it's not his real name." I smile at the waitress as she sets down my order and wait for her to move away. "Let's face it, we know nothing about him. Apart from the fact he arranged your murder and that he's maybe got links with a company your money's invested in. Broughton-Marley, you said. Let's google it."

Tilly's almost vibrating as I tap enter. "There!"

Broughton-Marley Ltd is a manufacturing company specializing in large drilling equipment and piping for South American oil fields.

Her jaw tightens as she reads. "This is wrong on every level, Jess. Old Mr Standish knows how I feel about fossil fuels; he'd never have gone against my wishes to invest in this company. Even worse, they aren't financially secure. Look! They've had to be bailed out twice in the last ten years."

"Says here they've been investigated by the professional standards agency too." I chase down my lunchtime meds with a bottle of super expensive water.

Tilly squints at the small print. "This is giving me a headache. Sometimes, I wish I'd been wearing my glasses when I died."

"You wore glasses?"

"Just for reading and showing off. Gorgeous Chanel ones, with little CCs on the hinges."

"Sound fabulous," I lie, clicking on the company website. "Wow. Is that him? Company director, Jonathan Markham." There's a photo but the man looks younger than the one we just saw. He's got way more hair.

"That's definitely him, the murdering bastard," says Tilly. "So Markham must be his real name. And here's some information about Broughton, sounds like he's the money man. Nothing about Marley, though."

"And absolutely nothing about them nicking your money and bumping you off. We need to find out what links him to you."

"Well, it's got to be Sebastian Standish," says Tilly. "We know he stopped the money going to Kidscope and I was murdered just *two weeks* after he took over from his grandfather. We don't even know why old Mr Standish is ill; maybe bloody little Sebastian was the one who put him in hospital!"

"Makes sense." A few weeks back, this would have seemed seriously farfetched, but now, sitting here with the ghost of a posh, dead heiress, I'm in no position to start dissing anyone else's conspiracy theories. "Was this the last statement before you died?"

"Yes, for the end of the quarter." Tilly nods. "But if you compare it with May, you can see some changes. I used to have shares in this property company called Sharma and Son, but there's no mention of them in the August statement."

I peer over her shoulder. "Is that normal?"

"Totally. If a company isn't doing well, the trustees move my money into something else. If you look back over the last year, there have been variations each quarter."

"So Broughton-Marley isn't on the May statement but rocks up in August once Sebastian takes charge?"

"That's right. Old Mr Standish wouldn't have touched them with a barge pole. How could the trustees possibly think they were a suitable investment?" Tilly thumps her knee in frustration. "If only I'd been able to get a clear look at those minutes yesterday—"

"Tilly." I try to interrupt. "Didn't you say the minutes were emailed to you after every meeting?"

"Yes, not that I ever bothered to read them."

"But they'll be here, won't they? In your unopened emails." I scroll back, searching for the end of August.

"Jess, you're a genius!" Tilly's eyes narrow as I locate and open the PDF. "Look! They've moved a massive amount of my money into bloody Broughton-Marley – almost eleven million pounds' worth of shares. There was a big discussion. Mr Chen from the bank advised against it and the trustees had to vote." She gestures impatiently for me to click to the next page. "Bloody hell! Two to one in favour of moving my money into Broughton-Marley."

"Two to one?" I say. "Only one of them listened to your bank manager? Who was it?"

"It doesn't say, but we hardly need ask. Aunt Lulu's always on my side. Bloody Sebastian Standish. Bloody Fox-Longley."

"Do you honestly believe your head teacher's mixed up in this?"

"Maybe." Tilly bites her lower lip. "She's such an old cow I'd love to say yes, but I can't imagine her deliberately doing anything illegal. Maybe he persuaded her in some way to vote with him."

"Like how?"

"Well, I don't know, sweetie, some financial incentive for the school, maybe? We know St Aggie's need money for their roof repairs. Having said that, she and Aunt Lulu simply can't bear one another – could have been more a matter of Fox-Longley voting *against* Aunt Lu than siding with Sebastian."

243

"Fair enough," I say. "I'd probably hold a grudge too if someone's daughter had put chilli powder on my loo seat."

Tilly tosses her head. "Some people have zero sense of humour. Anyway, The Fox was a total nightmare when they were dealing with my flat. If Aunt Lulu hadn't managed to talk poor darling Mr Standish round, I'd never have kept it. I'd be haunting some dump in Wimbledon instead."

"So what do we do now? Do we call the police?"

"And tell them what?" Tilly looks scornful. "They think my death was an accident and Leo's not going to tell them otherwise."

I point at the minutes of the meeting. "Yeah, but what about this?"

"It doesn't *prove* anything, Jess." Tilly's exasperated with me. "All it shows is that my trustees move my money around, which is perfectly normal practice. And these emails are supposed to be confidential. How do you explain having access to them? Officially, none of this has anything to do with you."

She's right. I'd probably end up getting myself arrested. "So what do we do?"

She shrugs. "Wait for Jonathan Markham to leave work and follow him."

"OK." Following is good. Not as good as staying out of trouble, but better than fronting up to an executive murderer any day.

41

It's growing dark by the time Markham leaves the office. We've already paid the bill, so we nip outside and loiter at a distance as he walks towards the station.

"Not too close," I beg as Tilly strains ahead. "We don't want him to see us."

"No, but we want us to be able to see him. Now look what's happened." Tilly grimaces as Markham is swallowed up by a surge of commuters at the entrance.

Bollocks. I dart past passengers, rubbernecking frantically, but when the crowd clears, he's completely disappeared. Chest burning, I head into the station as Tilly trails dejectedly behind.

"A whole afternoon of surveillance wasted," she says through gritted teeth. "What would Daphne and Velma say?"

"They'd say: maybe he stopped to buy a newspaper." My heart slows to a thud as I spot him in the queue at the newsagent stand. We smile at each other in relief as Markham moves off to board the train.

It's loads easier once we're onboard. It's too crowded to sit but a handy student with a huge backpack makes for good cover. I crouch behind him as Tilly pushes through to where Markham stands, reading his folded newspaper. The crowd part easily for her, rubbing goose-bumped arms in bewilderment, until she's directly in front of him.

"So!" she demands. "You think you're going to get away with sending people round to murder me, do you?"

Unfazed, he continues to read the football results. Tilly gives his newspaper an ineffectual smack and it flutters but doesn't fall.

Bristling, she returns to my side. "You know, Jess, I'm almost disappointed at how ordinary he is. A chinless wonder with a bald patch. Hardly the Godfather."

Once we swap back to the tube, there are plenty of other people talking to themselves so I don't feel self-conscious about joining them. "What if we're wasting our time here, Tilly? What if he's just going home?"

"Then we'll know where he lives, won't we? Anyway, you heard what Leo said. Markham does a lot of business

246

out of the office. He might even be meeting Sebastian Standish."

The tube stops and we hustle forward until we've joined Markham on the escalator, three people behind him as we ride down.

"Stand on the right. On the *right*. How many times do I have to tell you?" Tilly's annoyed. "It's like the city mouse and the bloody country mouse again. Are you trying to piss off the entire population of London?"

I shuffle over, keeping Markham's thinning crown in view. "I hope this is worth it. He could be going anywhere."

"Don't be so negative." Tilly tucks her chilly arm through mine. "Look, he's making his way towards the Central Line. That's good."

"Why?" I crane my neck. "Is that the way to the solicitors' office?"

"Totally," says Tilly as we follow him on to the busy platform.

Markham doesn't stand out in his grey suit, but his shiny bald patch is visible as we move towards the gaping doors of the tube. This time, he secures himself the last seat, seemingly oblivious to two strap-hanging pregnant women giving him filthy looks in stereo.

"Told you he was a bastard," says Tilly as the tube slows to stop. "Be ready to get off, Jess. If he's going to meet Sebastian Standish, he'll change here."

But Markham remains seated and the train rattles on.

"Oh! *Not* going to Chancery Lane." Tilly looks puzzled as we change at Holborn. "Where on earth's he going? I'll be totally pissed off if it's just Harrods to buy underwear for his wife."

Markham exits at South Kensington, weaving his way through the crowd.

"Don't lose him again for god's sake," Tilly calls, as I pant along in her wake. "Quick, he's flagging down that black cab!"

Mortified, I barge in front of an elderly couple to commandeer the next taxi. "Follow that cab!" I gasp as we leap inside.

The cabbie turns to grin at me. "What?"

"Follow that cab," I say, grateful to be sat down at last. "My uncle's in it and he's, erm, forgotten his mobile."

"Better not lose him, then." The cabbie chuckles, turning his attention back to the road. "Gotta love it! Twenty years I've been doing this job and no one's ever said 'follow that cab' until now!"

"I've always wanted to say it," I admit, flopping back against the seat.

"So have I." Tilly glares out of the window. "But I'll never get the chance now I've been murdered."

Markham's taxi is just a few metres ahead as we slow for a red light.

"Oi, mate!" The cabbie winds down his window and flashes his lights. "Yoo-hoo!"

"Shit," squeaks Tilly. "Do something, Jess! Don't let him stop them."

I leap forward to tap on the glass, but then the lights change and the other car draws away without seeing us.

"Never mind." Our driver's cheerful as he resumes the chase. "It was worth a try."

Tilly twists round as we move slowly through the traffic. "Do you recognize where we are, Jess?"

"Sort of." The posh terraces are super familiar.

Tilly presses her nose against the window. "We're almost at my flat. Any minute now, we're going to go past the turn off for Radley Square."

"We're not going past." Our taxi swings left and follows the one in front into the familiar tree-lined square. Tilly stares at me, biting her bottom lip in bewilderment as we draw to a stop next to the railings.

"Well, darlin'," says the cabbie, totalling the amount on the meter. "Looks like this is it."

42

"Hadn't you better 'urry up if you want to catch him?" The cab driver tilts his head as Markham strides away.

Shocked into action, I fumble in my purse for a twenty and shove it through the glass hatch. "Cheers, mate."

"Let's go," I hiss to a catatonic Tilly. She stumbles out behind me and we follow, keeping a clear gap between us and Markham. Chest thudding, I flatten myself against the railing as he turns, but he's just checking for traffic as he crosses the square.

"Where the *hell* is he going?" Tilly says.

"Erm, he's going to your house." I watch as Markham climbs the steps to the dark green door and presses the bottom bell. My heart gives an unpleasant skip. "And you said he didn't bloody know where we lived."

We hide behind a convenient hydrangea bush as Markham paces the wide doorstep. Eventually, he pulls out his mobile and speaks briefly into it.

"He's coming this way!" Tilly pulls me into the shade of a large beech tree. "No, no, he's going into the communal garden."

Markham crosses the road and pushes open the ironwork gate to the lawned area. We watch him stride in tight circles, constantly referring to his watch.

"He's waiting for someone," I say. "He's meeting someone at your flat and they're not here yet."

"But who?" says Tilly. "Who has a key?"

I nudge her. "Sebastian Standish? Surely your solicitor would have a key?"

"You're right, Jess. If we get inside before he comes, we can eavesdrop on what they're saying. It's the perfect opportunity!" Tilly's flushed with excitement.

"Yeah, right. The perfect opportunity for me to get murdered as well as you," I mutter into the tree trunk.

"We'll hide you somewhere safe, silly, while I go and listen. We have to be quick though, before Sebastian comes."

"Not a chance," I say.

"Come on, Jess, don't be such a coward. This is our one chance to find out what's going on! If you really want to get rid of me – "

"Jeez, don't start with that again. If he kills me, you're next." I sidle along the railings to reach Tilly's front door, hoping none of the neighbours are watching. It's that time of day when people are getting home from work. When Tilly signals that Markham's looking the other way, I unlock the door and we slip inside, scuttling across the empty communal hall to the relative safety of Tilly's front door.

"I can't believe I'm actually doing this," I say. "Locking myself in a flat with a man who pays people to kill other people."

"We'll open the French windows and hide in my bedroom," suggests Tilly. "If he finds you, you can always run into the garden and scream."

We skid across Tilly's oak-floored hall into the lilac bedroom.

"Where do I hide?" In Tilly's huge dressing table mirror, my wild-eyed expression is magnified times three.

"Get under the bed." Tilly tries and fails to lift the swathes of violet tulle. "They'll never spot you under there."

"Must go for a wee first." I charge into the white marble ensuite. I've been desperate to go to the loo all afternoon but didn't dare in case we missed Markham leaving the office.

"Hurry *up*," urges Tilly, as I pee frantically. "There's someone at the front door but I can't see who it is."

I tug down my skirt without flushing, lift the flimsy violet valance sheet and crawl underneath Tilly's bed. "I hope you've hoovered recently," I mutter through a mouthful of net. "If I start sneezing, we've had it."

"Manuela does the carpets every Monday." Tilly's voice floats under the frothy fabric. "But I expect she hasn't been in since I died."

I press my knuckles into my mouth as the front door slams. Footsteps echo on the wooden floor.

"Showtime, Jess. Oh, god!" Tilly kneels down and sticks her agonized face through a gap in the gauze. "It's not Standish at all. It's Georgie! With a watering can! She must have come to do the plants – you have to warn her, Jess!"

"How can I?" I whisper fiercely. "She'll wonder what the hell I'm doing here."

"You can't leave her in the flat with him. He's a murderer!"

"But it's OK for me to be here?" I mouth, listening to the click–clack of Georgie's heels as she potters around the hall. "She probably won't let him in anyway."

"This is all your fault!" Tilly's voice is shrill with anguish. "You were the one who reminded her about coming round to sort out my personal stuff. If he hurts her, Jess, I'll never forgive you. Never!"

As we scowl at each other, the doorbell chimes.

"Well, that's it," Tilly says coolly. "It's too late now."

I pull the gauze back into place, listening to muffled voices as Georgie answers the intercom. I can't hear what she's saying, but a moment later the front door buzzes.

"God's sake, she *is* letting him in. I'm going to keep watch – I need to make sure she's OK." Tilly's pointy boots disappear.

I shuffle closer to the edge of the bed. The front door opens and closes as I strain to listen. I can't hear what Georgie's saying but she sounds surprised.

There's silence for a moment. And then a high-pitched scream reverberates off the vaulted ceiling and resonates through the flat.

43

A faint echo hangs in the air as the screaming stops. I wait, holding my breath, before there's a new sound – raw, heart-wrenching sobbing.

Definitely Tilly. I strain to hear Georgie's voice too but, as the seconds tick by, there's nothing. What the hell has he done to her?

Shit. I can't just leave her there. Steeling myself, I lift the lilac gauze and crawl out from under the bed, looking around for anything I can use as a weapon. I'm just reaching for a heavy silver sculpture when Tilly runs into the bedroom.

"No, Jess!" Her cheeks are streaked with tears. "Get back under there right now."

"But—"

"Just do it." Tilly's cold hand is over my mouth as she propels me backwards. "Shh! Don't let them hear you, for god's sake."

I wriggle back under the bed as Tilly squashes in beside me, one shaking finger pressed to her colourless lips.

I point frantically towards the door.

"Is she OK?" I mouth.

"She's fine." Tilly grabs my arm, cold fingers digging into my wrist. "More than fine."

What? I frown and point again.

"It's *her,* Jess!" Tilly swallows, her trembling mouth a taut line. "Not Sebastian Standish. It was that bitch Georgie all along. She knows Markham; she arranged to meet him here and they're *laughing.*"

I widen my eyes at Tilly as the muted footsteps grow louder. Oh, jeez, they're coming in here. I tweak a swathe of tulle to make sure we're completely hidden and squash my face into the carpet, goosebumps prickling my skin. It's a good job I'm lying down because my knees are trembling so hard they wouldn't hold me up.

Two pairs of feet pause next to the bed: the polished brogues remain still, but the heels move away again. There's a clunk and a rummaging sound as the dressing table drawers are pulled open and closed. Tilly's pale face is utterly woebegone – instead of her usual opinionated running commentary, there's just silence. I reach for her hand and squeeze hard, barely daring to breathe.

Georgie's heels move back towards us and we both cringe as the mattress sags with her weight.

"Not here, darling!" Her warm laugh rings out. "Business before pleasure, Jonny. Plenty of time for that sort of thing later on."

Ew, yuck. A wave of nausea takes the edge off my terror. I seriously hope Georgie doesn't change her mind and decide to go with pleasure before business while we're still trapped under here.

Tilly's face is like thunder. "How *dare* she bring that terrible man into my home? Help me out of here, Jess," she says, commando-crawling towards the gauze.

I tentatively lift the fabric furthest away from their feet and Tilly tunnels under, her denim bottom disappearing from view.

Her boots blur past my eyeline and the bed jiggles as Georgie shivers. "Bloody chilly in here. I should have left the timer on for the central heating last time I came round."

"Did you ever find anything?" Markham's gravelly voice is less cultured than his bank manager appearance.

"I've told you I haven't," says Georgie. "I've been here twice in the last week and had a good search in the den upstairs. I can't find anything to give us cause for concern."

My stomach lurches at the thought of Georgie coming in and out of the flat. Thank god I was so on it about keeping my stuff tidied away.

"What do you think about waiting until the next

trustee meeting?" says Markham. "See if you can persuade Standish to move a few more shares our way?"

"Too risky, darling. Sebastian might be incompetent but he's not completely stupid. There are only so many times I can pull off the 'liquid lunch and buckets of flattery' trick. And now Tilly's gone, won't they dissolve the trust? They'll be selling not buying." She gives a nervous laugh. "We'd better pray old Grandpa Standish doesn't recover too soon. That clever old goat would never have fallen for it."

"I could make sure he doesn't recover." Markham laughs unpleasantly. Somewhere in the background, Tilly hisses like an angry swan.

Georgie clicks her tongue. "Don't be so bloodthirsty, Jonathan! Two deaths are quite enough to be going on with and probate could go through at any time. I say let's quit while we're ahead."

"Take the money and run?"

"Exactly. Twelve mill is plenty, Jonny; we don't want to spoil things by getting greedy. How soon can you do it?"

"I'll start moving the money this week. Can you be packed and ready to go by Friday?"

"Absolutely. Nothing to keep me here, darling."

The underside of the bed lifts and I watch their feet move away. There are distant footsteps on the oak floor before the front door clicks shut, but I've no idea if one or both of them have left. Without Tilly to give me the all-clear, I hyperventilate for a good five minutes before lifting the gauze to peer out.

Tilly's sitting on her heart-shaped stool, chin resting on her knees.

This time, I'm prepared for the storm of weeping. What I don't anticipate is the cold fury that follows.

44

"The bitch! The bloody traitorous bitch!" Tilly paces the room as I watch helplessly. "Do you know, she even took two lipsticks and a bottle of serum out of that drawer before she left?"

I shake my head, edging towards the door. It seems a bit insensitive to suggest we have this conversation elsewhere, but I'm seriously bricking it in case they come back.

"I was so frightened for her, thinking any minute that bastard Markham and Sebastian bloody Standish would show up," Tilly continues her rant. "Totally terrified she was in danger of death by plant watering. But it was her! Her, all along, Jess!"

"I guess at least we know Sebastian Standish wasn't involved," I say.

"Is that supposed to make me feel better? Don't you think I'd rather it was him?" Tilly demands, her voice shrill. "Don't worry, Tilly! Your solicitor isn't trying to kill you, he's just totally incompetent! It's your best friend in the world who arranged your murder."

Maybe this isn't a great time to point out that poor old Miss Fox-Longley probably wasn't the one who voted against the bank manager's advice either.

Tilly swings back to the sobbing stage. "I trusted her, Jess! She was my surrogate sister – the closest thing to family I had left apart from Granddad."

"I know, Til. It's completely horrible." I try to slow our heart rate as I squeeze her shuddering shoulders, swamped by a wave of homesickness for my own mum and dad. Suddenly, I'm so desperate for this to be over. But that would mean no more Tilly.

"I can't bear it. My parents are dead and the person I trusted most has betrayed me." Tilly sniffs. "Do you think Aunt Lulu is involved? God, do you think Georgie had anything to do with what happened to my parents as well?"

Maybe.

Probably.

Yes.

I can't add to her distress, so I shake my head. "Maybe it was all down to this Markham guy."

261

"But Leo said it was only supposed to be Mummy. What if she was trying to get my mum out of the way? Georgie adored my dad – she used to joke that if he'd married her mum in the first place, she wouldn't have had all those awful stepfathers. And when he died, she was devastated. I felt like she was the only person who knew what I was going through. She sat up night after night with me after the fire, said she'd always be there for me, just like we were real sisters. Did she mean it or was she after my money all along?"

"I don't know, Til, honest I don't." I flinch at a bumping noise from the flat next door. "I'm really sorry but do you think we could get out of here in case they come back?"

Tilly looks at her watch. "It's almost seven. I can't imagine them coming back tonight."

"Georgie said she'd been here twice already this week. I bet it was her who left your laptop out." I shiver to think how close we were to getting caught.

"We've been here the last few evenings, so it must have been during the day. What on earth was she looking for?"

"Something that might give them 'cause for concern' she said. What could that be?"

"No idea. Unless that bitch thinks two brand-new Christian Dior lipsticks might incriminate her in some way." She squeezes my hand. "Sorry, Jess. I'm whining on about being dead and you're terrified you're going to be next. How about we put the bolt on the front door and go up to the den? There's something I need to do."

"OK, but please hurry up," I say. "There's no way I'm sleeping here tonight."

"Agreed, sweetie, we'll go back to the hotel." She looks thoughtful. "But if you can bear to stay a tiny bit longer, I've got an idea that might just work."

The flat's like Fort Knox once I've followed Tilly's instructions to put on the deadlock, bolt and chain.

"First things first," Tilly says, hands on hips, as she strides around the den. "We make sure neither of those greedy bastards can get their hands on my money."

"They've already got their hands on some of it," I say. "If we don't get a move on, that money's just going to disappear."

"I might have a solution. They think I didn't make a will but what if I did? What if they just didn't know where it was? My eighteenth birthday was only weeks away and old Mr Standish was going to meet with me formally to 'hand over the reins'. Writing a will would have been part of all that."

"Yeah, but you died before that happened."

"I did," she agrees. "But Mr Standish knew I'd been checking out the ethical companies. What if I'd written a will as well? And just hadn't had the chance to show it to him?"

I nod. "Go on. What would the will say?"

"That apart from some money for Granddad, I'm leaving the whole bloody lot to charity! That'll put a stop to them."

"Would it be legal?" I'm confused. "I thought a will had to be witnessed."

Tilly smiles. "But it would be witnessed."

"By who?"

"By whom, you mean."

Jeez. Time and a place, Tilly. I roll my eyes. "Witnessed by *whom*?"

"You, Jess. My dear old mate from *Manchestoh*." Tilly puts on an appalling flat accent: Liam Gallagher does *Coronation Street*. "Both Kayla and that bitch Georgie think we've known each other for years. We just need to prove it. How about you write a couple of letters to me and we leave them amongst my stuff? As long as I don't leave you anything in my will, they'd have no reason to be suspicious."

"So we type it up and I sign it? It would need your signature too, Tilly."

She waves her hand dismissively. "You can have a go – it can't be that difficult to copy. Half a will's better than no will at all."

I'm beginning to think this could work. "We could try. But I'm only seventeen – would I count as a witness?"

"Let's google it," says Tilly.

I tap into my phone. "Says here it's not illegal. You can sign if you're under eighteen as long as there's an adult witness too."

Tilly bounces on her beanbag. "We'll ask Granddad."

I scroll down. "No, he can't witness the will if he's the beneficiary."

"Let's make a start and worry about that later. How about some handwritten letters from you to me? There's lots of different notepaper in that drawer – you can put different dates on and scrumple them up as if they've been read a few times."

"But everyone uses social media or email, Tilly. They'll think it's weird we've been writing proper letters to each other."

She gives me a patronising wink. "You're northern, sweetie. They'll probably think you haven't *got* a computer."

"I'm such a dur-brain," I say. "I've been in London so long I've forgotten that northerners don't have computers. Or mobile phones."

"That's the spirit. Look, we'll just say we've been writing to each other since we were little and the habit stuck."

Hands shaking, I start writing the letters while Tilly stands over me, prompting me to reference various midnight feasts, posh parties attended and ex-boyfriends supposedly shamed.

"Perfect," she says, reading over my shoulder. "Finish it off by congratulating me on dumping Tristan Rhys-Bartlett."

Jeez.

"Now use a different coloured biro and some of that blue Basildon-Bond," she says bossily. "Make this one from just before I died. Say how pumped you are about coming up to see me to visit the charity…" She trails off.

I look up in the middle of a sentence. "What?"

"Ooh," she says. "Light bulb moment. Carry on, sweetie, I'll be with you in a minute."

I hate it when she does this. "Please hurry up. I told you I don't want to hang around." I finish writing my old address in Sheffield while Tilly paces the room.

"How much longer until you go back to school, Jess?" She sounds innocent enough but I'm waiting for the punchline.

"After Christmas, maybe. Why?" I fold and unfold the blue note paper to make it look tatty.

She bounces on the suede beanbag. "Are you looking forward to it? Have you decided what you're going to do when you leave?"

"Why don't you just tell me what this is about?"

Tilly gives me a satisfied smile like a well-fed cat. "How do you fancy working in the new northern branch of a multi-million-pound kids' charity?"

45

I shake my head. "What the hell are you on about, Tilly?"

"It's been staring us in the face, Jess! We even used it as our cover story."

"Sorry, still don't get it."

Tilly rolls her eyes. "You've been pretending to everyone that I wanted to set up a branch of Kidscope in the north, yes?"

"Yeah."

"So let's make it true. We can put in the will that I'm planning to set up a further branch of Kidscope in Manchester and, in the event of my death, all my money goes towards setting up a national charity. Kayla can keep things going here in the south but when you leave school, you could work at the northern branch. We'll specify I want you to be appointed to the committee with Kayla as chief exec and we'll ask for Mr Chen, my bank manager, and Mr Standish. The original Mr Standish when he gets out of hospital, of course, not that useless Sebastian."

"Hang on, Tilly," I say. "They're not going to want me on some big executive committee. I'm only seventeen; I'm not qualified to have an opinion."

"Tell that to Greta Thunberg. When will you learn to value yourself, Jess?" Tilly looks stern. "Being seventeen doesn't preclude you from having a purpose or any influence. It never stopped me. You could make a big difference if you wanted to and, if you don't feel qualified enough, fine. *Get* qualified. Just get off your backside and do an apprenticeship or a degree in social work or something. You only get one life, Jess. Don't waste it."

"Your mum was right – you are bloody fierce." It's hard not to get sucked in by her enthusiasm. It'd be an amazing use of her money if we can swing it.

"The best thing is, you'd be perfect for it. I noticed how much you enjoyed the other day," says Tilly slyly. "When you weren't busy flirting with Wes, you were great with those kids – even little Darius didn't wipe snot on your backside. That's almost unheard of."

"Actually, I did notice that." I start to feel a tiny bit excited. Maybe I could do this.

"Worst case scenario and we really are stuck together for good, at least we can do something useful. Even if it's in bloody Manchester." Tilly looks hopeful. "Although, maybe in the future, you might come and live in London?"

"No chance," I say firmly. "I've spent my entire life moving around. Is it too much to ask to stay in one place for a bit? Anyway, I like being back in Manchester."

"Just some of the time then?" She gives me an innocent look. "You could always pop in and visit Wesley while you're at it."

"He's going off to uni, remember?" I try to sound casual but Tilly's not fooled. "He's applied to a couple of north west places. Liverpool. And Manchester, actually."

"Really? Fancy anyone wanting to leave London. Come on, Jess, it'd be brilliant," she wheedles. "I know lots of lovely places where we could do parties and fundraisers. We could even get a celebrity patron!"

"OK, I'll think about it," I say, grudgingly. "But if things go to plan, you and me will have parted company by then, remember?"

"Absolutely!" Tilly becomes businesslike again. "Now, the other thing we must do is ensure Granddad's properly looked after when I'm gone."

"Leave some money to an old people's charity," I suggest. "In honour of your Granddad. It looks more balanced than just giving all your money to Kidscope."

"Excellent idea. On the way back to the hotel, we'll nip to WHSmith and buy one of those do-it-yourself wills."

"What? Those crappy ones for like twenty quid?"

She gives me a withering look. "Not to fill in, you pleb. To give us an idea on how to set it out. We need it to look as authentic as possible."

"Fine, whatever." I'm starting to feel super twitchy. "Please can we go now? I really don't want to be here if they come back."

"Agreed. Let's leave the letters here and take the laptop back to the hotel. We can work on everything there. Tomorrow, we'll nip back, print off the will and leave it for them to find."

"Where do you want me to put these?" I hold up the two hastily written letters and a note on an old blank postcard Tilly found. We've torn off the corner to disguise the fact that there was no postmark.

"Put them in my desk drawer with these old birthday cards. And stick that postcard on the pin board under the theatre tickets."

My stuff's already packed. I pull my holdall from under the bed and we creep downstairs to the front door. I slide it open and Tilly does a quick recce of the communal hall before we go outside.

Only when we're in the taxi heading away from Radley Square, am I able to breathe.

46

The cab driver drops us off on the corner. The shop isn't far, but my exercise tolerance seems to be getting worse – anything faster than a walk and I feel like keeling over.

Not great when there's a greater than average chance of coming into close contact with a hitman.

"I didn't think they had any normal shops in Sloane Square," I say as we head into the busy newsagent's. We find what we're looking for in the business stationery section: *How to write your last will and testament.*

"Twenty-five quid!" I say.

"Ooh, look. It's buy one get one half price." Tilly's

amused. "With the state of your health, maybe you should treat yourself, Jess."

"Ha-de-ha. Like I've got anything worth leaving." The aisle's empty but I keep my voice low.

"Actually, you've got about a hundred and eighty grand, sweetie," she reminds me. "In cash."

Oh, yeah. I keep forgetting Tilly won't be spending "our" communal money once she's gone. But if she doesn't get a shift on to heaven and we keep staying in super posh hotels, it won't last long.

"Use cash not card," whispers Tilly when we reach the till. "We don't want this traced back to you. This has *got* to work."

Back at the hotel, I feel a million times better once I've kicked off my shoes and crawled on to the bed. We open the laptop and do another search on Broughton-Marley.

"There must be some link with *her*." Tilly avoids using Georgie's name. "Maybe we missed it last time because we didn't know what we were looking for. Try putting Morley, Markham and Broughton-Marley into the search engine."

I don't know where this is going, but I click "search" and it comes up straight away.

"*... the death of Malcolm **Morley**, founding partner of **Broughton-Marley** Ltd. Mr **Morley** was found dead in his family home after a suspected overdose of sleeping pills. It was reported that he had suffered heavy losses in the recent financial* *crisis. Mr **Morley** is survived by his ex-wife and daughter. His junior partner Jonathan **Markham** said he was 'saddened by the loss of a great friend and mentor'…"*

"Wow," says Tilly, leaning over my shoulder. "This is from donkey's years ago. You know who Malcolm Morley is, don't you?"

"I can hazard a guess," I say. "Georgie's dad? The one who killed himself?"

"He was Markham's business partner. Markham and Morley equals Marley. Yesss! I can't believe we didn't spot it before. Looks like Aunt Lulu had already left Malcolm by then so presumably he left his shares in Broughton-Marley to Georgie." Tilly speed-reads the rest of the article. "The shares didn't amount to much until an investor bailed them out a few years back."

"And that was?" I can guess the answer to this one too.

"My dad." Tilly's eyes fill with tears. "I think I remember it, Jess. I was only seven or eight, but I remember Daddy talking about financial responsibility and looking after those less fortunate than ourselves. He knew Georgie had shares in that company and he helped them turn it around. And this is how the bastards repay him."

I put both arms around her while she wipes her nose on my shoulder. I'm so used to the cold now it's going to feel super weird next time I hug a normal warm-bodied person. Like Dad or Mum. Or Wes. I sneak my mobile out of my pocket to look at the screen. No messages.

The rest of the article is financial stuff which goes way over my head. "I guess Broughton-Marley was doing OK until recently?"

Tilly wipes her perfectly made-up eyes. Clearly, ghost tears don't have the same ruinous impact on your mascara as real ones. She taps the screen. "I think so, although the share prices have dipped over the last two quarters."

"Maybe that guy Markham's already started to siphon money out of the business?"

"Probably. I wonder who this Broughton person is and if he has the faintest idea what's going on." She shakes her head. "I want to check something else, Jess. The last trustee meeting before I died. I want to know if it really was Aunt Lulu who voted against moving my money into Broughton-Marley."

"It didn't say, remember?" I remind her patiently as I search for the right email. "It just said two to one in favour – it didn't say who voted for what."

"It'll say who was bloody well present, though." Tilly scowls before putting on a silly simpering voice. "'I often stand in for my mother at meetings', remember?"

"Got it." I find the section at the top of the minutes.
Apologies: Mrs L. Summerfield.

I scroll down the *attending* list. There she is, right at the bottom.

Miss G. Morley on behalf of Mrs L. Summerfield.
Shit.

Tilly breaks the silence. "That's that, then," she says in a resigned voice. "You'd better get on with practising my signature. Where are those documents we found for you to copy?"

"Here." I pull out a sheaf of legal documents and insurance policies I've pinched from her desk.

"And the pen?"

"And the bloody pen." I rummage in my rucksack for the fancy silver fountain pen Tilly says she always used for important stuff. "Give me a minute to get used to the nib. I'm more of a biro girl."

I prop up one of the official documents bearing Tilly's full signature (Matilda Jennifer Linwood Spencer) and grab some hotel notepaper from the bedside table.

"God, Tilly, couldn't you just have two names or even three like everyone else?" I say as I scratch away, trying to emulate the rounded loopy handwriting.

"Don't you have a middle name? Mine were after Mummy."

"Cool. I was named after Jessica Fletcher."

"Is she a relative, sweetie?"

"No." I roll my eyes as I elaborate. "She's an old lady detective off the telly. My mum binge-watched *Murder She Wrote* the whole time she was pregnant. Could have been worse, I suppose – knowing Mum, I could have ended up with Moonbeam or Cosmic Karma or anything. Although apparently she wasn't such a hippy until after I was born – postnatal hormones, Dad reckons." I finish with a flourish, waving the paper so the ink dries. "What do you think?"

Tilly scrutinizes my handiwork. "Jess, that's terrible. You're not looping your ds properly."

"Why couldn't you just sign stuff 'Tilly Spencer'? Then I wouldn't have to do any ds."

"Have another go." She leans over me, her silky hair tickling my ear.

"Get off, Tilly, you're making me twitchy." I push her away and go again. "How about this?"

"No, no and no. Don't you realize how important this is? You're not even trying."

I grit my teeth. "I am trying, but the nib keeps catching on the paper. Can't I use an ordinary pen?"

"No, you can't. And the reason the nib is catching is because you're not holding it correctly. You're like a baboon brandishing a banana. Let me show you." She grasps my hand firmly to guide it and the weirdest thing happens. Her hand seems to shimmy into mine.

There's an intense stinging cold as Tilly grips the pen through my own fingers. It looks like one hand with two wrists attached. No way. I close my eyes, trying not to puke.

"Ugh." The connection is broken as Tilly snatches her arm away, looking pale and clammy. "That was *disgusting*; I could actually feel your fingers holding the pen!"

276

The warmth rushes back into my hand as we stare at each other.

"Try again," I whisper. "Try and do the signature."

Tilly hesitates then nods before placing her hand over mine. Blood surges into my frozen fingertips, throbbing in time with my hammering heart, but I close my eyes and let her take over. This time, my hand moves smoothly across the paper.

"Look, Jess," she says in an awed whisper.

I open my eyes to see the loopy authentic signature of Matilda Jennifer Linwood Spencer.

47

"Oh, yuck." Tilly stares at the signature. "It totally felt like your fingers were my fingers. How can you live with those bitten nails?"

"Ew. It was like that bit in *Ghost*." I exhale heavily. "You know, when Patrick Swayze takes over Whoopi Goldberg's entire body."

We eye each other with reluctance.

"Nah," I say immediately.

"Not a chance." Tilly shudders. "I bet Whoopi Goldberg didn't have bristly shins and big feet."

"I shaved my legs the day before yesterday, you cheeky cow." I give her a shove. "And I bet my feet aren't any bigger than Whoopi Goldberg's. Size six is completely average."

"If you say so."

"I do. Look, should we have another go? Just the hand bit, obviously," I add hurriedly.

"Well, it would totally solve the problem of the signatures. Even a handwriting expert would be hard pushed to say this one's not mine. And maybe I could write some letters to you, like the ones you did for me – as legal proof that we knew each other. If I can do it without puking, of course."

"Likewise. Let's have a look at this will first." I open the packet and spread the paperwork over the bed.

Tilly scans the various documents. "Well, this seems straightforward enough."

"I'll see if I can set up a template on the computer," I say, tapping away at the keyboard. "OK. Personal details first: full name, date of birth and address."

"Let's make the arrangements for Granddad," Tilly says, once we've filled in the basics. "I need to leave enough money for him to be comfortable for the rest of his life. Do you think two million will be enough?"

I try to keep a straight face. "How old is he?"

"Eighty-six next birthday."

"I think two million might just be enough."

"Good. We'll also give a donation to the nursing home, say five hundred thou? To be used for refurbishments and building a nice conservatory for Granddad to use in the winter months."

"Do I specify conservatory for his own personal use?" I say. "Or are the other olds allowed to go in there?"

Tilly finally gets it. "Stop taking the piss. Now we need an old folks' charity to support. It'll balance the kids' one and put them off the scent if they think you're just after a job. After all, you'll be the one who flags up the existence of the will."

News to me, but I keep searching until Tilly finds a charity she likes.

"Bless! This foundation helps old people look after their pets, even if the old person becomes too doddery to take them for a walk." Her blue eyes brim as she reads on. "And their nursing homes accept pets so the old person can keep their cat or dog until they die. Or the cat or dog dies, I suppose. Maybe Granddad should get a cat. I could write it into my will that they've got to let him have one, if they want the money for the conservatory…"

"Does he like cats? Did he have one before he went into the home?"

"Not that I remember. He used to keep ferrets, though."

I wrinkle my nose. "That's asking a bit much, Til, no matter how much you sub them. How much do I put down for the animal charity?"

"Same again? Do you think half a million is a reasonable amount?"

"Can't see them saying no, can you?"

"Good." Tilly frowns. "Now we need to sort out the Kidscope section. We need this document to be absolutely watertight."

"It's a homemade will, Tilly," I say with a yawn. "As long as they don't laugh at it, I reckon we're in business."

48

"Stay awake, Jess!" Tilly claps her hands as I slump over the laptop. "I want the rest of my estate used to set up a national charity for Kidscope with centres in the south and north. Note down that I've already had provisional discussions about office space in a deprived area of Manchester. Would that apply to where you live? What's it called, Fallowfield?"

"Only if you're talking skint uni students," I say, rubbing my eyes. "You could always add a beer and Pot Noodle fund, if you like. What else?"

"In the event of my death, I want Kayla Lawrence appointed executive director with support from Mr Chen. And old Mr Standish."

I look up from the keyboard. "I can't put that. What's his real name?"

Tilly looks vague. "Reginald, I think. Or maybe Roger. Just put Mr *R*. Standish. And I want them to appoint a celebrity patron. Tell them to get Kit for me."

"Kit Harington?"

"Of course, Kit Harington," she says narkily. "If I don't go to heaven, at least I'll get to look at someone pretty now and again. You can invite him to the trustee meetings and we can have charity balls and things! And if you can't get Kit, I want Robert Pattinson…"

"Not Harry Styles?" I try to keep a straight face. "Look, don't you think we need to focus on the actual charity, not the celebrity patron?"

"I'm getting to that bit. Are you ready?"

My fingers struggle to keep up as she dictates a surprisingly detailed outline for the development of the basic services offered in Battersea and how this could be applied to children living in other deprived areas of London and Manchester.

"I want new minibuses for each service," Tilly says. "A specialist support network for young carers. And a full-time crèche for teenage mothers so they can continue their schooling. Don't you have a lot of those in Manchester?"

"Crèches or teenage mothers?"

"Mothers, you pleb."

"Loads," I say. "It's a brilliant idea."

"Good." She scans down the information I've set out. "I think that's everything."

"What about personal bequests?"

"Hmm. Clothes and jewellery to be divided between Bea and Tanika. And money for Kayla to have a new car; hers is on its last legs."

"Anything else?"

Tilly sighs noisily. "I suppose we should leave a little something to my old school. Should we say five hundred grand for St Aggie's?"

"You're the boss. You want me to specify it's for the Tilly Spencer Memorial hockey pavilion or something?"

"No. Let the poor old cow spend it on whatever she wants. Whether it's solar panels for the staffroom or gold-plated loo seats in the prefects' toilets, I don't care. I haven't forgotten she was the only one to side with Mr Chen at that trustee meeting. Maybe she had my best interests at heart, after all." She peers over my shoulder. "Well, I think that's everything."

"Nothing for Georgie?" I daren't mention the Andy Warhol hanging above the fireplace in Tilly's den.

Her nostrils flare. "I'm not leaving a penny to that conniving cow."

"But won't it look weird? Everyone knows how close you were."

"I don't care." Tilly tosses her glossy hair. "If I get my way, everyone will find out what a bitch she is. Are we done?"

284

"We just need to leave space at the bottom for our signatures." I'm not looking forward to this bit. "Do you want to have a go at the handwritten letters we need?"

Tilly nods warily. "But then you've got to phone your parents, remember?"

"OK." I brace myself as her hand hovers over mine. "Ready?"

We spend the next half hour creating two backdated letters from Tilly to me on hotel notepaper. Tilly tries theatrically not to gag and I keep my eyes shut as my frozen hand moves across the paper. The results are amazing – pages of rounded, blue-inked scrawl which in no way resembles my own handwriting.

"Put one in your bag and take the other back to Manchester, just in case anyone questions the validity of the will. You can say we've been writing to each other for years, ever since—"

"Yeah, I know the script." I'm wiped out and the handwriting thing has given me a weird headache.

Tilly scrutinizes the letter detailing the raucous events of her seventeenth birthday party. "You know, I'm not totally sure this one should become public knowledge."

"We've got enough, even without it," I say with a yawn. "The Sheffield one dated July, with your ideas for the charity, is the one I'll show if I have to."

"It shouldn't be a problem," says Tilly. "The will's going to be found in my flat with my signature on it."

"How exactly?"

"Maybe I should write a little Post-it Note for old Mr Standish, saying this is my idea for a will, please take a look? You know, as if I was planning to take it along to that meeting?"

I need a sugar buzz to keep me awake. I open the mini bar and grab a can of coke. "Can I drink this first?"

"You should have something proper to eat and take your tablets," Tilly scolds, distracted by a mini bottle of champagne. "Ooh. I wonder if we did the whole body takeover thing whether I'd be able to taste that? Feel it go down into your stomach?"

"Feel me puke it back up again, you mean?"

"You're right." Tilly goes green. "Let's stick to the handwriting. Once we've done the Post-it Note, we can finish the will. We need to leave space at the bottom for three signatures. You just need to type the full names: mine and two witnesses."

"Yours, mine … and who else?"

Tilly smiles. "Let me spell it out for you. *Georgina Louise Morley.*"

"You're going to get Georgie's signature on your will?" I'm so sleepy, I must be missing something. "How? Do we forge it?"

Tilly shakes her head. "She'll only deny it and throw the veracity of the will into contention. No, Jess, she needs to *really* sign it."

"How the hell do we get her to do that?"

"Simple. I'm going to scare her into signing it." Tilly rubs her hands together with a vindictive grin. "I'm going to totally scare the shit out of her."

49

I open my eyes to find myself face down on Tilly's paperwork. I hope I haven't drooled on anything important. Then I realize the phone's ringing.

Tilly's face is anguished. "Jess! It's your dad!"

Crap. I'm super wide awake as I fumble for my phone. "Hi, Dad. Sorry I forgot to call earlier."

"Where the hell are you, Jess? And don't pretend you're staying with your mum because I know you're not. You haven't been there all week."

Double crap. I appeal to Tilly, but like me she's got nothing.

"I'm staying with Bex," I improvise eventually. "In Sheffield."

"Wrong again." Dad's voice is hard with anger. "I've already phoned Bex's mum. And Nisha's. They haven't seen you either. So you'd better tell me where you are *right now* so I can come and get you. You've got a hospital appointment tomorrow. Half past three."

"But that's not until Wednesday," I say.

"Tomorrow *is* Wednesday. I was worried sick when you didn't come home from Wales. Imagine how I felt when your mum said you hadn't even been there. All bloody week." His voice cracks. "I thought something terrible had happened to you. Are you OK?"

"I'm fine, Dad." My eyes prickle. "I'm really, really sorry."

"I don't want to hear it. I just want to know where you are. And don't even *think* about lying to me again."

I'm thinking, my brain and heart racing, when he starts up for round two.

"Who are you with anyway? Did you meet some boy when you were in that hospital?"

"In the *hospital?*" I have this ridiculous vision of me flirting outrageously over the top of my oxygen mask while looking like total crap. "When, Dad? Pre-op when I couldn't breathe or post-op when I was stuck in intensive care?"

"Don't get smart with me, miss. I won't ask you again – where are you and who are you with?"

I go for the truth. "I'm with a friend. In London. She

needed help and I knew you wouldn't let me go if I told you."

"Damn right I wouldn't." He sighs. "Bloody hell, Jessie, you'll be the death of me. Are you really OK? Eating properly and taking your tablets? No more of your … funny spells?"

Tilly nudges me. "He means: have you been talking to yourself again?"

I push her away. "I'm fine, Dad, honest."

"Right. Give me the address and I'll come and get you."

"You don't need to do that. I'll get the train in the morning." I swallow hard, turning my back on Tilly's open-mouthed protest. "I promise I'll be home in time for the appointment."

Finally, after a bit of negotiation, Dad agrees to stand down.

"Ring me from the station," he says. "And if you're not here by lunchtime, I'm phoning the police. I mean it, Jess."

"Got it." I end the call, staring at the blank screen.

"You can't go home yet. You promised me." Tilly shakes my shoulders, pulling me to face her. "You promised, Jess!"

"I know I did, but things change." I hesitate before giving her a rueful grin. "Don't worry. We're going to finish what we started. And when Dad grounds me forever, at least I'll have you to keep me company. Unless, of course, our cunning plan actually works and you can shove off to heaven where you belong."

"Thank you, Jess." She pulls me into a chilly hug. "I love you."

"Yeah, I love you too," I say grudgingly. "Now please will you let me go back to sleep? Big day tomorrow."

50

"So how are we going to work this?" I say, stuffing Tilly's silver laptop into my rucksack along with our stockpile of forged documents.

"Why don't you phone her? Georgie." Tilly pinches her lips, like she's got a nasty taste in her mouth. "Tell her you know where the will is, get her to meet you at the flat and once she's there, we make her sign it."

"You make it sound sooo easy."

"You have no idea how resourceful I can be." Tilly has an unpleasant glint in her eye. "I'm totally used to getting my own way and being dead won't stop me. She'll sign if it's the last thing she does."

"I don't know, Til. Georgie's got too much to lose. If all your money goes to charity, her business goes down the toilet. Why the hell would she sign?"

"Because if she doesn't, I'm going to haunt her for the rest of her life," Tilly says calmly.

"Yeah, right. Aren't you already signed up to me?" I grab my coat. "Anyway, if your plan works, you won't be hanging around much longer."

"*She* doesn't know that. I'll just do my usual stuff. I'm getting pretty good, have you noticed?"

I have. Tilly's been practising blowing, breathing on, tweaking and tormenting every member of staff in the hotel with her arctic hands. It's weird – some of them barely seem to notice her but others are super sensitive, like this morning's room service waiter who almost dropped his tray when Tilly stuck her chilly fingers up his waistcoat. ("Nice six pack, handsome.")

"It's a pain you can't do the rest of it," I say, zipping up my jacket. "I mean, that guy who brought my breakfast – he could obviously feel you perving on him but couldn't see or hear you like I can."

"It would be more convenient if I could talk to her." Tilly still refuses to say Georgie's name unless she has to. "Never mind, I'll do my touchy feely bit and you can translate, tell her it's me."

"Do you honestly reckon she'll believe it?"

"Yes, if you dish the dirt while I do the business.

There's loads of gossip about her you can't possibly be expected to know. You stand on the other side of the room while I do my stuff." Tilly wiggles her fingers vindictively. "And now we have the creepy handwriting thing. She'd recognize my writing a mile off so if she sees you doing it, she'll totally lose her mind. We can show her some scary messages — you know: *wooo, I'm going to haunt you forever* and *hey, I know you cheated in your A Levels.*"

"Did she?"

"Totally. And there are lots of other things. She bribed a policeman once to let her off for speeding."

OK, maybe this could work. "So, we get her to sign the will and then what?"

"We make her hand it in to the solicitor — you know: *duh! I'd forgotten all about this.* My money gets moved out of Broughton-Marley and into the charities instead."

"What about him? You know, Markham?"

"He won't be able to do anything if she's already handed over the will. But we need to act soon, Jess, before he starts moving that money."

"What about the other stuff they did?" My skin prickles. "Paying Leo to murder you and all that?"

"It would be cool to get her to admit it. Depends on how scary I can be."

"Depends on how irritating, more like," I say. "If it's a toss-up between being stuck in prison or having you blowing down my ear for all eternity, I know what I'd choose."

"Ha, *ha*. Let's see how it goes. Even if she admits to murder, the police might not believe her unless Leo and Markham back her up and I can't see that happening any time soon. The police might just think she's bonkers."

"Been there and done that," I say. "I don't fancy trying your haunting idea on that Markham. While you're blowing down his ear, he could have his hands around my throat."

Tilly agrees. "Too dangerous, sweetie. Let's go to the flat now – we can print off the will, stash it somewhere obvious for Georgie to find and then ring her to come and get it."

"What if she doesn't come?"

"Of course she'll come," scoffs Tilly. "She'll be desperate to get rid of it, before anyone else finds it."

I'm pretty knackered so we get a taxi to Radley Square.

"The end's in sight. Final push, sweetie." Tilly braces her narrow shoulders as we mount the steps to the dark green front door.

I unlock the door and she goes on ahead.

"All clear in the hall!"

I scurry across the wooden floor and stick the key in the lock. Tilly darts past like a Navy Seal and slides through the open door.

"We're safe," she calls. "The alarm's still on. There's definitely no one here."

Upstairs in Tilly's den, my hands shake as I fire up the laptop.

"I can't get into your documents." I panic as the desktop refuses to load.

Tilly leans over my shoulder. "Incorrect password, sweetie. Did you remember only one r in Harington?"

"Oh, bollocks." I retype the password. "Why couldn't you have stuck with Mrs Styles? At least I can spell that."

I switch on the printer and load the tray with expensive looking paper. We wait anxiously as it chugs into life and prints out the six-page document.

"You go first. Witness it in the space underneath and then we'll use the proper pen for my turn," says Tilly as I hunch over to write. We both take a deep breath as she slides her hand through mine to sign the bottom of the will with a flourish.

"Two down, one to go," Tilly says with a tight smile. "Ready to make that phone call?"

I nod. We touch knuckles before I reach for my mobile.

"Hi, Georgie? It's Jess Bailey, Tilly's friend."

"Hello, darling. Is this about the charity money?" Georgie sounds warm and friendly as ever. "Because if so, I've already been on to the solicitors, you know. About the payments being reinstated."

"Thanks, but this is something else. Sorry to bother you but I thought you should know."

"Go on then, Jess, but I am in rather a rush. I'm doing a celebrity baby shower this afternoon."

I take a deep breath. "I was talking to Kayla Lawrence from Tilly's charity—"

Georgie breaks in before I finish. "Gosh, whatever do they want now? Blood?" Her tinkly little laugh reminds me of Tilly. Then again, maybe not. Tilly hasn't done that annoying laugh for quite some time.

"They don't want anything." I keep my voice calm. "Kayla said Tilly hadn't written a will, but she had, hadn't she? I said you'd know all about it."

"Wait," cautions Tilly, her hand cold on my forearm. "Let it sink in."

Georgie's breathing quickens before her voice returns to the other end of the line. "Darling, are you absolutely sure about this?"

"Definitely." I'm almost enjoying myself. "I was telling Kayla about the money Tilly planned to leave to the charity. You must know all about it, what with you and Tilly being so close. I mean, if she told me, she'll have said it to you as well."

"I really don't recall her mentioning it."

"Wow, good job I told you. Tilly had it ready for the next meeting with her solicitor so it must be somewhere in her flat. Sorry, I know you don't fancy the idea of going round there yet. Forget it, I'll just phone the solicitor's office instead."

Tilly gives me a thumbs up. "Good one, Jess."

Georgie clears her throat. "No, no, don't bother them. I'll deal with it later, but I must go. Ciao, darling."

Tilly bounces on the beanbag beside me. "Do you think she took the bait?"

"Hook, line and sinker."

51

"She's coming, she's coming!" shrieks Tilly from the den window.

I peer through the blind. "Jeez, I can't believe she fell for it. I'd better hide."

"What's the point?" Tilly shakes her head. "You have to face her when I do."

No way. "I hide first and let's see where she goes."

We compromise on her parents' peacock-blue bedroom. I crouch behind the door and Tilly hovers on the landing, giving me a running commentary as Georgie lets herself into the flat and pounds up the stairs towards us.

"She's going into the den. Now she's opening the top drawer of the desk."

Even I can hear Georgie's audible gasp. I raise my eyebrows at Tilly, wishing I could see what's going on.

"She looks totally stunned," Tilly updates me. "Ha, ha, that envelope wasn't there last time you looked, was it, dear? Oof, now she's opening it and she does not look happy. I think she's found the space for her own signature. Right, Jess, you're up."

I stand on shaky legs and go out on to the landing. Georgie doesn't notice me; she's too busy skimming through the will. As I watch, she turns to ram the whole document into the shredder.

"Stop her!" Tilly's voice is like a train whistle in my ear.

I step forward. "Don't bother. I know where there's another copy."

"Jess!" Georgie spins around from the desk, looking flustered. "What the hell are you doing here?"

"Same as you. Looking after Tilly's interests. I see you found the will."

She stares down at the papers in her hands. "When did she ask *you* to sign it?"

"Ages ago."

"You're just a kid." She gives a nervous laugh. "It wouldn't hold up in a court of law."

"You're right," I say. "That's why she needed you to sign it as well."

"I'm fairly certain it's not valid to witness someone's signature after their death."

300

"I reckon you should," I say. "There are plenty of pens in that jar on the desk."

"What's in this for you?" Her pretty face hardens. "Money?"

I shake my head. "It's more about what's in it for Tilly. She's not thrilled about the idea of you using her money to buoy up your failing business and then diverting it into your own pocket."

Her face is smooth. "I've no idea what you're talking about."

"You bloody do!" shouts Tilly in frustration. "Bitch!"

"Tilly knew all about it," I say, keeping my distance. "She knew you'd nicked her money and arranged to have her killed."

"Murdered," says Tilly. "Tell it like it is."

"What? But I didn't … she couldn't … how could she know?" The pages fall from Georgie's fingers and she sinks down into the office chair, pale under her perfect fake tan. "I see. It's blackmail, is it?"

"I've told you, Tilly just wants her money back. To give to someone more deserving than you and your creepy boyfriend, Markham."

Georgie cringes back into the chair. "You talk about her as if she's still here."

I smile. "Maybe she is."

"Boo! Guess who?" says Tilly, blowing hard on the back of Georgie's neck.

52

Georgie's rigid, her face drained of colour. Tilly avoids touching her but takes another breath and blows harder this time, ruffling the faux-fur collar of Georgie's jacket.

"Is there a window open up here?" Georgie whispers.

"No. But there is a super angry ghost." I lean against the door frame, miles too far away to be held responsible for any of the breezy activity. "Knock yourself out, Tilly."

Tilly wrinkles her nose in reluctance before placing both cold hands around Georgie's throat. She slides her fingers into the thick piled up hair at the nape of her neck and tugs. Georgie winces as a hairclip pings out and drops to the floor.

"Look how good I am." Tilly blows hard across Georgie's face, making her screw up her eyes.

"This is some sort of horrible trick," Georgie croaks, turning her face away. "I'm going to call the police and tell them you're trespassing."

"Good luck with that." Tilly seems to have got over her aversion to the hands-on stuff. She scratches her fingernails up and down Georgie's freckled wrists as her god-sister sits paralysed in the office chair.

"Tilly says 'good luck' with the police," I translate. "She reckons I should tell them how your boyfriend paid off Leo Rossini to crash that car into a stone wall. Gambling debts of one hundred and fifteen grand, yeah? By the way, that's her doing that chilly thing to your arms. Now she's moving up, ooh, she's got her hands around your neck and she's starting to squeeze. Now, back to your hair."

The red hair blowing across Georgie's eyes can't disguise the terror in them. "Stop, please!"

I hold out my hands. "But I'm not doing anything."

"It's some sort of trick!" Georgie repeats.

Tilly rolls her eyes. "God's sake, what does she want? White nighties and clanking chains? I know. Tell her I was with her when she bought that dress in Marc Jacobs. Tell her she tried it on in the lime green, but she thought it made her chest look flat. It totally did but the grey she's got on isn't any better."

As I relay the information, Georgie looks faint.

303

"Just clever research," she says.

"OK. Tell her she got drunk at New Year and snogged her friend's fiancé in the men's toilets. She was totally mortified the next day." Tilly giggles. "Not because she felt bad about stealing her friend's man but because the boyfriend looked like Elon Musk. Tell her that."

I do.

Georgie sags in her seat. "How on earth—"

"This is kind of fun." Tilly dances around the chair, flicking her fingers through Georgie's hair and tugging on the fur collar of her jacket. "Tell her she returned an evening dress to Harvey Nicks after she'd worn it twice and she'd already been photographed in it coming out of The Ivy. Tell her she dyes her eyelashes because otherwise they're totally white like an old sow's. What else? Tell her…" Tilly pauses, her rosebud mouth set in a hard line.

I wait. "Tell her what?"

"Tell me what?" Georgie rotates her head, clearly terrified.

Tilly speaks directly into Georgie's ear. "Tell her I know she killed my father."

I look up and she gives me a firm nod. "Say it, Jess."

I step nearer to the stairs in case I have to leg it. "Tilly knows you killed her dad."

Georgie breaks down. It's hard to hear what she's saying as she sobs into her clasped hands.

"That was never meant to happen. Tilly knew how

much I adored Uncle Ollie. He should have married Ma, but she never stood a chance once he'd met that Jennifer. Oliver Spencer could have had anybody but who does he choose? A jumped-up postman's daughter from Pudsey." Georgie wipes her nose on the back of her hand, her mouth quivering with anger. "I was so jealous of Tilly sometimes. Her father spoiled her rotten and she never had to worry about anything, especially money. But Uncle Ollie's death had nothing to do with me, I swear. That was all Jonathan's idea, same as it was with Tilly. I never knew a thing about that fire until it was too late."

"Liar!" shouts Tilly. "You chose a night when my father was away because you wanted to get rid of my mother. Did you think you could all play happy families once she was gone? That he'd forget my mother and marry yours?" She leans over Georgie, her voice heavy with contempt. "Or were you actually deluded enough to think he'd marry *you*?"

"Tilly doesn't believe you," I summarize. "She thinks you were crushing on her dad."

"Why are you doing this?" Georgie lifts her chin. "What's in it for you? And where are you getting your information from?"

"God's sake," says Tilly, hands balled into fists. "Show her, Jess."

I step forward, unbuttoning my shirt. "See this? I had a heart transplant seven weeks ago. My new heart came from a girl who'd been killed in a car accident and when

I woke up from the operation, Tilly was in the room with me. She's been here ever since, trying to find out why she was murdered. She told me all about you, all about Leo and how to find him."

Georgie's head snaps up. "That was you? *You* went to see Leo last week?"

"Yes. Tilly even told me how to get into her flat and where to find the will."

Her hands shake as she picks up her handbag to leave. "I don't believe you."

"Fine. If you don't believe me, watch this." I pick up a pen from the desk and nod to Tilly. I shut my eyes as her cold hand closes over mine, but this time there's no nausea as the pen slides across the paper. When I open my eyes again, there's a neat row of rounded handwriting: *Tilly's still here, Tilly's still here, I'm still here...*

"Oh god. That's her writing. That's Tilly's handwriting." Georgie looks up, red-rimmed eyes darting from side to side. "She's really here?"

Finally. "She's standing right in front of you."

"Ask her if she can feel this," says Tilly, smacking Georgie across the cheek.

Georgie shrinks back in her seat. "Was that her, touching my face?"

"Oh yes." Tilly swoops back in, this time to tug and twist at the silver ring on Georgie's left hand. "And tell her I want my ring back."

306

As I relay the message, Georgie fumbles with the ring, holding it out to me. "Tell her I'm sorry. I'm so sorry."

"She can hear you." I tuck it into my jeans pocket. "Tell her yourself."

"I don't want her apologies," says Tilly. "I want her to sign the bloody will and give me back my money *right now*."

"She wants you to sign." I hold out the paper and pen.

"I can't." Georgie's trembling. "Jonathan will kill me. You don't know what he's capable of; he's killed once over this already—"

Tilly rolls her eyes. "Don't you think we already know that?"

"I've told you," I say. "We *know* about him arranging Tilly's murder."

Georgie shakes her head frantically. "Not just Tilly. Leo Rossini."

My stomach plummets. "Leo's dead?"

"Dead." Georgie's cracked voice rises to a shriek. "Jonathan knew all about you going to see him last weekend. Leo told him on Tuesday. He said he wasn't going to take the rap for Tilly's murder – he even made a ridiculous veiled threat about some local gangster being involved. He said if he was going down, Jonathan was going down with him."

"What happened?"

"He was found dead yesterday morning. Suspected

overdose, drink and drugs. All very convenient. I'm surprised you haven't heard; it was all over the local news."

"Maybe it *was* an overdose?" I say. "He was drinking a lot."

Georgie swallows, shaking her head. "Jonathan's very good at making things look like an accident. You know: 'Tragic driver wracked with guilt over heiress death'."

"How many times? He was a chauffeur – not a *driver*," snaps Tilly. "Can't anyone get it right?"

Georgie rattles on feverishly. "I made a terrible mistake getting involved with Jonathan Markham. One I will regret for the rest of my life. God knows what he has planned for me when my usefulness is over…"

"Whatever it is, she bloody well deserves it. Tell her if she doesn't sign the will, I'm going to haunt her forever. *Forever*, tell her." Tilly pulls at the roots of Georgie's red hair. "And she's got to tell the police about me and Leo – tell her if she's in prison, she'll be safe from Markham, but she'll only be safe from me if she does as I say. Make her believe it, Jess."

"OK." I set the will in front of Georgie. "Tilly says you have to sign. Make sure you backdate it to August. And then you've got to go to the police and tell them about her and Leo. Maybe Markham can't get to you in prison, but Tilly can. She'll never leave you alone for a minute unless you do what she says. Another thing," I add truthfully. "She doesn't ever go off duty."

Georgie flinches as Tilly grips her upper arms. "Fine, just give me the pen. I'll sign the damn thing, but then we have to get out of here."

"Why?" I say.

"Because he's coming!" Georgie scribbles her signature, dates it and throws down the pen. "Don't you get it? Jonathan Markham is on his way here, right now!"

53

"What did you say?" I whisper, my throat suddenly dry.

"I told Jonny I was coming here." Georgie's hands are trembling. "He was always concerned there might be some paperwork we'd overlooked and he sent me here a few times to check. When you rang to say there really was a will, I called to let him know. He said he'd meet me here to help search."

"We need to leave." Tilly pulls on my elbow. "Let's take the will and go straight to the police station. Let her go out first in case he's already on his way up."

"Right." I relay the instructions to Georgie and stuff the brown envelope containing the will into my rucksack.

310

We hurry down the cinnamon stairs to the hall and wait as Georgie opens the front door.

"Too late!" she says. "He's already here!"

"Shit! Tell her to say nothing!" Tilly grabs my hand, pulling me backwards. "We'll just hide until he's gone."

"Tilly says: tell him you can't find it and get rid of him," I hiss, running through the door into the lounge.

"Not here! It's the first place he'll come." Tilly doubles back into the hall, before returning. "He's here. She didn't even have time to close the front door. Quick! Into the garden, Jess."

I creep across the wooden floor, thankful that I'm wearing trainers and not Tilly's favourite heels. The key turns noiselessly and I edge the French door open.

"Hurry!" Tilly runs back to peer into the hall. "They're coming."

I slide through the glass door, pulling it towards me as Tilly slips through the gap. She looks pale and frightened.

"I'm so sorry I got you into this, Jess. No, don't close it completely," she warns. "We need to hear what's going on."

I leave the door open but draw the thick tapestry curtain across to cover me as I flatten myself against the outside wall.

"Calm down. I can hear our heart." Tilly places her palm against my chest. It's thudding so hard I'm terrified Markham can hear it next door.

"He's asking where the will is and she says she doesn't

311

know," Tilly says, pushing her face through the crack in the curtains. "She's a rubbish liar. Can't believe I didn't spot it years ago."

Tilly makes space for me as I edge closer – through the gap, I can see most of the living room.

Georgie is white, her shaking hands clasped together. "I've looked everywhere, Jonny. It isn't here; I'd have found it if it was."

Markham has his back to us. "But the girl told you it was here."

"Then she got it wrong. Or maybe Tilly changed her mind or, or … maybe she's already sent it to Standish's office and it hasn't been found yet—"

"Too much information," murmurs Tilly.

Markham strokes Georgie's collarbone with his thumb. "I think there's something you're not telling me."

She flinches away. "No, I promise there isn't."

"There's something going on. What is it?" His calm voice is edged with menace and the hair lifts on the back of my neck.

"I can't!" Georgie's eyes dart from side to side. "It's just that—"

"God's sake," says Tilly. "She's going to spill. I'd better remind her what's at stake here."

"No!" I clutch her arm, but she's gone. The French doors creak slightly as Tilly breezes through them. Both Georgie and Markham look round.

Tilly stalks forward and tugs at Georgie's hair. "Remember me?" she says, blowing hard against Georgie's neck.

"Leave me *alone*!" Georgie twists away and stumbles into Markham, pressing her face into his waistcoat. "Oh god, she's here! Tilly's here!"

Tilly steps back, frowning. "Oh, shit."

Markham pushes Georgie away from him. "What are you talking about, you stupid woman?"

"Tilly's here! She's haunting me!"

"The Spencer girl? She's dead. She's not haunting you, for Christ's sake."

"She is! She made me do it!"

"Do what?" He grabs Georgie's upper arms. "What the hell have you done now?"

"I signed it. I had to." Georgie stares around the room in terror, entirely bypassing Tilly standing on the left. "She was here, the girl who went to see Leo. She knows everything!"

"How does she know everything?"

"She got Tilly's heart in a transplant," babbles Georgie. "Tilly was haunting her but now she's haunting me instead! She's here, Jonathan!"

Markham's head whips around to look directly at the French doors. "The girl's still here? Where is she?"

I press myself against the wall as Tilly moves protectively in front of me, arms outstretched.

There's a pause before Georgie speaks. "No. After I signed, she left, taking it with her. It's Tilly who's still here."

Tilly exhales. "At least she has some shred of common decency left."

I return to the crack in the curtain as Markham turns on Georgie.

"You stupid, paranoid bitch. What exactly have you signed?"

"Tilly's will. She's left everything to charity. We have to give it back, Jonny." Georgie cringes away as Markham removes his rimless glasses and places them in his top pocket.

"Where's the will?" He strikes her hard across the face. "Where is it?"

Her lip's bleeding. "I had to sign it, I had to."

Another slap. "I *said* where is it?"

Georgie sinks to her knees, the condemned prisoner awaiting execution. "I can't tell you, Jonathan. She won't ever leave me alone if I do."

He hits her again, harder this time, and she slumps face down on to Tilly's oak floor.

I start forward but Tilly blocks my way. "You can't help her, Jess. We've got to get you out of here. God only knows what he'll do if he finds you."

54

I slide along the high garden wall towards the side gate, but it's locked. "Where's the key, Tilly?"

"Kitchen drawer, I think."

The wall's at least three metres tall – there's no way I can climb over so I creep back towards the windows. Inside, glass smashes as Markham strides around the room, pulling books down from shelves and swiping photo frames from the mantelpiece.

"You need to call the police," says Tilly. "Where's your phone? In fact, where's your bag?"

We both look around but there's no sign of my rucksack.

"I must have left it inside," I whisper. "God, Tilly. It's got the will in it."

"We'll find it." Tilly creeps into the lounge as far as she can until my chest starts to strain. "It's under the chair in the hall, Jess, he's just walked past it. He's taken the key from the front door and he's going up to the den. Quickly!"

I slip back through the French windows, legs wobbling as I sprint past Georgie's unconscious body into the hall.

"He's coming back." Tilly grabs my arm as I scoop up the rucksack with its precious contents. "Get in here."

We run into the bedroom and I close the door softly. I push the envelope containing the will far underneath the trailing gauze of Tilly's bed and dial 999 with shaking fingers. "Ambulance to 18 Radley Square. A girl with head injuries. Quickly, please." I speak as loud as I dare.

"Ask for the police as well," urges Tilly.

Before I have the chance to speak, the bedroom door bangs open.

"Well. Who do we have here?" Markham stands in the doorway, his shiny forehead beaded with sweat. I run to the window, struggling with the sash, but it won't budge.

"Help us!" I scream into my phone as Markham draws closer. Tilly throws herself against him, scratching and clawing, but he seems immune to her fingernails. He grabs my arm, dragging me away from the open window, shaking me until I drop the phone. His heel grinds down and the screen cracks, the casing shattering into a thousand pieces.

"You stupid little cow." He yanks my hair, throwing me against Tilly's bed. "Where's the will?"

I slump down to the thick carpet and draw up my knees protectively. "I don't know what you're talking about."

"Don't play games with me, little girl. You've seen what happens to people who cross me." He jerks his head towards the open door and smiles.

"Get away from her!" Tilly launches herself at him, both hands raking at his throat, but he doesn't seem to feel anything. She falls to the floor, watching with frightened eyes as Markham bends to run one finger down my cheek.

"I'll ask you one more time." His sour breath makes me gag. "Where's the will?"

I shrink back against the bed. "I don't know."

He flicks cold grey eyes around the room. Without stepping away, he pulls open the top drawer of Tilly's dressing table. Make-up still in its packaging cascades to the floor as he drags the drawer out completely and lets it fall with a thud, millimetres from my scrunched-up toes.

He sweeps his arm across the dressing table and bottles of perfume and jars of cream hurtle towards me. He upends Tilly's jewellery box and the large swing mirror on the top of the dresser is next – I cower as shards of glass land on my hair and shoulders.

"Tell me where it is."

I swallow. "I don't know what you're talking about."

He leans forward, grabbing the roots of my hair and yanking me to my feet.

Tilly inserts her body between his and mine, her panicked face level with my chin. "Tell him, Jess, for god's sake! He's going to kill you!"

No way. I freeze as he ramps up the grip on my hair. Tilly deserves better. Anyway, it won't matter if I tell him or not, he's going to murder me anyway. My best bet is to drag it out and hope the police get here first.

"Up." Markham pulls me back into the living room. "Is it in here?"

He drags me past Georgie who lies very still, blood pooling beneath her head on to the oak floor.

Tilly bends and places her fingertips to Georgie's throat. "She's not dead."

Georgie responds, moaning and turning her head. As Markham turns to swing a kick into her ribs, I pull away, a handful of expensive highlights coming out in his hand as I scramble towards the French doors. I slam the door in his face, buying me seconds as I lurch into the garden, my legs like lead. But the gate's locked; there's nowhere to go.

"The treehouse, Jess!" Tilly points to the wooden ladder.

I nod, too out of breath to speak. If I get up there, maybe I can shove the ladder away.

As I grab the middle rung and lever myself up, I

hear Markham's ragged breathing close behind. I kick backwards, catching him in the face. With a grunt of rage, he grabs me by the ankle and yanks hard. I body slam into the top rung, the burning in my sternum indescribable – worse than Tilly straining at me, worse than having the chest drain out after my operation. Stars burst before my eyes as I haul myself up on to the platform, but it's no use. Markham vaults up behind me and rolls me over so I'm facing up.

Standing astride me, he rips open my shirt to show the puckered scar beneath.

"Interesting. You really are the transplant girl? Tilly Spencer's heart in there?" He's detached rather than surprised. His probing fingers press against my wound and I swallow, unable to speak with the pain.

"I guess it would hurt quite a lot if I did this?" He raises one foot and stamps down on the right side of my ribs. I let out a single shriek of pain and Tilly rushes at him again, furious but impotent.

I rock from side to side, biting my lip. Through a crack in the decking, the lawned grass below looks a million miles away.

"Where's the will?" Markham's foot is poised directly above my breastbone. "Ready to tell me yet?"

"For god's sake, just tell him," sobs Tilly. "They're not coming. One life is enough to waste. I don't care if they get away with it, I only care about *you*. Please, Jess! I'm sorry I called you a coward. You're not a coward, you're the bravest person I know."

"Last chance," says Markham calmly. "Tell me where the will is."

I think of the envelope in my rucksack under the bed. "In the den upstairs."

"We've already checked the den. I hope you're not wasting my time." He smiles down at me. "I'd hate to have to do something like this." He grinds the heel of his shoe against the left side of my ribcage. The pressure climbs until there's a crack and my head swims.

Is this where I'm going to die? A posh treehouse in a Chelsea garden? Dry-eyed, I blink through a canopy of red and gold leaves to the grey sky, imagining familiar faces in the clouds. Dad cheering on United. Mum with her crystals and terrible cooking. Their first Christmas without each other might be their first Christmas without me. And what'll happen to Tilly if I die? She'll never cope, left here all by herself.

Markham looms over me, blocking out the sky. I try to protect my chest with my arms, but they're like rubber – I can't even lift them from the decking.

"Come on, don't give up." Tilly reaches for my limp hand, her frozen fingers morphing into mine. "Please, Jess, you've got to *fight*."

Through the black patches scudding across my eyes, I see her jaw clench in fierce determination as she draws our entwined fingers towards the back of Markham's ankle. With surprising strength which isn't mine, my hand closes and jerks forward.

For a long second, Markham is suspended above me, his face a strange combination of shock and rage. Then he stumbles, arms windmilling, as he lurches backwards over the edge of the platform. There's silence, then a sickening thud as he hits the ground below.

My arm flops on to the decking as Tilly unlinks her fingers and leans over the wooden platform. "Take that, you *total* bastard."

In the background, there's the swoop of an ambulance siren as Tilly returns to bend over me, her long hair tickling my face.

"Hold on, Jess." Her anxious smile swims in and out of focus as I try to get my breath. "Just hold on."

55

When I open my eyes, the garden is swarming with people. Police, paramedics and, according to Tilly, the nosy neighbours from two doors down. I try to sit up but a sharp pain zings through my chest and my left lung feels like it's been pulled inside out. Tilly holds my hand while the paramedics assess me and then a super-hot policeman carries me down the ladder. Tilly scampers down ahead and, by the time we reach the bottom, she's sitting cross-legged on Markham's chest.

"I'll tell you if he tries to move, sweetie," she says. "But this paramedic seems to think he's broken his neck. How fabulous is that?"

Inside the house, Georgie's being loaded on to a stretcher. Another paramedic checks me over while two police officers hover in the background, asking questions I can't begin to answer. Tilly prompts me with outlandish suggestions as I try to cobble together a brief and breathless fabrication of the official version of events.

I'm just about running out of ideas when the paramedic rescues me by sticking an oxygen mask over my face. "That's enough. We need to get her to hospital now. She might have a collapsed lung."

As they wheel me out, Tilly reassures me that Markham's still in the garden, my cute copper standing guard as the paramedics strap him on to a spinal board.

Handily, Georgie and I end up in adjacent cubicles at the A&E department. While I have an ECG monitor strapped to my chest, Tilly nips between the thin flowered curtains to give me a running commentary, although I can hear most of what's being said.

"She's come round!" Tilly says gleefully. "They've said it's just concussion. I'm going to blow on her neck. Remind her I'm still here, won't you, Jess?"

I nod. Until she's given that statement to the police, Georgie could backpedal at any time, although it would be pretty hard to explain away her signature on the will.

"Tilly's still here," I call out, earning me a super weird look from the porter who's come to wheel me off to X-ray.

When I come back (four fractured ribs on the left, a broken bone in my right hand but both lungs fortunately intact), Georgie's spilling her guts to a frantically scribbling policewoman. I try to tune out the details about Leo's death. Tilly darts back and forth through the curtains, subjecting Georgie to numerous ear blowing and hair ruffling interventions.

"The good news is you don't need a chest drain. And the fractured ribs aren't a worry, but the ECG showed your heart's working a wee bit hard," says the cheerful male nurse taping my ribs. "We don't think there's any real damage, but we'll keep you in for observation. You'd better see your own specialist once you get home. Now, how does that feel?"

I inhale cautiously. There's less pain than before but I'm completely exhausted. Every breath feels like a battle.

"All right there, Jess?" A motherly looking police officer pops her head through the curtains. "Your mum and dad are on their way."

"Both of them?" I squeak. God knows how I'm going to explain all this. "Are they seriously fuming?"

"Hard to say. Your dad said to tell you you're grounded and then he burst into tears." She gives me a stern look and shakes her head. "Kids, eh? While you're waiting, are you up for having another chat? Whenever you're ready."

"I'm ready."

"Me too." Tilly fingers the collar of her blue jacket with

324

dissatisfaction. "Could be anytime now, Jess. I just wish someone could tell me what the procedure is. And, more importantly, whether I can change into some new clothes when I get up there. This jacket is *so* last season."

56

The early morning sun streams through the blinds on to my pillow and I wince, turning my face away from the bright light. Someone's fingers are threaded through mine but, weirdly, they're warm not chilly.

Oh. It's my mum. She's scrunched up in the plastic chair next to the bed, her brow furrowed in sleep. I sit up, stiff and sore but with a strange sense of weightlessness. Apart from Mum, the room's completely empty. I extricate my fingers and look around, hardly daring to believe. *Where the hell is Tilly?* I scan the four corners of the room and, feeling silly, lean over to peer under the bed. My chest is as tight as ever, but that could be down to the strapping on my fractured ribs rather than being ghost related.

No way. She's gone.

She's *gone* and she didn't even say goodbye.

I can't believe I won't ever see her again. Hear her again. Smell her precious posh perfume. My eyes prickle and my bruised heart aches with emptiness at all the things I left unsaid. All the times I was mean to her (even if she was meaner to me first). I sniff fiercely, scrubbing my eyes with the back of my good hand.

Get a grip, Jess. It's what Tilly wanted.

Hell, it's what I wanted. I've just got to get used to being on my own again, that's all, but the idea of my old pre-transplant life seems grey and colourless without Tilly in it. I flop back against a pile of pillows which seem way more comfortable than the ones in the Manchester hospital, imagining what Tilly would say if she was still here. ("We're in Kensington, sweetie. Of *course* the pillows are softer.")

The door creaks open and a health care assistant pops her head round.

"Oh, you're awake, dear. Ready for breakfast?"

"Yes, please." Anything but bloody porridge.

Mum doesn't stir as the nurse brings in the tray.

"Are you going to manage OK with that splint on?" She points at my right hand.

I nod. "I'll be fine with my left." My strapped-up chest

gives a sudden stutter as I register the forlorn blue-jacketed figure standing behind her. Tilly trembles in the doorway, eyes red-rimmed. She looks vulnerable and very young. My heart aches with pity for her, mixed with guilt at how relieved I am.

With difficulty, I wait until the nurse has left the tray and closed the door behind her.

"I thought you'd *gone*," I whisper, trying not to wake Mum.

Tilly shakes her head, the picture of misery. "I waited all night, but nothing happened, Jess. Then early this morning, I heard a noise in the corridor and when the night staff came to check on you, I nipped out to see what was happening. I thought it might be … well, never mind. Anyway, she'd already closed the door. I've been sitting out there for ages, waiting to be let back in." A tear slides down her cheek and disappears before it reaches her chin.

"Oh, Til." I open my arms and she rushes forward to rest her cold cheek against my strapped up chest.

"I'm never going to heaven, Jess," she sobs. "I just haven't been good enough. I'll never get to see my mum and dad again."

I swallow, divided between disappointment and relief. "There's still time." I keep my voice low. "Maybe it won't happen until they get found guilty. For now, you'll just have to stay here with me."

"Thank you, Jess," she says humbly. "I'll be good. I won't be bossy, I promise."

I smile. "Yeah, right. I'll believe that when I see it."

57

Next day, handcuffed to his hospital bed in the spinal unit, Jonathan Markham's charged with grievous bodily harm (me and Georgie), murder (Leo), conspiracy to commit murder (Tilly) and conspiracy to commit fraud (trying to shift money out of Broughton-Marley).

It's a slight worry when the detective warns me that, even with Georgie's confession, there might not be enough evidence to link Markham definitively to Tilly's death.

Tilly seems resigned rather than angry. "Oh, well. I can't see Jonathan Markham walking out of prison any time soon. In fact, with that broken neck, maybe he won't be walking anywhere at all, ha, ha. At least that bitch Georgie has been charged with conspiracy to commit murder and fraud as well." She stands in the doorway, watching as the police leave. "It doesn't look as if I'm going anywhere either."

I squeeze her hand as she returns to the bedside. "I'm sorry."

"I'm sorry, too. You'd better get used to the idea of me coming back up north with you. And your mum and dad."

My parents are in the corridor, chatting to the ward sister as they sort out my medication ready for discharge.

"Could be worse," I tease. "At least Mum's heading back to the commune soon."

"Do you think she will?" Tilly gives me a sly grin. "Maybe she'll stay for Christmas. They seem to be getting on pretty well."

"Not that well," I say, fidgeting to get comfortable. It's so hard to breathe right now. "It's only because I'm ill. Once I get better, they'll be back to arguing again."

Tilly looks sadly at the borrowed wheelchair and the portable oxygen cylinder waiting for me by the door. "I won't give you any trouble, I promise. You know, not get upset and use up too many heartbeats. It's your heart now, not mine."

"We can share. Maybe if we calm down and do less running around solving murders, our heart won't have to work so hard. I've got an appointment with Mr Khan next week; I bet he can fix us up." I'm not sure who I'm trying to convince – her or me.

"Totally." She grins again. "Hey, if we're going to be housemates for good, maybe it's about time you introduced me to your dad."

"Yeah, right. You were the one who kept saying he wouldn't believe me."

"Yes but look what's happened since." Tilly ticks off her fingers. "Swiss bank accounts, hitmen, wicked god-sisters, fake wills and a heroine who just happens to be a ghost – let's face it, sweetie, you couldn't make it up."

"Dad says I can have Bex and Nisha to stay in the Christmas holidays. I'll introduce you to them instead."

"I'd like that," Tilly says, turning as the door creaks open.

I'm expecting Dad but it's someone else.

No way. "Wes?"

He leans round with a tentative grin. "OK to come in?"

"Yeah, yeah." I push myself up against the pillows, super conscious of my shiny nose and bedhead hair. "What are you doing here?"

"Mum heard what happened. She feels terrible, you putting yourself in danger because of us."

I'm seriously confused. "What do you mean?"

"You know, you trying to find out what had happened to the charity money."

"It wasn't your mum's fault, Wes." I shake my head. "I was doing it for Tilly."

"Well, I heard you smashed it, man. Tracking down the

scammers. Can't believe the nerve of Tilly's bestie trying to nick all her money."

I glance at Tilly who's looking puzzled as me. The police have only updated us this morning. "How do you know all this?"

"Mum rang the solicitor and that secretary lady told her. Mum said I shouldn't disturb you, but the nurse said I could have five minutes as long as I promised not to tire you out." He looks embarrassed. "Or get you too excited."

My heart gives a little ricochet and Tilly bursts into peals of laughter. "Careful, Jess. Remember what we agreed about conserving those heartbeats."

I try to zone her out and focus on Wes. "It's cool you came. I might be going home later today."

"Back up north?"

"Yep."

"OK." Wes shoves his hands into his pockets and looks down at his trainers. "So I'm coming up to Manchester after Christmas. Looking around the uni, you know? Maybe we could meet up for a Nando's while I'm there?"

"Classy," says Tilly but I can see she's smiling.

"That'd be good," I say. "Yeah, I'd like that."

"It's a date, then." Wes leans in, blocking out the light. Soft stubble scrubs my cheek and there's a tantalizing tang of citrus. My heart goes into overtime as warm lips brush mine and then he's backing away, a big grin splitting his face. He turns, almost bumping into my dad coming through the door, before loping down the corridor on long legs.

"You look very pleased with yourself," says Dad. "Who the hell was that?"

"Just a friend from the charity," I say, ignoring Tilly's muffled snigger. Nothing can wreck my buzz now, not even the bloody wheelchair and the oxygen cylinder.

Dad looks like he's going to say something but changes his mind. "We've got the all-clear to take you home. I'll go and give your mum a shout."

"Looks like we're off, sweetie." Tilly reaches for my hand as Dad exits the room. "Before we go, can I ask you one last favour?"

"Not another one, Tilly." I snort in mock outrage. "Go on, then. What is it this time?"

58

"Remind me what we're doing here?" Dad says, turning the car into a tree-lined street. The gutters are littered with red and gold leaves.

"I want to say goodbye to Tilly's granddad before we go home."

"I still don't understand how you managed to track down this girl and work out she'd been murdered." Mum leans around the passenger seat, looking super excited. "Perhaps you've developed some sort of psychic ability since your surgery?"

"I dunno, Mum. It was just, you know, stuff on the internet." I'm being vague. "It's a long story. I'll explain properly later."

Dad looks sceptical. "Are you also going to explain why a load of parcels have arrived at our house with your name on them?"

Crap. We seriously need to do some work on our cover story.

Tilly bounces beside me in the back seat as we arrive at the nursing home. "I can't wait to see Granddad."

Dad parks his Peugeot between a Ferrari and a Porsche. "How far is it to walk, Jessie? Do you want me to wheel you inside?"

"Best not, sweetie." Tilly watches me struggle to unbuckle with one hand. "They might mistake you for one of the residents."

"Thanks a lot," I say. "I mean, thanks, Dad, but it's only a few steps." I smile, trying to disguise how out of breath I am.

"We'll wait in the car then." Dad gets out his newspaper. "Don't be too long, love, or we'll hit the traffic."

Tilly looks sad as we crunch our way up the gravel path to Greendale.

"We'll come back," I promise. "But now that *nearly* everything's been sorted out, it's time for me to go home, Tilly."

"I know," she says. "I've already reconciled myself to becoming a Man United fan – red is totally my colour. Hey, wasn't Mr Standish funny when you showed him the bit we'd written in the will about asking Kit Harington to

336

be the celebrity patron?"

"I don't think he'd ever heard of *Game of Thrones*," I say, ringing the bell. "But it was nice of him to say he'd see what he could do. Poor old sod looked even more knackered than me."

Tilly links my arm. "I expect he's still trying to make sense of the monumental cock-up Standish Junior made while he was stuck in hospital. Still, better to find out your grandson's incompetent rather than corrupt."

The door's opened by the same smiley lady who was on duty last time. "Tilly's friend! What a nice surprise. Have you come back to see Stanley?"

"If that's OK?" I say, as we step inside.

"Oh, yes." She leads the way through the sunny day room. "It really perked him up last time you were here. He's out in his usual spot, wrapped up nice and warm." She points to a striped steamer chair positioned under the same tree. "He might be having a little nap."

I have to stop again at the French windows to get my breath. Tilly watches me with anxious eyes.

"I'm fine," I say, waving her forward. "It's just these broken ribs. You go and see your granddad."

I lag behind as she hurries across the grass.

"Hello, my flower." Stanley holds out his arms and she skips straight into them. "I've been waiting for you. Did you get all your jobs done?"

"Yes, we've sorted everything out, Granddad." Tilly

presses her pink cheek against his woolly jumper. "We saw the solicitor today. Guess what? He's managed to get nearly all my money back."

She doesn't mention Georgie but chatters on about the charity as she perches on the edge of his lounger, swinging her legs. "Jess's going to help out at the northern branch when she leaves school. She lives in Manchester, you see, so I might not be able to visit quite so often." Her lower lip starts to tremble and I step back to give her some space.

Stanley laughs, shaking his head. "You don't want to worry about all that now, Tilly. All that matters is you're here. I told our Jennifer you'd be back in no time."

Tilly stares at him. "You've seen Mummy?"

He crinkles his eyes. "Every day for the past week. She's been waiting for you."

Tilly's mouth drops open. "Why didn't you tell me last time I was here?"

"It wasn't the right time, Tilly." Stanley nods wisely. "You had things to do before you were ready to go. But now you're finished, she'll be along to collect you."

"Mummy's coming to collect me?" The longing in her voice makes my heart tighten.

Stanley squeezes her hand. "That's right, flower. You just stay here with me for a while. Your Mam won't be long; she always was an impatient lass. She's been that desperate to see you again."

"Did you hear that, Jess?" Tilly's voice is very high.

"My mother's coming to get me."

"That's amazing, Tilly." I'm happy for her, honest I am. But how do we even do this? Can I leave or do I have to wait for her mum to get here first?

Tilly looks as confused as me. "Do we try this?"

I nod. She stays put and I edge backwards across the lawn until we're further apart than we've ever been. I'm waiting for the chest pain to kick in any second but, despite the complication of my fractured ribs, it doesn't come. Tilly keeps her eyes fixed on mine, both hands clasped over the place where her heart should be.

"You OK?" I whisper, but she's too far away to hear the undertone we use in public places.

Crap. This is it and I'm seriously not ready. I swallow, raising my hand in silent farewell and suddenly she's hurtling back across the grass towards me.

She throws her chilly arms around me, sobbing into my neck.

"What's wrong, Til?" I stroke her silky hair. "I thought it was working?"

"It *is*." She nods vigorously, gulping down tears. "I just wanted to say thank you."

I inhale her familiar orange blossom scent and then hold her at arm's length to get a proper last look. She's not at her best, nose pink and tears trickling down her face, but she looks so happy.

"You daft thing." I run my thumb down her cheek to

catch the drips before they disappear. "Just as well you're going off upstairs to heaven, or wherever, because you're useless down here. You didn't even learn to walk through walls in the end."

She sniffs, giving me a sly smirk. "Didn't need to when I had you to open doors for me."

"Bloody upper-class ghosts." I try to smile but my voice comes out wobbly. "Too posh to push."

"Something like that." Her voice cracks. "Oh, Jess. How lucky I am to have something that makes saying goodbye so hard."

"Who is it this time, Shakespeare?" I say but she shakes her head. "Jeez, not Spider-Man again."

"Winnie-the-Pooh," she says gravely. "I'll never ever forget you, Jess."

"You'd better bloody not," I say to cover the fact I feel like howling. But I never cry and I'm not going to start now. Instead, I touch my fist to my chest. "I won't forget this. I never did say a proper thanks, so here goes: thank you, Tilly. Thank you for giving me this second-hand heart."

"Pre-loved, remember?" Tilly looks back wistfully towards her granddad. "It *was* loved, wasn't it, Jess?"

"It really was. I'll look after it, I promise." I bite my bottom lip and taste salt – puzzled, I reach up to find my cheeks wet. I turn away, hoping Tilly hasn't noticed, but the treacherous tears just keep on coming. To distract

340

myself, I dig into the pocket of my jeans. "Almost forgot. I've got to give this to your granddad."

My heart twists as I hold out Tilly's silver ring. It feels like I'm ripping off a plaster, severing the last connection between us.

She shakes her head, curling her fingers over mine. "You keep it. Something to remember me by."

"Oh, Tilly. I don't need anything to remind me of you," I say, but I push it on to the middle finger of my left hand anyway. Tilly holds up her right hand and we press our palms together, rings glinting in the low autumn sun, silver leaves merging as our fingers intertwine.

We smile at each other for a long minute until her grandfather beckons.

She unlinks her fingers from mine. "Do you think it's time?"

"I reckon so." I swallow hard, my throat tight with tears. "Take care, Tilly."

"And you, Jess. Use that money to do the things I never got a chance to. I've been to Rome, Barbados and Florida but I never did swim with dolphins, you know." She rolls her eyes in an endearing familiar gesture. "Or snog Harry Styles."

"Harry Styles? Nah, he is so not my type." I give her a shaky grin. "I'll see what I can do about those dolphins, though." I watch her run back towards the tree where a small shadowy figure waits, arms outstretched. I blink as they embrace and, a heartbeat later, they're both gone. It's just Stanley now, waving into the low sunlight, his eyes bright with tears.

All at once, it's easier to breathe. I unzip my jacket, taking large gulps of welcome air as the warmth tingles back into my fingers and toes. Arms pumping and legs striding out, I hurry back to the car where Mum and Dad wait.

"All done?" Dad smiles up from his newspaper as I open the back door. "Are you ready to go home, Jessie?"

"Ready," I say, my pre-loved heart light.

ACKNOWLEDGEMENTS

The first thing I asked Scholastic was: how many pages can I have, please, because I have a LOT of people to thank.

First up, my awesome agent, Rachel Petty, who is wise, patient and hugely supportive. Thank you for having faith in me.

My fabulous editor, Yasmin Morrissey, who has been the best champion for Jess and Tilly, and Julia Sanderson who provided great follow-up support.

The wider team at Scholastic with special thanks to Sarah Baldwin (who designed the stunning cover), Sarah Dutton, Tierney Holm, Harriet Dunlea, Holly Clarke, Alice Pagin, Emily Landy, Ruth Middleton and Sarah Bardell.

The best bit about writing is the friends you make along the way. Much love to all the amazing groups below and the gorgeous Venn diagrams which resulted as people overlapped.

My longstanding critique group, all talented writers

in different fields. The amazing Allie Reynolds who has had my back from day one (*even after* reading my terrible first novel). Wonderful Gail Richards who taught me about paired commas and helped Jess and Tilly navigate the London underground. Linda Middleton and Julia Anderson who have always provided fantastic support.

Sara Grant and the fantastic Undiscovered Voices team, volunteers who generously gave their time to support us 2022 finalists. Working Partners who sponsored the anthology. My brilliant fellow UV finalists and writing buddies.

The fabulous NW SCBWI group with special thanks to Helen Lapping for organizing us, Anna "show me the stakes!" Mainwaring and lovely Mel Green for her razor-sharp beta reading skills.

The multi-faceted support system™ that is WriteMentor with huge thanks to the ever-generous Stuart White and marvellous Melissa Welliver.

The wonderful #WMClassof2020 summer mentees who have remained friends, some of whom overlapped with the brilliant #2023debuts group – yay!

Lovely industry people: Liz Flanagan and Will Mackie from New Writing North, Rachel Leyshon, Tilda Johnson, Caroline Ambrose and Alice Williams.

Critique partners who cheer-led for Jess and Tilly: Jan Dunning, Ali Clack and Shannon Cowan. Other writers who supported me along my journey include Amanda

Sellet, Nancy Werlin, Lou Finch, Clare Harlow, Joanna Moran, Sharyn Swanepoel, Lee-Anne Farebrother, Anna Britton, Cynthia Murphy, Tasha Harrison, Rachel Owen and anyone I haven't mentioned (so sorry).

Grateful thanks to Laura McGarrigle and Michaela Bailey from the Transplants and Cardiothoracic teams at Wythenshawe Hospital who helped make Jess's transplant journey as authentic as possible (despite the ghostly goings on). Any mistakes are my own (including Mr Khan's orthopaedic vibe!). Thanks to The British Heart Foundation for helpful advice.

Coming into the home stretch now.

To Col, who makes me brave enough to share my stuff. Without him, this story would still be in my head, possibly on my laptop but never ever on a page. This is for you.

To Joshy, who'd make an awesome editor if he ever fancies a career change from being a rock god. And Nathan, who gave advice on teen speak, sustained me with homemade brownies and gives the best hugs ever.

To my mum and dad who always encouraged me to read.

And to Joyce who encouraged me to write.